DUEL OF HEARTS

Twenty-seven and unwed! Beautiful but lonely Sarah Stanborough had all the disadvantages of marriage, with none of the advantages. She was kept a spinster by her mother's choice for her, the dissolute Lord North, who drove all her other suitors away.

She would rather die than marry such a loathsome man! But when Lord North, in a fit of jealous rage, threatened Edward Middleton, Sarah realized she had to make a choice; she had to wed the man she hated, in order to save the man she loved . . .

Berkley books by Elizabeth Mansfield

DUEL OF HEARTS
HER MAN OF AFFAIRS
MY LORD MURDERER
THE PHANTOM LOVER
A REGENCY MATCH
REGENCY STING
A VERY DUTIFUL DAUGHTER

Elizabeth Mansfield
Duel Of Hearts

BERKLEY BOOKS, NEW YORK

DUEL OF HEARTS

A Berkley Book / published by arrangement with
the author

PRINTING HISTORY
Berkley edition / November 1980

ISBN: 0-425-04677-X

A BERKLEY BOOK® TM 757,375

PRINTED IN THE UNITED STATES OF AMERICA

Prologue

IT WAS QUITE a pretty little cap, really. Hardly the sort of trifle a lady should stare at with such a troubled frown. It lay on Sarah's lap, resting on the bed of tissue paper in which it had been wrapped, looking quite innocent and charming—a frivolous confection of pure white dimity trimmed with rows of satin ribbon and edged with the finest Alençon lace. But Sarah's fingers trembled slightly as they played with the ruffled lace, and she looked down at the cap with an expression of dismay. Yet she herself had ordered it just a week ago—on the occasion of her twenty-seventh birthday—from one of London's finest milliners. There seemed to be no reason why its arrival this afternoon should have caused any agitation of the spirits.

A little cap could not be, of itself, an object to be feared. What, then, was the problem? Sarah knew the answer. Shaped very much like the mob caps worn by housemaids while doing their cleaning, this delicately trimmed head-piece (often erroneously called a widow's cap) was an item of clothing meant to be worn indoors, but not only by widows. In households in which proper attention was paid to tradition, this type of cap was worn by married women as well—indeed, it was appropriate dress for *all* females of mature age. Only young girls were exempt from covering their hair with headpieces of this sort. As soon as a girl married, she took to wearing a cap about the house as a symbol of her new maturity. As such, it was usually donned with a feeling of delight.

But Sarah was not married. There was the rub.

Sarah looked from the cap in her lap to her reflection in the mirror of her dressing table with a wince of pain. She was well aware that, at the advanced age of twenty-seven, most women had long since been claimed in matrimony. She, however, had been left on the shelf. It was of small comfort to her to realize that most people considered the situation to be her own fault; a woman, they said, whose appearance was so extraordinarily pleasing must surely have been spoken for by this time. A refined young female with a slender, graceful form, a pair of intelligent eyes, a well-modelled face and a head of thick, warmly auburn hair could not possibly be passed over in the matrimonial stakes *unless she herself had wished it so*. That was what everyone said. And although Sarah felt that the encomiums to her appearance were exaggerated, she had to admit that her single state was as much her fault as anyone's.

The abrupt opening of the bedroom door interrupted her ruminations. Her mother, Lady Laurelia Stanborough, bustled in with her customary disregard for her daughter's privacy. She was dressed for the outdoors in a fur-trimmed pelisse and a bonnet bearing a number of enormous plumes, and she carried an oversized muff of the same fur which edged the pelisse. Lady Stanborough, a woman of remarkable style and charm (but rather *un*remarkable intellect), stood under five feet tall even in her highest-heeled shoes, a fact which had irritated her since her salad days and for which she attempted to compensate by wearing the tallest hats she could find. The hats, while they did nothing to disguise her lack of stature, nevertheless inspired many admiring comments and did much to give her a reputation for possessing a daring sense of fashion. To her mind, the success of her hats signified that *other* items of her wardrobe should be made oversized as well, and she ever afterward dressed herself in the widest scarves, the largest rings, the broadest muffs and the longest gloves she could find.

Struggling to fasten the many pearl buttons of her lavender gloves, she barely glanced up at her daughter as she spoke. "I'm off to Lady Howard's. Are you determined not to come? If you should ask me, an afternoon of cards is just the sort of diversion you need."

"No, thank you, Mama," Sarah answered promptly. Her mother would have been surprised by any other response. Sarah never went to card parties.

"Mmmmph!" her mother grunted with habitual disdain. "Very well, I'll convey your regrets to La—" Her eye fell on the open package in Sarah's lap. "Good heavens! What's *that*?"

"You can see very well what it is," Sarah said defensively, holding it up for her mother's inspection.

"Surely you don't intend to . . . to *wear* that thing!" Lady Stanborough exclaimed, aghast.

"But of course I do."

"Over my bruised and broken body!" her mother declared, trying to snatch the cap from Sarah's hand.

Sarah, who took after her deceased father in the matter of height, stood more than six inches taller than her mother. She jumped up from the dressing table and held the cap aloft, well out of her mother's reach. "But why should I *not* wear it?" she asked reasonably. "It is certainly appropriate costume for someone my age."

"Give that cap to me at *once*," Lady Stanborough demanded furiously, "and don't be such a green-head! Putting on a cap is like admitting to all the world that you're . . . you're—"

"That I'm an old maid? But that's just what I am."

Lady Stanborough glared up at her daughter. "Don't talk such drivel! You're a mere child!"

Sarah had to laugh. "Really, Mama, be sensible. A woman of twenty-seven is hardly a child. I'm sorry to upset you, dearest, but at my age I can't even be called a *girl* any more."

"Sorry to upset me, indeed!" her mother responded with a pout. "You upset me all the time! I declare, I shall have an attack of apoplexy if you don't stop this foolishness. And *look* at what you've made me do—my hat is completely askew . . ."

"That's because you insist on wearing bonnets that are much too large for your head to carry. Sit down here, and I'll set it right."

"Never mind," the older woman said curtly. "I'll do it myself." And she sat down at the dressing table and proceeded to repair the damage the altercation with her daughter had done to her appearance. "Old maid!" she muttered. "You don't look a day above nineteen!"

"*Nineteen!*" Sarah giggled and knelt beside her mother so that their two faces were reflected side by side in the mirror. "Take a good look at me, Mama, and try not to tell yourself—or me—a rapper. Is that the face of a nineteen-year-old?"

"Of course it is," her mother said promptly, looking more carefully at her bonnet than at her daughter's face. Lady Stanborough was given to self-deception. She found it pleasant to believe whatever made her most comfortable. But Sarah could not fool herself so easily. The hazel eyes that looked back at her from the mirror had an unmistakable world-weariness that would never be found in the eyes of a girl of nineteen. Her auburn hair, while still thick and rebellious, had lost the reddish gleam it used to have. And there were tiny smile-lines at the corners of her mouth. *Oh, Mama*, she thought with a sigh, *it's been a long while since I had the face of a girl*.

Lady Stanborough, intent on her own appearance, patted a recalcitrant strand of hair into place. "You'd not *be* an old maid," she scolded, more out of habit than conviction, "if you'd listened to me *once* in all these years and married North."

There it was again, the same old refrain. Sarah was heartily sick of hearing her mother harp forever on the same string: *John Phillip North, the Marquis of Revesne, so handsome, so well-placed, so rich, so impressive, so important!* Her mother tended to latch on to an idea and hang on to it forever, no matter how mistaken it was. "Oh, Sarah," she'd moaned repeatedly over the years, "*why* were you so foolish as to have *refused* a man like that!" Nothing that Sarah said could convince her mother that her evaluation of Lord North was misjudged.

"And you *still* can have him, if you will only exert yourself in that direction," Lady Stanborough was saying as she rose from the dressing table. It was a remark she made every time she brought up the subject of Lord North.

"Hasn't he remained single all these years?"

Even though Sarah and Lord North barely spoke to one another except in the coolest civilities, it was generally whispered about that Lord North still wore the willow for her sake. What her mother—and the other London gossips—could not seem to understand was that he was utterly detestable to her. Anything in the world—even spinsterhood—was preferable to being married to Lord North.

The trouble, Sarah admitted to herself with a deep sigh, was that she was an idealistic dreamer. All she'd ever wanted was a quiet life—a life with some purpose, some meaning, some sense. The society of London—the London of opulent ballrooms, of card games and cotillions, of scandals and marital infidelities, of debauchery and deceit, of duels and dishonor—was not a likely breeding ground for the sort of man who would prefer her style of life, but she'd always hoped that *somehow* she would find one man of honesty, valor, dignity and common sense. She had not found him. But it seemed to her that John North, the Marquis of Revesne, was the complete *opposite* of the sort of man she wanted.

Lady Stanborough gave herself a last, quick look in the mirror and turned her attention back to buttoning her gloves. "I know it's a waste of breath to speak to you about North," she said, "but I hope you'll listen to me about that cap. Wearing it is a good as admitting you've taken yourself off the Marriage Mart."

"And so I have, Mama. At twenty-seven, it is time to face the facts," Sarah said firmly.

Lady Stanborough stalked to the door. "If I see you wearing a widow's cap," she threw over her shoulder as she took her leave, "I shall have the megrims! The *megrims*, I tell you! You'll be the death of me yet!"

When the sound of her mother's footsteps had faded away, Sarah sank down on the edge of her bed and stared at the inoffensive little frippery in her hand. Such a to-do over nothing . . . over merely the making of an overt admission (by the donning of an innocuous little white cap) that the days of her youth were over, as were the rituals of courtship. Cap or no, those days of girlhood had passed. She had not had a suitor for a long while. Why couldn't her mother recognize and accept that fact?

For the first time in a long while, Sarah fell to wondering if she had been wrong to have refused matrimony. Surely in the nine years since she'd been presented there must have been *someone* whose attentions she might have encouraged! If only Lord North had not frightened away so many potential suitors with his fierce possessiveness. If she were to be absolutely truthful with herself, she would admit that it was quite her own fault that her suitors had been a rather sorry lot.

It was not shyness which had kept her from the great social success her mother and the rest of the *ton* had expected from a young woman of her physical, mental and financial advantages, although most of the gossips blamed everything on what they called her shyness. She did not usually feel shy; it was just that she always felt decidedly out of her element at the huge, ostentatious social gatherings which single young women were forced to attend. She did not care to make the simpering, foolish little remarks which young girls were expected to utter: "Oh, think *shame* on yourself, Mr. Stiffback! I am *not* the prettiest girl in the room (tee-hee)!" Or, "Yes, indeed, this is the most enjoyable *squeeze* of a party I've attended all season!" And yet again, "Now, *really*, Sir Hotbreath, I've stood up with you for two country dances and the gavotte. We would *not*— (entrancing giggle)—wish to set the tongues *wagging* about us, would we?" In order to avoid the necessity of uttering such inanities, she tried to keep herself quietly in the background.

Her reputation for being shy and withdrawn had spread quickly (probably encouraged by the tongues of jealous mamas of girls who were less advantageously placed), but her good qualities were evidently sufficiently attractive to entice some eligibles to look in her direction. However, it had come as a considerable surprise to most onlookers— and to Sarah herself—when Lord North indicated his decided interest. North was everything a Matchmaking Mama would wish for her daughter. Tall, handsome, with an impeccable lineage and an income fit for a King, he embodied every quality the ton considered admirable: he was cool in his enthusiasms, he was a sportsman of considerable talent, he gambled at cards and horses with icy control, he looked at strangers through his quizzing glass with such practiced hauteur that it gave the object of his scrutiny a case of the fidgets, he was acquainted with the Regent, and he knew how to keep his numerous paramours hidden with admirable discretion. In short, he was considered a nonpareil. What more could one wish from a gentleman?

For Sarah, however, there was little in this list of attributes which she could like. Even before she'd met North, eight years earlier, she'd heard rumors about him that made her take him in dislike. He was said to spend a great deal of his time at gambling. It was whispered that he'd been involved in a number of duels—all at his instigation. And she'd heard that a married lady had attempted suicide for his sake, and that one of his fancy-pieces had complained publicly that, once he was done with her, he had treated her with extreme cruelty.

When North, without the slightest encouragement from Sarah, became her suitor, there had been nothing in his arrogant demeanor to make her feel that the gossip she'd heard about him was unjustified. He'd taken one look at her and—in spite of her protestations that she had no wish for his attentions—he'd adopted the most infuriating attitude of possessiveness toward her. Frightened and angry, she'd attempted to encourage several other young men to court her, more in self-defense than in real attraction toward them. But no sooner was she seen three times in the company of any one gentleman than Lord North would pick a quarrel with the fellow and challenge him to a duel.

Lord North's prowess with either pistol or sword was legendary. It was not very surprising, therefore, to learn that two of the gentlemen who'd courted her had promptly become engaged to other, safer females; another had fled the country; and a fourth (even though he went through with the duel and suffered a minor wound) eventually had found it expedient to give up his pursuit of her. And the lesson had not been lost on the other eligible gentlemen. Sarah had soon found herself completely bereft of beaux.

The only course left to her was to go into seclusion. But if truth were told, that course suited her quite well. Sarah had taken little pleasure in the carousel-like whirl of social amusements. She disliked the superficial chatter, the noisy gaiety, the shallow flirtations which were part and parcel of London's social life. She was quite content to withdraw, to spend her time at the pianoforte, at her books, exchanging quiet visits with one or two good friends and seeing to the domestic concerns of the household. Her mother, whose interests were completely frivolous, protested loudly against her daughter's hermit-like existence, but in reality Lady Stanborough was quite content to leave the burden of the household and money management in the capable hands of her quietly authoritative daughter. What bothered Lady Stanborough more than anything else was the fear that her daughter might—Heaven forbid!—turn into a spinster.

For her part, Sarah had long since accepted her spinster state. Even Lord North had eventually become convinced that she would have none of him, and he'd left her alone. By that time, Sarah had grown accustomed to her withdrawn, reclusive style of life and would do nothing to change it. The little white cap in her hand was merely the symbol of her complete withdrawal from the mating rituals of London society. Why, then, was she so hesitant to put it on?

She got up from her bed and returned to the dressing table, the cap still in her hand. Her reluctance, she supposed, came from the ending of the dream. She would have liked to be married, if she could have found someone like . . . like . . .

Like whom? she asked herself, staring at the hazel eyes that looked back at her from the mirror. In all these years, had there been *no one* she'd met whom she would have liked for a husband? Alain du Bois had been charming, but too weak to stand up against North's assault. Bertrand Quayle had been considerate but a bit of a bore. Lord Osterend was cultured and loved music as she did, but he was close to fifty and admitted honestly that he was much too old to change his bachelorish ways. North, although her mother's set considered him the best catch, was too debauched and unscrupulous. No, there had been no one whom she could honestly say she should have wedded. In fact, she'd not met *one man* whose acquaintance she would have liked to pursue. *Except . . .*

Except . . . the gentleman who'd come to her rescue at Corianne's come-out. He had seemed to be just the sort— But it was foolish to speculate about him. She didn't even know his name!

She closed her eyes. Sometimes, just before she fell asleep at night, she would think of him, and his face would flash before her mind's eye in complete detail. It was a quite astounding phenomenon, especially since she couldn't bring her own father's face nearly so distinctly to mind. But even now, sitting here in the daylight at her dressing table, she could see the stranger's face almost as clearly as she'd seen it that evening two years ago: his short-cropped, dark hair lightly sprinkled with grey; those eyes so piercingly light in a dark-skinned, weathered face; a pair of heavy brows; a strong nose and a mouth, thick-lipped and firm, that had altered radically when he'd flashed a grin— a smile that gave him a look of surprising sweetness.

Of course, she was quite ready to admit that the circumstances of their meeting might have distorted her impression of him. If she saw him today, she might very well find him disappointingly ordinary. Considering the circumstances of that dreadful night, it was entirely possible that she had endowed him with an aura of heroism he really didn't have.

It had all come about when her uncle Roland, the Earl of Daynwood, had written to his sister, Sarah's mother, to assist him with a problem. He had been widowed when his daughter Corianne was a child, and he had brought her up in the quiet of his Lincolnshire estate. But the child was about to come of age, and she wanted nothing so much as to be presented to London society. Roland himself hated London and knew nothing about such things as come-outs. He hesitantly and humbly begged his sister Laurelia to be good enough to present the girl.

Laurelia Stanborough had been delighted to agree. There was nothing she'd more enjoy than taking her niece about on a whirl of parties, balls, dances and fêtes. And Sarah, on whom all the responsibilities of the complex arrangements had fallen, had accepted with equal willingness because of her great affection for her uncle. Thus, for one hectic month, she had been brought back into the social maelstrom.

For most of the period of her cousin's come-out, Sarah had managed to keep in the background, but the presentation ball had been held at Stanborough House, and Sarah, as one of the hostesses of the occasion, could scarcely fail to appear. She'd unpacked her most elegant ball-gown, she'd permitted her mother's hairdresser to arrange her hair in the latest fashion, she'd taken her grandmother's pearls from the safe and, thus accoutered, had emerged from hiding.

To her dismay, she'd discovered that Lord North was among the hundred-and-fifty guests her mother had invited. She could feel his eyes on her wherever she moved. Twice he asked her to dance, but each time Sarah managed to fob him off. Shortly before the late supper was announced, however, he found her taking a brief respite from her duties in a little, secluded sitting room. "At last!" he sneered triumphantly as he came up behind her chair.

She jumped up and made for the door, but he was too quick for her. He grasped her hands and, pinioning them behind her back, he pulled her to him. "Still trying to avoid me, my dear?" he asked, looking down at her with what she could only describe as a leer. "Then why did you bother to invite me?"

"But I *didn't*," she said hastily, trying to free her hands. "My mother must have—"

"Oh, yes, your mother! Of *course!*" he said with a smile of patent disbelief. "*You* knew nothing of it."

"I tell you, I *didn't*—!"

"Never mind. It's a mere detail. And quite irrelevant. The *important* fact is that we're here together. And you are looking as beautiful as ever. It's quite remarkable, really, to find you still in such high bloom."

"Well, I'm not yet ninety," she answered with asperity, twisting her wrists painfully in his unyielding grasp.

He laughed. "No, a ripe twenty-five, if my calculations are correct. An age of female perfection—no longer green, but not yet on the road to decay. At the very point, from the look of you, of luscious sweetness." He might have been speaking of a plum or a pear! His eyes gleamed, and he inclined his head as if he intended to ascertain the correctness of his judgment by taking a taste of her.

She gasped and pulled away as far from him as she

could. "I trust you've not completely forgotten, my lord, that you are supposed to be a gentleman," she said, turning her head away. She tried to keep her voice steady and her nerves calm. "It would be unfortunate if I were forced to scream."

"Unfortunate for whom, my dear?" His smile was so smugly complacent that she would have loved to slap him. "An episode of this sort is what people have come to expect of me. But you, on the other hand, would be bound to suffer excruciating pangs of embarrassment. So scream if you must, my sweet. You have more to lose by it than I."

Sarah looked up at him with contemptuous loathing. "What have you to *gain* by this, my lord? You surely can't believe that such arrogant behavior will enhance your standing in my eyes."

"Are you certain, dear girl? I've known many women who've responded very prettily to just this sort of physical persuasion."

"I assure you, sir, that *I* shall *not*!" Sarah declared disgustedly, trying in desperate anger to wrench her hands free of his grasp. "Let me go, my lord, *at once*!"

His lordship merely laughed again and bent his head toward her once more. She struggled fiercely, crying out, "No, *please*! Let me *go*!" in a choking gasp as his face moved inexorably toward hers. But before his mouth could touch hers, someone loomed up behind him, grasped him by his neckcloth and whirled him around. "I think I heard the lady ask you to let her go," the man said quietly.

Sarah, so abruptly freed, tottered a step backward and stared at her rescuer. His face was vaguely familiar, and she suddenly remembered that she'd been introduced to him earlier in the evening—he was Corianne's neighbor who had come down from Lincolnshire for this occasion. He was sturdily built and broad in the shoulders, and although he was not quite as tall as Lord North, he seemed not in the least daunted by the furious glower which North fixed on his face.

"By what right do you barge in here, damn you?" North demanded, trying to shake the man's grasp on his neck. "Do you realize that I'm *North*?"

The stranger only shrugged, one corner of his mouth

turning up in a tiny suggestion of a grin. "North or south, you seem to have been moving in the wrong direction *here*, old fellow," he said pleasantly, not loosening his hold. "I suppose you're foxed. Why don't you sit down on the sofa there until you've sobered up a bit?" And to the astonishment of both Lord North and Sarah, the man propelled his lordship firmly to the sofa and pushed him down upon it.

A shocked oath broke from Lord North's throat. The stranger ignored it and turned to Sarah. "I hope this little brangle hasn't upset you, ma'am. A man will sometimes take on like a tom-doodle if he's cast away." The startlingly sweet smile lit his face as he offered her his arm. "May I escort you to the supper table?"

Floundering somewhere between tears and hysterical laughter, Sarah found herself unable to utter a word. She gulped, nodded and took the stranger's arm. But before they could take a step, Lord North leapt from the sofa with the growl of a strangling animal. He pulled them apart, grasped the stranger by the shoulder and pulled him round. "Interfering dolt!" he hissed between clenched teeth. "You'll pay dearly for your presumption. What's your name and direction? You'll be receiving a call from my second!"

"Your *second*?" the stranger asked with a tinge of amusement in his voice. "What are you talking about? A *duel*?"

Sarah tensed. Lord North seemed not to have outgrown his hotblooded habit of trying to kill or maim those who crossed him. He was rapidly recovering his equilibrium and, in this mood, could easily turn dangerous. The stranger was taking the entire matter to be rather a joke, but Lord North was not noted for possessing a sense of humor. "Of *course* I mean a duel," his lordship barked, glaring at the stranger with cold superiority.

The unknown gentleman laughed out loud. "Don't be a clunch," he advised the smoldering Lord North, drawing Sarah's arm through his again and leading her to the door. "If you had any sense," he added as they crossed the threshold, "you'd put your head under the pump." With that, he closed the door in Lord North's face.

Sarah, unable to find her tongue, said not a word as the stranger led her to the banquet room. There, with a bow and another of his remarkable smiles, he left her. She knew quite well that he'd left an indelible impression on *her*, but apparently she'd made only a passing impression on *him*. It was soon clear that he had eyes for no one but Corianne. Sarah couldn't help noticing how his eyes seemed to follow the girl wherever she was. Sarah had had the pain of realizing that the gentleman from Lincolnshire had completely forgotten her existence by the end of the evening.

Lord North had spent the rest of that evening watching the stranger, his eyes narrowed and his lips compressed. But he'd soon discovered that the fellow was a mere bumpkin from the country, and his vengeful interest had faded. The next day, the stranger had called to take his leave of Corianne and had returned to Lincolnshire. Sarah had not seen him again.

But she knew he was more than a mere country bumpkin. He had shown signs of humor, courage and strength of character. She would have liked to know him better. But there was little profit in dreaming of the might-have-been. She would show better sense to pay attention to the here-and-now.

And the here-and-now meant a twenty-seventh birthday and a little lace cap. Facing herself squarely in the dressing-table mirror, she asked aloud, "Shall I wear it?"

"It's time," her reflection seemed to say.

Decisively, she pulled the cap over her hair. "There!" she said bravely. "That wasn't so bad, was it?"

"Bad enough," her image admitted.

Sarah stuck out her tongue at her reflection. Then she stood up and executed a deep curtsey. "How do you do, ma'am?" she murmured to the mirror with formal politeness. "I'd like you to meet the new Miss Sarah Stanborough."

The face in the mirror corrected her. "Miss Sarah Stanborough, *spinster*," it retorted with a mocking grin.

Chapter One

A HEAVY AND steady rain streamed down on the Lincoln-shire hills, but the inclement weather had evidently not daunted the young girl who was running down the muddy road leading out of Daynwood Park. She wore nothing to protect herself from the elements except a rather thin pelisse, and although she held up the front of her gown with one hand (a crushed and rain-soaked letter was clenched in the other), the back of her dress was becoming sadly begrimed as it trailed wetly behind her.

She soon left the road, crossed a wide field, climbed with tomboyish agility over a stile, circled a small wood, and in a very few minutes was dashing up the drive of a neat, square-shaped country house whose weathered stone edifice seemed remarkably indifferent to the onslaught of the rain. The girl scampered up the wide stone steps, tossed a dripping strand of hair back from her forehead and hammered at the front door. As she waited for a response, she shifted her weight impatiently from one foot to the other. After a few moments, the door was opened by an elderly man in a butler's coat who gaped at her, uttered a shocked exclamation and stepped hastily aside to let her in. "Miss *Cory*!" he scolded. "Ye *never* ran all this way dressed so . . . in such a downpour!"

"Never mind that, Chapham," the girl answered, brushing by him and hurrying across the wide hall. "Is the Squire in the library?"

"No, Miss, he ain't. He's gone to the stables."

"Oh, *blast!*" She stopped in her tracks, momentarily nonplussed. The thought of going out into the rain again was not pleasant.

"I'll send Robbie to fetch 'im, if ye like," the butler offered.

"No, no. I'll run over there myself," the girl said.

"No, ye'll not." The butler had known Corianne Lindsay since her childhood and didn't stand on ceremony with her. "Ye'll seat yerself by the fire and dry off."

Corianne found his lack of deference extremely provoking. "Really, Chapham," she said with irritable hauteur, "can't you learn to mind your saucy tongue? I'm not a child, you know. I'm in the devil of a hurry, so I'll use the back door, *if* you don't mind." Without waiting for what was bound to be a disapproving reply, she ran to the back stairs, dashed down to the lower floor, swept through the large kitchens (blundering into but ignoring the shocked scullery maid who happened to cross her path), flew out the rear door and across the kitchen gardens to the stables.

She pushed the wide doors open just enough to squeeze through. As soon as her eyes grew accustomed to the dim light, she saw, directly opposite her, two men kneeling before a huge black stallion. One man wore a striped dust-jacket, and the other was in his shirt-sleeves. Both were completely absorbed in applying a poultice to the horse's left foreleg. "Well, *there* you are, Edward," the girl said breathlessly.

The man in shirtsleeves looked up in surprise. "Corianne! Good lord, girl, you're soaked through!" He jumped up and crossed to her in three quick strides. "Is something amiss?"

"No, nothing. But I had to see you. Can we go somewhere to talk?"

"Yes, of course. But I think we'd better dry you off first. Hand me one of those towels, will you, Martin?"

"Aye, I will," the groom replied, tossing it to him. "And ye'll be needin' a blanket, too, I'd say."

"If you think I'd let you wrap me in one of those filthy horse-blankets," the girl objected haughtily, "you're fair and far off."

"Filthy!" Martin exclaimed in outrage. "They're as clean as the ones on yer bed!"

"Just so," Edward agreed with a grin. "Therefore, my girl, you can dispense with your missish ways. Take this towel to your hair, and when you've rubbed it dry enough, you can wrap this blanket round your shoulders like a sensible little chit. You don't want to come down with a lung infection, do you?"

Corianne knew better than to argue with Squire Edward Middleton when it came to matters of her health. Ever since she could remember, he'd treated her with the concern of an elder brother or an uncle. Although her friend Belinda often claimed that Corianne could twist poor Edward round her little finger, Corianne knew that the claim wasn't strictly true. He was a dear, and he found it hard to refuse her anything, but refuse he did if he thought it was for her good. There was something immovable about Edward when he thought he was right. Therefore she must handle him especially carefully today. She couldn't afford to annoy him now, not if she wanted him to agree to the enormous favor she was about to ask of him. So she meekly took the shabby towel he handed her and rubbed her hair.

Edward removed the wet pelisse from her shoulders and put the blanket over her. "Well, Martin," he said to the groom, "I'll leave you to finish with the fomentation. Just keep the leg bound, and we'll take another look at it in the morning."

"Is there something seriously wrong with Bolingbroke?" Corianne asked in sympathetic concern. The black horse was Edward's favorite.

"Nothing nearly as wrong as there'll be with you, if we don't get you near a warm fire," Edward answered lightly, steering her out of the stable. In short order, he established her comfortably before the hearth of the large stone fireplace in his library, gave her pelisse to Chapham to dry and press, and ordered the butler to bring her a glass of hot milk laced with honey. "Now, my foolish child, you can tell me what brought you out in this weather so inadequately protected," he said to her, taking a seat in the wing chair opposite her and lighting a pipe.

"It was this," she said, leaning forward to hand him the letter she had clung to all this while.

He unfolded the soggy missive, now almost unreadable, and strained to make out the words. "What is *this*? An invitation from your Aunt Laurelia?"

"Yes, isn't it *wonderful*? She asks me to come for a nice, long stay."

Edward cocked an eyebrow at her suspiciously. "Strange, isn't it, that she should have written after all this time?"

"Strange?" Corianne lifted her chin belligerently. "Why is it strange to receive an invitation from one's very own aunt?"

"You haven't had a word from her since your presentation, have you?"

"Well, no, but—"

"That was *two years* ago, wasn't it?"

The girl tried to stare him down. "Yes, but what has *that* to say to anything?"

"Come now, Cory, don't take me for a flat."

"I don't know what you mean," she persisted, but her eyes wavered.

"Yes, you do." He tossed the letter onto her lap, leaned back in his chair and put his booted feet up on the hearth. "Your aunt probably hasn't given you a passing thought in all this time. *You* wrote and *asked* her for this invitation, didn't you?"

Corianne was about to phrase a heated denial, but she thought better of it. "Well, what if I *did*?" she demanded defensively. "I see nothing so very terrible in that."

Edward stared into the flames, frowning. "Don't you? I should have thought— Well, never mind. It's not my place to lecture you."

"Don't look like that, Edward," Corianne pleaded, leaning forward and looking at him with worried eyes. "You *know* how much I want to go back to London. It's the only thing I've ever really wanted."

He sighed. "Yes, I know."

"Then say you're glad for me."

He tossed her a quick glance. "I don't see why I should. In fact, I don't see why this news should have brought you rushing over here in the first place. What's behind all this?"

"Nothing. Really! I was just so excited that I had to come and tell you—"

"Nonsense. You know perfectly well that I'm expected at Daynwood this evening to play chess with your father. You could have told me then."

"I couldn't wait!"

He shook his head. "I've never known you to be so eager to bring me news that you'd run out into the rain and spoil your coiffure. It's not like you, my girl."

She put her hand to her hair which was hanging in limp tendrils about her face. "I *did* spoil my coiffure, didn't I! I must look a *sight.*"

He didn't bother to reassure her. If Corianne was aware of anything, she was aware of her beauty. She had heard it praised since she was a dewy-eyed, dimpled infant. She was one of the few fortunate females who had never gone through an awkward phase. Even in her adolescence she'd been breathtaking. Her hair was of a gold color which was deeper and richer than ordinary blond. Her eyes were of a blue just bordering on violet. Her complexion was the envy of all her friends, so unblemished and creamy that it put other skin to shame. She had a tantalizingly full mouth and fascinating dimples that appeared just before she smiled. And now that she was fully grown, her shapely form had reached the perfection that her face had always had.

There was scarcely a man or boy in the county who had not been captivated by her appearance. Edward was no exception, but he would never tell her so. He disliked to see her so self-satisfied and spoiled, and he had no intention of adding to her rapidly developing sense of power over men. Because her beauty had brought easy gratification of all her desires, she was showing signs of setting too great store by appearances and of neglecting the more important facets of character and intellect. It troubled him that her personality was being adversely affected by her outward appearance, but, in truth, her maturation and development were not his affair. She might think of him as an elder brother, but he was no relation to her at all.

This London madness troubled him, too. Ever since her come-out, the girl had been wild to return to the scene of her triumph. That first London season had been a spectacular success. She had certainly made a mark. Why, there were several of her London admirers who *still* made their way to Lincolnshire to gape at her. They would appear without warning on the doorstep of Daynwood on the pretext of "being in the neighborhood." Corianne very much enjoyed these surprise visits, although Edward could notice no young man of whom she seemed especially fond. He couldn't help wondering if perhaps she'd met one *particular* young man in London—one who had not come to Lincolnshire—whom she wished to see again.

He hoped it wasn't merely jealousy that made him dislike the idea of her returning to London. Although he had long ago realized how deeply he cared for the girl, he knew that he could never have her. He was thirty-five years old—fifteen years her senior—and she'd never looked at him with other than sisterly affection. The dearth of society in this secluded area, and his close friendship with her father, had brought them much in each other's company and had given them the habit of easy companionship, but he'd trained himself to control his feelings and to treat her always with no more than brotherly interest. He was sure that no one but her father guessed the extent of his emotional involvement.

But his objection to this eagerly anticipated London trip had deeper foundations than jealousy. He had met her Aunt Laurelia only briefly (when he'd gone down to London for Corianne's presentation ball), but he'd received the definite impression that Laurelia Stanborough would not be a stabilizing influence on the girl. She had seemed to him to be a woman of shallow intellect and flighty interests—the very sort who would encourage Corianne's already dangerous propensities for self-indulgent vanity. And the only other member of the Stanborough household was Laurelia's daughter. He had no recollection of Miss Sarah Stanborough, but he'd heard she was standoffish and reclusive. No, Stanborough House was not a place which he would like Corianne to visit for a protracted stay.

"I *do* look a sight, don't I?" Corianne asked again, interrupting his brooding thoughts.

"Like a drowned kitten," he said heartlessly. "But let us not stray from the point, Cory. I want to know what you've come to say. You'll have to broach the matter sooner or later, won't you? So out with it, girl."

Corianne made a face at him. "You're the most irritating know-it-all, Edward! Yes, I do have something to discuss with you, but if you're going to frown at me in that disapproving way, I shan't say another word."

"I am doing no such thing. Why should I be disapproving?"

Corianne shrugged. "I know you don't want me to go to London. I'm not such a fool that I can't tell *that.*"

"Whether or not I want you to go has nothing to do with this. You didn't come all this way in the rain just to ask my approval, did you?"

"Well, yes . . . in a way."

He looked at her keenly. "But whatever for? It's your *father* you should be talking to."

"I've already done so. He's *refused* me," she admitted in sepulchral tones.

Edward sat back in his chair and puffed at his pipe in considerable relief. "Did he? Good for him. Now I understand the whole. You want me to intercede for you. Well, you've spoilt your hair for nothing, my little one, for I have not the least intention of trying to persuade him to let you do what I myself would disapprove of, if I were he."

Corianne chortled in satisfaction. "There, you *see*? You think you know *everything*! Well, you're quite out in your reckoning, my friend. I did *not* come to ask you to intercede for me."

"Oh? Then what *did* you come to ask?"

She gave him a measuring look and got up from the chair. "What makes you assume I've come to ask you *anything*?"

"We are not going to start *that* game again, are we?" he asked drily.

She walked to the fireplace and peered down into the flames. "All right, you win. I *did* come to ask you something."

There was a long pause. Edward merely puffed at his pipe and waited. At last, Corianne turned away from the fire and came up beside his chair. "I came to ask you to . . . to . . . come to London *with* me," she blurted out.

Immediately, she sensed that she had not done well.

He looked up at her in amazement. "Come *with* you? Have you taken leave of your senses?"

She had to be careful. He would need very special handling if she were to succeed. She knelt before his chair. "*Please*, Edward . . . ?" she murmured.

Her hair was drying, and the firelight behind her lit the little tendrils that had begun to curl around her face. She looked so young and endearing that he felt a distinct pang in his chest. How easily the girl put him at a disadvantage! But he was no callow youth—he was a man of maturity and sense. He had taught himself to say no to her. "You are being a goose, you know," he said gently. "In the first place, I *hate* London. In the second place, I have a great deal to do right here. In the third place, I can't possibly go *with* you to London when you yourself are not going. Your father refused you, remember?"

She sat back on her heels and smiled at him. Her face was shadowed, but he thought he saw her eyes gleam, catlike, as she studied him. "He's refused to let me go *alone*," she said, "but—"

He had the feeling she was about to pounce like a cat. "But . . . ?"

"But he would not refuse if . . ." She leaned closer to his chair and looked up at him coquettishly. ". . . if I told him you had agreed to come along as . . . well, as a sort of . . . chaperone."

So *that* was it! The little minx had worked out quite a foolproof plan. Edward was the one person Lord Lindsay would accept as a substitute for himself. But Edward had no intention of agreeing. "Chaperones are *women*," he said coldly.

She made a sound of disgust at such a trifling irrelevancy. "All right, a . . . a *guardian*, then."

"I don't want to *be* your guardian. You're too much of a nuisance."

"I would be a pattern-card of virtue, I promise! I would do exactly as you told me, every minute!"

He snorted. "A likely tale. Don't be silly, Cory. The whole idea is out of the question."

"But *why*?"

"I've told you why. I hate London. I haven't the time
to fritter away. And in any case, your father would never
agree to such a wild plan."

"Let's ask him."

"We'll do nothing of the sort!" Edward declared quickly,
knowing quite well that Lord Lindsay might easily *accept*
the proposal.

The girl was quite skilled at getting her own way. She
wasn't in the least discouraged by his objections. She
reached out, took his hand and rubbed it against her cheek.
"Please, Edward, don't refuse me this. It's the one thing
in the world I want."

Her cheek was smooth and warm, and the firelight made
a halo of her hair, and he couldn't help imagining how
pleasant it would be to take her to the opera, to show her
the Elgin Marbles at the museum, to buy her trinkets at the
Pantheon Bazaar . . . But he caught himself up and snatched
his hand from her grasp. "It's no good using your wiles on
me, my girl. I wouldn't go to London for all the tea in
China. The answer is no, no and no. And that, Miss Lindsay, is my final word!"

Chapter Two

BUT IT WAS not to be Edward's final word. Later that evening, when he called at Daynwood Park for his weekly chess game with the Earl, Lord Lindsay brought up the subject of Corianne's London invitation immediately. (Evidently Corianne, when she'd found that she couldn't move Edward, had promptly set to work on her father.) But Edward quickly told Lord Lindsay his position, and the Earl obligingly dropped the subject. They set up the chessboard and began to play, but it soon became evident that Lord Lindsay's mind was not on the game. First his lordship completely missed an opportunity to capture an unprotected bishop, and then he failed to check Edward's king which had been left wide open to attack. Surrendering to the inevitable, Edward sighed and pushed his chair back from the board. "Very well, Roland, let's discuss this London business. You'll never manage to concentrate on the game while this matter presses on your mind."

"You're right, my boy," his lordship said glumly, running agitated fingers through his thin, white hair. "That girl has a most unfortunate way of cutting up my peace."

Roland, Lord Lindsay, was a small, spare, nervous man with sharp, keenly intelligent features and a head that was much too large for the small body which carried it. It was hard to believe that he had fathered the strikingly lovely Corianne. The only feature the girl had inherited from her

father was the remarkably deep blue of her eyes. Lord
Lindsay was past sixty years of age, and he secretly felt
too old and unworldly to handle a beautiful, volatile daughter. She'd been born when he was forty-two—his first and
only offspring. During the child's infancy, his adored wife
had protected him from the trials of fatherhood, but the dear
woman had passed away when Corianne was only eight,
and he'd had to deal with the girl ever since. It had not been
easy, for she was willful and impetuous and not above
indulging in emotional scenes to get her way. Poor Lord
Lindsay was not the man to withstand tempestuous out-
bursts. He was suited to the quietest kind of life, a life
undisturbed by unexpected storms. At the least sign of any
household disturbance, his pulse would become agitated,
and his fingers would tremble. He would quickly withdraw
to his study in the hope that the problem would have passed
by the time he emerged.

Fortunately, he had the assistance of a sensible and capable housekeeper who could withstand Corianne's tantrums, and he had the advice and support of his dearest
friend and neighbor, Edward Middleton. These three had
managed, among them, to raise the child and to make of
her a lively, charming, passably well-educated and accept-
ably accomplished young woman. Lord Lindsay realized
that his daughter was somewhat spoiled, but, after all,
who on earth was perfect?

"You can't seriously consider letting Corianne go off to
your jingle-brained sister, can you?" Edward asked bluntly.
"You've said time and again that Lady Stanborough thinks
of nothing from one week to the next but clothes and cards."

"I know, my boy, I know," his lordship said, getting up
from his chair and beginning to pace about the room, his
hands clasped nervously behind him, "but the child has
nagged at me for two years about the matter. I'm very much
afraid there will be no end to it unless she is permitted to
have her way."

"She is permitted to have her way much too often,"
Edward muttered impatiently.

Lord Lindsay paused at the fireplace and gazed abstractedly into the flames. "I wish I knew what to do. I would

not have an easy moment if I left her in Laurelia's care for any length of time, but if I knew *you* were there . . ." He looked over his shoulder at Edward, his eyes deeply troubled. "I shouldn't be asking this of you, I know. If I were any kind of father, I should go with her myself. but I'm really too old to be gadding about town like a damned court card. Truthfully, I was too old for it when I was twenty."

"I don't see why you can't simply *refuse* her. Tell her it's out of the question."

"But she'll be *heartbroken*. I hate to see the child made miserable—"

"She'll get over it," Edward said unsympathetically. He picked up an ivory knight from the chessboard and played with it absently. "I don't see what she hopes to find in London that she can't find here at home."

"A husband, I expect."

"There are at least a half-dozen likely young fellows here in Lincolnshire who would be glad to offer for her."

"Well, she won't have any of *them*. Not that I blame her. A sillier set of mooncalves I've never seen. I'd always hoped . . ." The Earl poked morosely at the fire with the toe of his boot.

"Hoped what?"

"That she would have you," his lordship admitted with a sigh.

Edward laughed mirthlessly. "Don't be a gudgeon. I'm too old for her."

"Only fifteen years older. I was *eighteen* years older than my Elspeth, and we were as happy together as grigs."

"Well, Corianne has not her mother's tastes—or disposition." Edward gave an impatient toss of his head and frowned unseeingly at the little knight in his hand. "It's not a matter worth speaking of."

"Tell me, my boy, have you ever asked her?"

"To marry me?" He looked at Lord Lindsay in surprise. "No, of course not. Why should I?"

Lord Lindsay looked back into the flames. "Well, they do say that nothing ventured—"

"You're letting your wishes outstrip your judgment in this case, Roland," Edward said with a rueful smile. "Cor-

ianne has no interest in me except as a brother. She wouldn't
be so eager to dash off to London if she cared a whit about
me, would she?"

"No, I don't suppose she would. What fools women can
be sometimes!" He resumed his pacing, his shoulders sag-
ging in discouragement. "Then what can I *do* but permit
her to go? She ought to be given a chance to make a suitable
match, I suppose."

"I can just imagine the sort of match she'll make with
that Stanborough woman to guide her," Edward muttered.

"That's just *it*," Lord Lindsay said, turning to Edward
earnestly. "That's the crux of the problem. Who knows
what impulsive, unsuitable entanglements my little girl will
get herself into under the guidance of my ninnyhammer of
a sister? But if *you* were there to watch over her . . ." He
looked at Edward with a pathetically imploring expression.

"Oh, confound it, Roland, don't show me that hang-dog
look!" Edward burst out impatiently. "I'll *do* it! I'll *go*!"
He tossed the ivory knight onto the chessboard angrily, his
face a study in self-disgust. "I shall dislike every minute
of it, I suppose, but I'll go."

Lord Lindsay stared at him in surprise, relief and gratitude. "Edward, you . . . you *brick*! You're a veritable Tro-
jan, you truly are! How can I *thank* you? I . . . I don't know
what to say!"

"Don't say anything," Edward said disagreeably. He
shook his head in disbelief at his own impulsiveness and
got up from his chair. "I don't know what maggot's got
into my head. To agree to go to London, a place I utterly
abhor, to assist Corianne to find herself a husband, a position I would rather have myself, is an act of . . . of lunacy.
Absolute lunacy." He bade his host an abrupt goodnight
and started for the door.

"But shouldn't you inform Corianne of your decision
before you go?" Lord Lindsay suggested tentatively, not
wishing to push him too far.

"I'll leave that to you," Edward said. "I'm going home
to drown myself in rum."

Corianne, although not in the least *surprised* that she
had got her way again, was nevertheless quite delighted.

She immediately set about packing a number of trunks and bandboxes with all her worldly goods, an occupation that took days. In this task, she was often assisted by her friend Belinda, a tall, awkward girl with prominent teeth and a rather neighing laugh, qualities which made her unkind younger brother call her "horsey." But nature had compensated Belinda for these shortcomings by endowing her with a keenly observant eye, a sense of the ridiculous, and a large helping of common sense. And the combination of all these qualities made her stare at Corianne's numerous and ill-packed pieces of luggage with amused disapproval. "You are taking enough apparel to keep you for a *year*! I thought you said you'd been invited for only a couple of months."

"Do you think I'm taking too much?"

"No, if you intend to change your clothes six times a day," her friend said sarcastically.

"Well, they *do* change often in London . . . morning dresses, and walking dresses, and riding costumes, and dinner dresses and so on."

Belinda shrugged. "I can't pretend to know much about it—never having been invited to London myself—but *I* would find it embarrassing to arrive at *my* aunt's house with four trunks and a mountain of bandboxes and portmanteaux."

"Would you really?" Corianne surveyed the assembled luggage with sudden apprehension. "Perhaps you're right. I wouldn't want my aunt to disapprove . . . Very well, then, let's go over everything and decide what to leave behind."

"But you've just spent three days *packing* all this!" Belinda objected as, with a sigh of resignation, she knelt beside a trunk and began to pull out the contents. The girls engaged in long and serious debates over the importance of each item, and before long Corianne's bed was covered with discarded clothing. "I don't know what I shall do with myself when you're gone," Belinda sighed, looking over the shambles they'd made of the room. "Life will be quite dull without you. I shan't be able to waste my afternoons straightening out messes like this."

Corianne stretched wearily. "I'll miss you, too, Belinda. I shall have no one to advise me on problems of the heart."

"As if you need such advice," Belinda said scornfully.

"You *have* no problems of the heart. All the men take one look at you and fall right into your pocket."

"Well, that may not hold true in London, you know," Corianne said with unaccustomed modesty.

"Then why go? I can't say I really understand you, Cory. You can easily find yourself a husband right here. You can have your pick of anyone—even Thomas Moresby."

Corianne giggled. "I'll leave Thomas Moresby to you. I saw the way you looked at him at the assembly ball last month."

Belinda gave her braying laugh. "Perhaps I *did* take notice of him. He's far and away the most sensible of the sorry lot who attend those balls. But much good it did me to notice him—he didn't take his eyes from you during the entire evening."

"Then you should be glad to see me go. You may have him all to yourself at the next assembly."

"That's true," Belinda agreed, grinning. "It will be an interesting experience for *all* the girls at the assembly, not having you there to take the shine out of us all."

"There, you see? You won't miss me at all."

Belinda's grin faded, and she shook her head. "Nevertheless, Cory, I don't see why you find it necessary to go all the way to London to find a husband. If *I* were you, I'd stay right here and marry the Squire."

"Do you mean *Edward*?" Corianne blinked at her friend in astonishment. "You must be joking! Why, he must be well past *thirty*!"

"What does *that* signify? Have you ever really looked at him? I think he's the most attractive man in the entire county."

"Attractive? *Edward*?"

"Yes, Edward. All that sort of sinewy muscularity . . . it makes him almost handsome, if you ask me."

"Do you really think so?" Corianne asked wonderingly.

"Of course. If he'd take the notice of me that he does of you, I'd be in *transports*."

"Really, Belinda, I've never known you to talk like a goosecap before. Edward is like . . . like an *uncle*. One doesn't think of marrying one's uncle!"

"But he's *not* your uncle."

"And besides, he isn't even a *baronet*!" She looked across the room at her friend, a mischievous twinkle in her eye. "I have my eye on bigger game."

Belinda frowned. "Cory, I know that look. What are you up to? Is there someone in London you've set your eye on?"

Corianne laughed and got to her feet. Lifting her skirts, she twirled around her friend with dancing steps. "Yes, there is," she chortled, "and *he's* a *Marquis*!"

"I might have known!" Belinda shook her head in disapproval. "If you think to impress me with titles, Cory, you've mistaken your girl. Mama says that titles all sound very well on the announcements, but one has to live with the *man*."

"*This* man is quite up to his titles. He's handsome and rich and . . . oh, Belinda, he's *terribly* romantic."

Belinda's interest was caught in spite of herself. "Romantic?" she asked with a touch of eagerness. "In what way?"

"Well, if you promise on your honor not to breathe a word—!"

Belinda snorted. "Even slivers of bamboo pushed under my fingernails won't drag from my bosom the secrets of my best friend!" she declaimed with mock-heroic gestures.

Belinda sat down on the floor beside her friend and leaned close. "First," she said in a dramatic whisper, "his name is John Philip North, the Marquis of Revesne. And he's a positive *prize*! They say his fortune is *enormous*, and he's so magnificent to look at that he makes Edward Middleton look a *bumpkin* in comparison."

"I don't believe you," declared Belinda staunchly.

"True as I sit here! But the romantic part is that he's quite unattainable."

"Unattainable? Then, why—?"

"Unattainable so *far*," Corianne answered smugly. "*I* have not yet had a chance at him."

"I'm not sure I understand any of this, Cory," Belinda said, puzzled.

"Well, you see, it seems that he holds all ladies of fashion in dislike. A woman in his past must have angered him a great deal. I don't know all the details, but I've heard that, although he's taken a succession of opera dancers and other 'fancy pieces,' he treats ladies of quality with utmost disdain."

"Why, he sounds to me like a *rake*!" Belinda said, revolted.

"Yes, isn't it *delightful*? I've been told that any number of real beauties have set their caps for him, to no avail. He's said to be completely cold to their lures. In fact, they call him Frozen North."

"Good heavens! *Frozen North*? Do you call that *romantic*? He sounds to me to be positively forbidding!"

Corianne shook her head pityingly. "You haven't a touch of the romantic in your nature, have you, Belinda? What a shame. You'll miss so much that is exhilarating in life."

Belinda ignored the criticism, her mind occupied with sudden misgivings about her friend's impetuosity. "Cory, I think you're making a huge mistake. It sounds to me as if you're heading into dangerous waters."

"Thrilling, isn't it?" Cory answered, her eyes dancing.

Belinda had a strong urge to give her friend a shaking. "Thrilling! You goosecap, what makes you think *you* can melt this . . . this iceberg, if all the others could not?"

"But that's the *challenge*, don't you see? I feel like . . . like an explorer—"

"Good God, Cory, something's addled your *brain*! An *explorer*?"

"Yes, that's just the right word—explorer!" Corianne declared, striking a pose before her friend, one arm raised bravely to indicate the far horizon. "I shall sally forth with flags flying and attempt to conquer the frozen wastes where so many before have failed." She dropped her arm, giggled gleefully and gave her friend a broad wink. "And before two months have passed, I shall have planted my standard firmly in the ground and made the territory my own!"

Belinda was unimpressed. "If you ask me, Corianne Lindsay, you are about to take a wolf by the ear. Just have a care that you don't wind up being eaten alive!"

Chapter Three

On a chilly, late-September night, a tired and tight-lipped Edward tipped the footman of the Fenton Hotel, sent his man Martin off to bed and shut the door of his hotel room with a firm slam. He cast a quick look about him and groaned. The room was decorated with just the sort of baroque femininity he most disliked. Perhaps he should have taken himself to Long's, a hotel he'd heard of which was located in Clifford Street, but the Fenton was situated somewhat closer to Stanborough House (where he'd just deposited Corianne) and had therefore seemed the better choice. *Oh, well,* he thought, *this room will probably do as well as any other. I'm not likely to find any room in London to my liking.*

He tossed his portmanteau on a low chest, took off his coat and sat down at a small, uncomfortable writing table. He lit an oil lamp which stood at his elbow, trimmed the nib of the pen that stood waiting in the inkstand and began to write: *To Lord Lindsay, Daynwood Park, Lincolnshire— My dear Roland, This will be a brief report, for we have been travelling all day, and I am at the point of exhaustion. I wish only to assure you that your daughter has been deposited safely into the arms of your sister at Stanborough House. The trip brought no catastrophe, but thanks only to my assiduous guardianship of your impossible offspring, for she attracted an alarming amount of masculine admi-*

ration at every stop we made. The postboy at the Swan in Peterborough was so instantly smitten with her he dropped a trunk on his foot. Two young coxcombs in the taproom of the inn came to blows over which one of them was to open a door for her. And she actually flirted with a complete stranger who blundered into our dining room, which was supposed to be private. Can you imagine the havoc she'd have wrought if we had gone by the mail, as you suggested? I'm thankful that I followed my instincts and came in my own carriage, for it would have been the outside of enough to have had to sit in the mailcoach for two days and watch the other passengers ogling her. In any case, it will be convenient for me to have my own carriage available here in town.

I have put up here at the Fenton on St. James Street. I've been told it is a very fine hotel, but in actuality it is a noisy place with small, cramped rooms containing so many chairs and tables and furnishings that there's not a bit of bare wall to be seen. And the furniture is so elegantly dainty in design that a man of my size and bulk can approach it only with extreme caution. I sincerely hope the bed is long enough to permit me to stretch out my legs. The mattress is of the overstuffed, feathered kind that I detest, but in my weary state I shall undoubtedly find it passable enough. We shall soon see, for I am headed for it as soon as I write my name. Hoping you keep in good health, I remain yours, etc., Edward.

He threw the pen aside and sealed the letter, uncomfortably aware of its ill-humored tone. But since he was too tired to attempt to rewrite the message, and since he knew that Lord Lindsay would be eager to learn of his daughter's safe arrival (even if the letter in which the news was contained was decidedly morose), he rang for the hotel footman and arranged for the note to be dispatched. Then he rummaged in his portmanteau for a nightshirt and quickly readied himself for bed.

In spite of the feather mattress, he was almost instantly asleep. If it were not for the fact that he had a most unpleasant dream—in which he lost Corianne in a crowded city street full of leering men—he would have had to admit that he'd passed a surprisingly comfortable night.

Corianne's spirits on *her* first night in London were a good deal happier than those of her guardian. Her aunt Laurelia and her cousin Sarah welcomed her most affectionately and gave not the slightest sign that they felt any resentment at having been coerced into inviting her. Sarah was most kind when she showed Corianne to the lovely rose-colored bedroom in which she'd stayed two years before, chatting pleasantly about some of the people Corianne had met on her earlier visit and complimenting her most flatteringly on her appearance. Then, after she'd washed up, her aunt called her down to partake of a late supper, during which both her hostesses made every effort to make her feel at home.

Aunt Laurelia described to Corianne in some detail the numerous plans she'd made for the girl's entertainment—a program which was to begin the very next day with a luncheon at Lady Howard's and an evening at the opera in the company of a few of Lady Stanborough's friends. The girl nearly burst with excitement but had to admit that she was not certain she would be permitted to attend.

"But why not, my dear child?" Lady Stanborough asked in surprise.

"You see, Edward made me promise I would not go out until he'd had a chance to speak to you."

"Edward? Who's Edward?" her aunt inquired. "Is he the gentleman who brought you?"

"Yes, he is."

"Well, what has *he* to say to anything, may I ask?"

Corianne made a face. "He has *everything* to say, I'm afraid. You see, Papa would not permit me to come to London unescorted, and he asked his friend—he's Squire Middleton, you know, whose land marches along with ours—to come with me as a sort of guardian."

"*Guardian?* I never heard of such an arrangement! Do you mean the man will be supervising your activities during your stay?"

"Yes, I suppose so," Corianne admitted.

Lady Stanborough's finely pencilled eyebrows rose in offended dignity. "Does your father think that *my* guardianship will not be good enough?" she demanded.

"Come now, Mama, don't get on your high ropes," Sarah

put in. "My uncle has quite understandable qualms about permitting his lovely daughter to gallivant about London with only two weak females to protect her. I think it was very wise of him to provide Corianne with a masculine protector."

"Nonsense," her mother said, refusing to be mollified. "I don't see why he found it necessary to do so *now,* when he didn't do it two years ago when Cory came here for her come-out."

I don't see why, either," Corianne said with a sigh.

"But I do," Sarah insisted. "You see, Cory, now that you've been presented, you have more freedom to go about than you had before. Not only that, but your last visit was for a month only, and part of that time your father was here with you."

"That's true," Corianne said. "And Edward, too."

"Edward?" Sarah asked, looking at Corianne interestedly. "This Edward—did he come down for your presentation ball?"

"Oh, yes. He's a very old friend of the family, you see."

"Well, I certainly don't like this arrangement," Lady Stanborough grumbled. "He'll probably be a crotchety nuisance, telling us where we may or may not take you."

"Oh, Edward isn't like that, I assure you, Aunt. Besides, I can handle him."

"I hope so, child," her aunt replied. "There's nothing I detest so much as being plagued by an overbearing old man."

Sarah kept silent, but a little smile played about the corners of her mouth. If her suspicions were correct, Corianne's "guardian" was not nearly so old as her mother believed.

Before she went to sleep, Corianne, like Edward, penned a letter to Lord Lindsay. *Dear Papa,* she wrote, *It is very Late, and I should be abed, but I shall take only a Moment to write a few lines to tell you that we've Arrived Safely. It was a most Enjoyable Trip, everyone along the way being very Kind and Attentive to me from the lowliest postboy to the very grand Gentleman who happened into our dining room at the Swan and exchanged a few Pleasantries with us. I am only sorry that we didn't travel by Mail as*

*you suggested, so that I could have had more People to talk
to than only Edward, who was usually in the Sullens and
answered my remarks with only Monosyllables. But I didn't
mind, because there was so much to See and to Think about
that the time really flew. And now I am Here at last!*

*Aunt Laurelia and Sarah have been most Kind and Wel-
coming and have given me the Rose Bedroom again, a room
which I particularly like for its Ornate Furnishings and
wonderful feather bed. I'm sure that they would have sent
their Best if they had known I was writing you.*

*Well, Papa, I shall say Goodnight, even though I don't
think I shall sleep a Wink knowing that London lies right
outside my window. Thank you again for Letting me Come.
Your Most Loving Corianne.*

By the time Corianne climbed into bed, the clock in the
hallway was striking two. She was asleep before the sound
of the chimes had faded away.

Sarah, in the bedroom down the hall, found sleep more
difficult to capture. She couldn't keep herself from wondering if Corianne's *Edward* was indeed the fascinating
gentleman who had come to her rescue that night two years
ago and whose face was so indelibly etched on a page of
her memory. Edward Middleton. If Corianne's escort were
truly the man she remembered, the name suited him. But
why had she jumped to the conclusion that Edward Middleton and her erstwhile rescuer were one and the same?
Just because in each case the man had been described as
"a neighbor from Lincolnshire"?

Of course, how many neighbors could one have in such
a remote, thinly populated area? And of the few neighbors
one might have, how many would be *bachelors*? (The man
was obviously a bachelor if he was free to leave his home
to jaunt to London in Corianne's wake.) These were the
clues that led Sarah to believe that Edward Middleton was
the man.

On the other hand, the gentleman she remembered had
been completely besotted over Corianne. Would such a man
be likely to escort the girl to London to help her accomplish
what was obviously her purpose—to catch herself a husband? No, it was not at all reasonable to think a man would
cooperate in a program designed to destroy his hopes.

Therefore, it was quite possible that Sarah was lying awake and troubling her mind about nothing.

But if Edward Middleton *did* turn out to be the man, it could certainly be an awkward moment for Sarah when they met again. If he *remembered* the humiliating situation in which they'd last met, she would be hideously embarrassed; if he did *not* remember it, it would be even *more* painful to her, for it would be devastating to realized that she'd made no impression on the man at all!

She tossed about in bed, realizing that she was upsetting herself for very little cause. Nevertheless, if Edward Middleton *should* turn out to be the unknown rescuer, and if he *should* show signs of remembering the dreadful scene at which they'd met, Sarah felt the need to prepare herself. If she could only find the right words to say when she greeted him on the morrow—something carefree and witty and casual—she could ride smoothly over a potentially mortifying moment. But how *should* she greet him? Should she use the straightforward, direct approach? ("How do you do, Mr. Middleton? It's been so long since you rescued me from ravishment in a back room. *Do* let me offer you my belated thanks.") Well, *that* would hardly do.

Should she pretend to have forgotten the entire matter? ("Squire Middleton, you say? No, I'm sorry, but I can't say I remember you at all. *Where* did you say we'd met before?") But she couldn't carry that off. She disliked that sort of insincerity.

Should she brazen it out with a joke? ("You say you rescued me from the advances of a *bounder*? Oh, *la*, my dear man, someone's *always* doing that!") She giggled to herself, but she knew that such a remark was too unladylike.

Nothing she could think of seemed suitable. After struggling with the problem for most of the night, she decided to banish the subject from her mind. She would leave the entire matter to fate . . . where in truth the matter had always been anyway.

Chapter Four

CORIANNE WAS IN a state of quivering agitation the next morning. If only Edward would make an appearance before noon, so that she would have a chance to convince him to permit her to go to Lady Howard's luncheon! If he did not come in time, Lady Stanborough would leave without her, and she would be forced to spend the afternoon either at home with her cousin Sarah or on a sightseeing tour with Edward. She didn't know which of those two choices would be the greater bore! At the luncheon, on the other hand, she would be able to meet Lady Howard's splendid guests, she would play a card game or two, she might find an opportunity to begin a flirtation, and she'd undoubtedly receive an invitation from someone for some other festivity. It was a chance to begin the social "round"—and *that*, after all, was the reason she'd come to London.

Calculatingly, Corianne dressed herself in her best jaconet round-gown (its ruffled collar admirably accenting the curves of her breasts, and the azure color accenting her remarkable eyes), knowing that Edward particularly liked this dress and would more easily be persuaded to permit her to go. Then she waited in the drawing room in agonizing suspense for the sound of his carriage to arrive at the door.

As noon approached, her nervousness increased. With a kind of desperate optimism, she picked up her hat and went to the mirror which hung over a table near the door.

It was the perfect bonnet to wear at an elegant luncheon: a straw-colored bergère hat with a thick, softly curled blue feather pinned to the front. She put on the hat, tied it in place with a blue satin ribbon and smiled at her reflection with satisfaction, Edward would never be able to refuse her now! If *only* he would *arrive*!

She resumed her pacing, crossing from the window to the doorway (stopping at the former to look out for Edward's carriage and at the latter to listen for her aunt's footsteps), the enticing little plume on her hat bobbing impatiently as she moved. The clock in the hallway struck noon, and shortly afterward she heard a step on the stair. The sound made her wince—her aunt was ready to leave. She flew to the doorway to try to persuade her aunt to wait a few more minutes, but it was only Sarah who was descending the stairs. "Oh, Sarah!" Cory cried in perturbation. "He hasn't yet arrived!"

Sarah patted the girl's shoulder sympathetically. "Don't worry about it, Cory. If you *should* have to miss the luncheon, it will not be so dreadful. I always find Lady Howard's luncheons to be quite tedious."

"*Tedious!* How can you say so? The one I attended when I was last here was perfectly *thrilling*!"

Sarah smiled and shook her head. "Well, you were much younger then. It is quite possible you will feel differently now that you're a grown-up young woman of twenty."

Corianne looked at her cousin doubtfully. "Will I? That is hard to believe. Sarah, do come into the drawing room with me and keep me company. I'm as nervous as a cat."

Sarah hesitated. "Well, I *had* intended to go to the study to work on the household accounts . . ." she demurred. The truth was that Sarah intended to hide away until Edward had paid his call and left. She had not had a pleasant morning and had finally decided that the better part of valor was to retreat.

She had arisen earlier with every intention of dressing with special care and facing the meeting with Edward with all the charm and self-confidence at her disposal. But when she'd looked into her mirror and had seen the damage her sleepless night had done to her appearance, she'd been considerably discouraged. Her eyes were darkly underlined, and her cheeks seemed almost ghostly. To add to her frustration, her hair resisted all attempts to tame it into a semblance of neatness. She'd tried three different arrangements, all without success, and had finally given up in discouragement, piled it on top of her head, pinned it firmly and covered it over with her cap. Then, since she already looked so old-cattish, she had pulled out of her wardrobe the morning dress she liked least in the world—a loosely fitting, faded yellow muslin—and had made up her mind to hide from the world for the rest of the day.

She'd breakfasted in her room, spent the morning with the housekeeper mending linen in the little sewing room on the third floor, and had then determined to pass the entire afternoon with her account books. Now Corianne was asking her to sit with her in the most public room of the house, where Edward Middleton would be certain to be shown the moment he arrived! It would be quite rude of her to refuse Corianne's request for her company, but surely fate did not intend for her to have to face the gentleman looking her very worst!

But fate is not to be anticipated easily. Her mother's footsteps on the landing above them gave her a blessed reprieve. "Oh, there's Mama," she said to Corianne in relief. "She'll keep you company, I'm sure." And without giving Corianne a chance to reply, she whisked herself down the hall to the study.

Lady Stanborough appeared at the top of the stairs, her costume indicating that she was quite ready to leave. Her bonnet was in place, her velvet spencer had already been thrown over her shoulders, and she was buttoning the last button of her glove. Corianne's hopes were completely dashed. But the knocker sounded at that very moment— Edward had arrived in the nick of time! He handed his hat to the butler just when Lady Stanborough reached the bottom step. "*Edward!*" Corianne clarioned ecstatically.

Lady Stanborough stared at the gentleman in considerable surprise. "You *can't* be Squire Middleton!" she exclaimed.

Edward grinned broadly. "That news comes as a great shock to me, ma'am. I've spent many years under the impression that I was."

"But . . . Corianne gave me to understand that you were quite *elderly*."

Edward's grin became mocking as he threw Corianne a sardonic look. "Did she indeed?" he asked drily.

Corianne giggled and ran to him eagerly. "I *never* said you were elderly," she whispered as she enveloped him in a hug of delighted relief. "I'm so *glad* you've come. I was beginning to be afraid I would have to spend the entire *day* at the window watching for you."

Lady Stanborough, while waiting for her niece to complete her effusive greeting, used the time to examine the Squire from the top of his cropped hair to the bottom of his blunt-toed boots. The man was certainly a surprise to her. In spite of his coat (which had obviously *not* been cut by a London tailor), his britches (which were far from being in the latest mode), and his boots (which were so worn that they might almost have been termed *shabby*), the man was really quite presentable. Very attractive, in fact. If he could be made a little less "countrified" in his manner of dress, he might be very useful to have on call. It was always far more pleasant to attend evening functions under the escort of an impressive man than to arrive unescorted. Perhaps his presence in London might be less of a nuisance than she'd thought.

The gentleman having acknowledged Corianne's puppy-like greeting with avuncular propriety, Lady Stanborough advanced on him with her hand outstretched. "Well, well, Mr. Middleton, how delightful that you've come in time. I understand you wish to speak to me before Corianne and I go out this afternoon."

"Yes, Lady Stanborough, if you can spare me a moment or two."

"Several, my dear sir, several. Come into the drawing room, and we shall have a comfortable coz. You must tell me how my brother does. I've not had a word from the man in months."

Edward hesitated. "I wonder, ma'am," he said, throwing a look at Corianne which told her plainly he wanted her to leave, "if our . . . er . . . interview could be private."

Corianne, who had already crossed the threshold of the drawing room, pouted. "I don't see what you have to say to my very own aunt that I can't hear."

Edward glared at her and then turned to Lady Stanborough. "You must excuse Corianne, your ladyship. I only hope you will not believe, from her example, that country manners are so unequal to those of town."

"Mr. Middleton is quite right, my dear," Lady Stanborough told Corianne flatly. "One must take the greatest care not to appear in the least vulgar."

Corianne lifted her chin haughtily. "I was not aware that expressing one's feelings was vulgar. I apologize, Aunt Laurelia."

"There's no need, my love," Lady Stanborough assured her. "Just excuse us for a few minutes. I'd be much obliged if in the meantime you'd try to find Sarah and tell her I wish her to make herself known to Mr. Middleton."

Corianne nodded and curtseyed, but her expression remained piqued. Edward ignored it and followed his hostess into the drawing room, turning to close the door behind him and flashing a teasing grin at the irritated Corianne before shutting her from view.

Lady Stanborough sat down on her favorite striped-satin loveseat. "Well, sir, what is it you wished to tell me that Corianne should not hear?" she asked frankly, motioning Edward to the wing chair opposite.

He took his seat and looked at her in some awkwardness. "I feel you deserve some explanation of my position here, Lady Stanborough. I've escorted Miss Lindsay here at her father's request. He feels that she is too young and inexperienced to be left to her own devices in London, and he's asked me to . . . how can I put this? . . . keep a fatherly eye on her."

Lady Stanborough fumed. "My brother is an overstrung, jittery *fidget*! Doesn't he think *me* capable of taking proper care of his precious babe?"

Edward had anticipated just this sort of reaction and was quite prepared to deal with it. "Of course he does, ma'am. You misjudge him. You see, he surmised—being quite familiar with Cory's little tricks—that the girl had wormed her invitation out of you. He wishes me to tell you how grateful he is to you for your kindness in granting her this London holiday, but the last thing in the world he wants is for you to take on the same burden you so obligingly assumed during the month of her presentation."

Lady Stanborough visibly softened. "But I *enjoyed* supervising her. I told him so a dozen times!"

"Nevertheless, Lord Lindsay was extremely reluctant to ask you to put yourself out a second time. It was only when I offered my services as a sort of . . . guardian, you might say . . . that he agreed to let her come."

"Well, I suppose one could consider it thoughtful of him, but I don't see, Mr. Middleton, how this business is to be contrived. I hope you don't expect me to ask your approval for every invitation I accept in Corianne's name or for every outing on which I take her!"

Edward smiled at her reassuringly. "Of course not, ma'am. I don't mean to be in your way at all. But I *would* like your permission to call on Corianne every few days, to take her riding or to escort her on any little errands you may wish her to execute for you. In that way I can learn about her activities and report to her father that all is well. And, of course, I am instructed to handle all matters of expense which she may incur. Lord Lindsay is quite aware of the problem involved in the supervision of a volatile young girl. He hopes that my presence nearby will make dealing with them easier for you. I'm staying at the Fenton, which is not far from here. You may count on my assistance or advice whenever you have need of it."

Edward had accented the positive advantages to her of his presence, and though she was not quick-witted, Lady Stanborough could see that he might be an asset to her. "Would you be willing also to lend us your company for an occasional service as escort?" she asked, looking at him measuringly.

"I am entirely at your service."

She smiled. "Well, then, Mr. Middleton, I must say you have quite won me over. I admit that when I first heard about you, I was considerably put out. But perhaps things may turn out very well indeed."

"I hope so, ma'am." He rose to leave. "Please feel free to call on me at any time," he assured her, bending over her hand.

She looked up at him with a sudden impulse. "*Tonight,*
then!" she said, half to herself.

"Tonight?"

"Yes. The opera. Can you escort us tonight?"

"Well, yes, if you wish."

"Delightful. Eight-thirty?"

He bowed. "My carriage will be at your door."

"Oh? You have your own carriage?" She bit her lip as
her momentary euphoria dissolved in a wave of doubt. What
if the man's carriage were as shabby as his boots? "There
is no need for you to trouble, you know. *My* man can pick
you up."

"It's no trouble at all, Lady Stanborough," Edward said,
eyeing her shrewdly.

Lady Stanborough became distinctly uneasy. She would
rather *die* than be discovered at the entrance of the Covent
Garden Opera House alighting from a hired hack or an
outmoded, lumbering equipage! "Will you . . . er . . . have
room for us *all*, Mr. Middleton? My daughter intends to
make one of the party, and that, I believe, makes four."

Edward understood just what troubled her and, being too
kindhearted to tease her on the subject, decided to set her
mind at ease. "My coach is quite capable of carrying four,
ma'am," he assured her. "I had it from Tattersall's, you
know, only a year ago. I think you'll find it to your liking."

"I *will*?" she asked in considerable relief. "How lovely."
But as her daughter had often noted, she tended to latch on
to an idea hammer and tongs once it struck her. Mr. Middleton had shabby boots, and therefore he might be guilty
of committing other solecisms. While she didn't mind his
country clothing *now*, she might find it objectionable before
her friends. As she rose to show him the door, she couldn't
resist remarking, "Of course you *do* realize, Mr. Middleton,
that full dress is required at the opera."

A corner of his mouth twitched. "I believe that I'd heard
something to that effect up in Lincolnshire, ma'am," he
said.

The irony passed over her. She merely smiled and patted
his hand. "Good," she said, hoping his dress clothes were
better than his daytime rig.

* * *

In the meantime, Corianne was having a good deal of difficulty trying to persuade her cousin to come to meet her guardian. Poor Sarah had tried every excuse she could think of, but Corianne had an answer for each one. At last, she'd pointed out that she was not properly attired to receive visitors. "Oh, pooh!" Corianne insisted. "No one cares about that. I'll wager Edward won't even notice."

He undoubtedly won't, Sarah thought in self-disgust. Next to the dewy loveliness of her cousin, she looked positively insipid. But it was too late to improve matters now, and it seemed impossible to avoid giving in to Corianne's importunities. With a helpless shrug, she put away her papers and rose from her desk. "Very well, Cory, I'll go with you," she said dolefully.

Corianne had little patience with her cousin's reluctant pace. She grasped Sarah's hand and pulled her down the hall. Lady Stanborough and Edward were just emerging from the drawing room when the cousins came upon them. "Oh, you're *finished*," Cory chirruped happily. "Good. If we hurry, Aunt Laurelia, we shan't be very late."

"Don't worry, love," Lady Stanborough said calmly. "Everyone arrives late at London gatherings. Ah, there you are, Sarah. Don't stand there in the shadows like a gawk. Come and meet Corianne's Squire. Mr. Middleton, my daughter Sarah."

Sarah tried to keep her head lowered, even though her posture reminded her of the dreadfully awkward granddaughter of their cook who, when she'd been brought up to the drawing room to "meet the family," had come forward in miserable shyness and had hung her head in this very same way. Of course, *that* girl could be excused for her behavior—she was only fifteen and getting her first glimpse of the "nobility." Sarah, on the other hand, was twenty-seven, a woman of considerable sophistication, who had met the *Prince Regent* on more than one occasion without the least inner perturbation. What excuse had *she* for standing about like a frightened housemaid?

"How do you do, Miss Stanborough?" Edward said politely, noting that the young woman seemed to be even more withdrawn than he'd expected.

Sarah dropped a curtsey and gave him a quick, sharp glance. She'd noticed at once that he *was* her rescuer, and the knowledge made her even more tremulous. She'd listened carefully to his voice when he'd greeted her, but she couldn't determine from his words whether or not he remembered her. The one sharp look, however, was enough to reveal that he had not a spark of recognition in his eyes.

Surprisingly, this fact relieved her tension. She straightened up, feeling quite capable of responding to his greeting at last. But before she could say a word, Corianne stepped between them, throwing her arms about Edward's neck. "We've got to *go*, Edward," she said impatiently, planting a kiss on his cheek. "Thank you for coming. I hope you aren't miffed with me for dashing off like this, but if we don't go soon, we will be dreadfully late, won't we, Aunt Laurelia?"

He laughed and removed himself from her clutches. "Go ahead, Miss Prattlebox. I shall see quite enough of you tonight at the opera."

"She's a veritable whirlwind, isn't she?" Lady Stanborough said indulgently as Corianne pulled her to the door. "Good afternoon, Mr. Middleton. Until eight-thirty."

They were gone. Left alone with Edward, Sarah's heart began to hammer as if she were a green girl again. Should she ask him to stay to tea? Perhaps in the quiet of Corianne's wake, she could recover her senses and become capable of making adult conversation with the man.

She glanced up at him again. He was looking at the door through which Corianne had just disappeared, a faint smile still playing about his lips, as if a little bit of Corianne still lingered in the hallway. Sarah almost sighed aloud . . . the poor fool was still afflicted with the same besotted affection for that silly and selfish girl that he'd displayed two years ago.

Sarah took a deep breath to steel herself to invite him to remain for a cup of tea or even a bite of luncheon, but he suddenly turned and smiled at her with abstracted politeness. "I'm afraid I've taken you from some occupation, Miss Stanborough," he said.

"Oh, no, no," she said hastily. "Not at all—"

"You are very kind, ma'am, but I fear I *have* disturbed you. Let me not take any more of your time. I wish you a very good day." He made a hasty bow, picked up his hat from the table near the door and left.

Sarah stood motionless for a moment while a quick succession of bewildering emotions swept over her. The first was a wave of inexplicable anger. The fellow had treated her as if she were a veritable dowd! She might just as well have been a strip of faded wallpaper hanging in the corner of the room! But she immediately realized she'd brought it on herself. It had been *her* choice to hang back as inconspicuously as possible, so why should she be so angered at *him*?

Her illogical anger was soon followed by an assault of self-pity. It was no wonder he'd cut her—what could one *expect* when one's bloom was gone, when one was past twenty-seven and dressed in a shapeless, faded gown and an old-maidish cap?

But finally, from some inner wellspring of resourcefulness and good sense, a laugh bubbled up to the surface. The entire scene was quite funny, really. The drama which she'd rehearsed with such agitation the night before had taken place, and it had proved anti-climactic in the extreme. For all the notice her *hero* had taken of her, that dreadful occurrence at the come-out ball might never have taken place!

She laughed aloud—a somewhat bitter laugh, to be sure—as she crossed the hallway to the stairs. All the adroit, sophisticated, self-assured remarks she'd rehearsed—how ridiculously futile that sleepless night had been! He'd said his how-d'ye-dos, and she'd said . . . *nothing*! She laughed again and started up the stairs. In her room, she dropped wearily on the little bench before her dressing table and looked at herself in disgust. "Well, Miss Stanborough," she told her reflection, "I must congratulate you. You were brilliant, positively brilliant."

Her eyes lit upon the innocent little cap perched on her head. Suddenly it seemed unspeakably offensive. "As for you," she said aloud to the irritating headpiece, snatching it off furiously, "you've brought me no good at all! Where is the maturity, the serenity, the acceptance of reality which you're intended to symbolize? Do you know how I intend to punish you? Nothing less than *banishment*!" She threw the cap into a lower drawer and slammed it shut.

"For a couple of months, anyway," she added sheepishly.

Chapter Five

LADY STANBOROUGH'S DRESSER emerged from Sarah's bed-room with a look of startled satisfaction on her face—Miss Sarah had suddenly requested her services to dress her hair this evening! Miss Sarah had always dressed her own hair except on one or two occasions of very special importance. But what was so special about tonight, the dresser wondered, to have caused Miss Sarah to ask for her assistance? It was only the opera, after all.

Of course, this often-wished-for development *would* come at a time when she was terribly rushed, what with having to attend to her ladyship and the visiting niece as well. Nevertheless the pleased dresser looked forward to the challenge. If any dresser in London could handle three heads in one evening, she could!

The energetic little woman called herself Madame Marie, but the French appellation was only recently acquired. The closest Madame Marie had ever come to France was an outing to an eastern suburb of London. But Madame truly believed that everything French was more stylish, more elegant, more chic than its British counterpart. Paris was the *beau monde*, the *dernier cri* . . . and the determined Miss Mary Dabbs of Finsbury, who was gifted with a talent for styling hair and had an eye toward improving her station in life, had become Madame Marie Antoinette Honore Dabbs when she'd applied for her first post.

If the various ladies who employed her were bemused by the French name and the French words which were interspersed in her vocabulary (for Madame Marie had acquired a French dictionary which she studied in her spare time) and pronounced with a native Londoner's accent, they made no comment. For whatever her eccentricities, Madame Marie was a *find*.

The culmination of her career was her present post as dresser to the stylish Lady Stanborough. Except for the housekeeper and the butler, she was the highest-paid member of the household staff. Her ladyship found Madame's services completely indispensible. She'd often confided to friends that she wouldn't know how she'd get on if she lost Madame Marie. She'd sooner do without her cook!

Madame Marie was quite content with her post, but she had to admit that she'd been finding it somewhat dull of late. Lady Stanborough insisted that her hair be dressed in the same way each day—a complicated arrangement in which the popular curls-over-the-ears were kept to a minimum, and the rest of the hair was piled on top to make her ladyship appear taller. At first, the styling had been challenging, but it was no longer so, and Madame Marie yearned for a chance to exercise her considerable creativity. How delightful that tonight she would have that opportunity. What a *bon chance*!

But as she walked down the hall to the back stairs, she rubbed the side of her very English nose in bafflement. She must discuss this matter with Cook. There *had* to be a good reason for Miss Sarah's about-face. What was so special about a night at the opera to cause Miss Sarah to feel this sudden *souci* about her appearance? After wearing that hideous old-maid's cap for almost a month, why was Miss Sarah suddenly desirous of blossoming out? If Madame Marie knew anything about life, she'd wager there was a new man in the picture. *L'amour*. It was always the cause.

Earlier that afternoon, Sarah had seriously considered changing her plans and remaining at home. Facing Edward Middleton's disregard once that day was quite enough to bear. But the opera that evening was to be Handel's *Radamisto*, an opera she had not heard, and she'd looked forward to it eagerly. Why should she permit herself to go into a taking over an incident which no one else had even noticed—and miss the music because of something she'd merely built up in her own mind?

No, she would not change her plans. She would attend the opera, hold her head up and enjoy herself. She must not let Edward Middleton (blast him!) upset her equilibrium. Since he was to escort them this evening, Sarah determined to make as impressive an appearance as possible. She knew that she was not in her first bloom, nor would she win his notice beside the radiant appearance of the bewitching Corianne, but neither would she cringe in the shadow as she had earlier this afternoon. She was Sarah Stanborough, a person of considerable worth, and she intended to behave as if she believed it.

Madame Marie, having decided with Cook that Miss Sarah had taken an interest in a likely gentleman at last, gave the others short shrift that evening so that she could devote herself to turning Miss Sarah out in proper style. She entered Sarah's bedroom shortly after six, bearing a tray of soup, cold meat and tea. She'd informed Lady Stanborough that it was unlikely that Miss Sarah would have time to come down to dinner if she was expected to be ready to leave at eight-thirty.

If Lady Stanborough had been surprised at her daughter's sudden desire to beautify herself, she had given no sign. "Do what you can with her, Madame," she'd said placidly, and she'd dismissed the dresser apparently without another thought.

Madame Marie found Sarah still undressed, staring indecisively at a number of gowns which she'd laid out on her bed. "Oh, wear the burgundy, Miss," the dresser urged eagerly. "It's *tres belle*! It'll bring color to y'r cheeks, which, if ye don't mind me *parleyin'* to ye, you sorely need."

"Do you think the *burgundy*?" Sarah asked dubiously. "It's a bit too rakish, isn't it? I was thinking of this one." She held up a gown of lustrous Persian silk the color of deep topaz.

The maid put her head to one side and considered the gown carefully. "It's darker than *I'd* choose, but let's see it on ye." And she bustled Sarah into it and hooked it up in a twinkling. Then, stepping back and squinting at Sarah for a long moment, she nodded admiringly. "Ye've a good instinct, Miss Sarah. It's a proper eye-catcher. *Charmant*! Makes y'r pale color look . . . well, *ravissant.*"

The dress had puffed half-sleeves which cunningly enhanced the provocativeness of the low-cut bodice. Madame Marie decided at once that the most effective hairstyle would be one in which Sarah's thick hair was drawn up and away from the neck, so that, by being left completely bare, its slender grace would be emphasized. "Now, Miss, just leave everythin' else to *moi*," she ordered, urging Sarah to take a seat beside the dressing table but facing away from the mirror. She touched the thick hair here and there with her special pomade and brushed it in. She bound the now-shiny tresses tightly at the back of Sarah's head, twisting them into one thick curl which she permitted to fall over Sarah's left shoulder. Then she freed a number of little tendrils of hair around the face and let them curl as they would.

"May I use a *soupçon* of blackin' on y'r lashes, Miss?" she asked, tilting Sarah's face up to scrutinize it with professional dispassion.

"I am entirely in your hands," Sarah said, throwing caution to the winds.

A few other touches, from various pots and jars which Madame produced from the pockets of her voluminous apron, and she nodded with satisfaction. Then she added only a pair of topaz earrings to Sarah's costume, tossed a gauzy shawl over her shoulders and pronounced her ready.

Sarah turned and stared into her mirror in considerable astonishment. She found it difficult to believe that the face looking back at her was the same one she'd seen that morning. This person had pale skin and shadowed eyes, too, but they seemed strangely luminous. Her hair and dress, in dark contrast to her skin, gave her an air of drama and mystery. There was a bit of the Lorelei in those eyes, a touch of the tantalizer in the shadowed curves of her breasts. "Madame Marie, you are a *genius*!" she breathed.

Madame Marie, looking at her handiwork with satisfaction, almost said absently, "That I am." But she caught herself in time, smiled broadly and bobbed a quick curtsey.

However, before she left the room, she couldn't resist remarking, "If anyone was to ask me, Miss Sarah, I'd say you look a proper *Parisienne*, and that's a fact."

Edward had already arrived when Sarah came down the stairs. He'd been carefully checked by Lady Stanborough, who found—to her immense relief—that his evening clothes, while obviously not cut by a tailor the caliber of Weston or Stultz, fit him well; that his shirt points, while not high enough to be the epitome of fashion, were properly stiff; that his neckcloth, while not tied in a fold of particular originality, was presentable; and that his evening shoes were completely beyond reproach. If only his coach turned out to be satisfactory, her evening would be made.

So eager was her ladyship to get a glimpse of the carriage that she took hardly any notice of her daughter's altered appearance. "Ah, Sarah," she said, crossing to the foot of the stairway impatiently, "there you are at last. Hurry with your cloak, my dear, for it will not do to keep the Squire's horses standing."

"Good *Lord*," Edward exclaimed, sotto voce, to Corianne, who was standing just behind him looking into the mirror near the door, "that can't be Miss Stanborough, can it?"

Corianne, whose blonde curls had been gathered up in charming profusion at the nape of her neck and bound with a chaplet of tea roses, was studying in the mirror the effect on the flowers of a toss of her curls. Preoccupied with the problem of the stability of the wreath, she merely cast a look over her shoulder at the stairway. "Of course it's Sarah," she responded uninterestedly. "Who else should it be?"

Edward, however, couldn't help but gape. The young woman descending the stairway looked remarkably lovely and self-possessed. It was hard to believe that the unobtrusive, retiring, awkward Miss Stanborough he'd met earlier could have so transformed herself.

As the butler helped Sarah with her cloak, Lady Stanborough found time to look at her. "Well, I must say, Sarah, Madame Marie has done well by you. Your hair is charming."

This caught Corianne's attention. "Why, so it *is*!" she

exclaimed. "It's very becoming, Sarah, really. I must ask
Madame to fix *mine* so one of these days."

As Edward ushered the ladies down the stone steps to
his waiting carriage (which turned out to be most acceptable
to Lady Stanborough—she was almost ecstatic to see the
spotless sheen of the side panels, the gleaming brass fittings
of the lamps, and the plush grey velvet luxury of the upholstery inside), he found himself wondering about the conversation he'd overheard. The ladies had merely complimented Miss Stanborough on her hair. Could that be all?
Was her transformation merely the result of a new way of
dressing her *hair*? He couldn't credit it. This afternoon,
Miss Stanborough had seemed to him almost ungainly.
Could a hairstyle transform a gawkish insipidity into *that*?
He must have been blind, earlier.

He took his place in the carriage and glanced at her
again. She was smiling faintly at Corianne's incessant and
excited chatter, her head erect, her body leaning back
against the squabs in poised relaxation, her eyes dark and
intriguingly secret. He shook his head in amazement.
Women were always and ever a mystery to him.

Lord North had many acquaintances, but few intimates.
Of late, however, the gossips noted that he appeared every-
where in the company of young Anthony Ingalls, second
son of the impecunious Lord Bentwood. Ingalls, a fellow
of loose morals and a hedonistic disposition, had made
himself notorious for his debts and his excesses by the
remarkably young age of twenty-four. Those gossips who
were not well acquainted with Lord North may have wondered why he'd taken up with an unsavory character who
was almost ten years his junior, but those who understood
North's character were less puzzled. Lord North had always
been susceptible to sycophancy, and Anthony Ingalls knew
well how to play the courtier. He had the not-inconsiderable
ability to show constant admiration to the older man without
the slightest touch of self-abasement; and he could make
himself agreeable without the least air of the lackey in his
manner. In return for this pleasant companionship, John
Philip North, the wealthy Marquis of Revesne, could be

counted on to foot the bills for their various activities and amusements.

Their amusements tonight were to begin quite late, and to pass the time they put in an appearance at Covent Garden. Before the curtain rose on the spectacular Handel opera, the two gentlemen looked up from the pit at the occupants of the boxes to determine their targets for the first intermission. "I *say*, Jack," Ingalls remarked eagerly after a moment, "who's the little beauty in the box next to the Howards?"

John North lifted his pearl-handled opera glasses and turned them in the direction his friend had indicated. Suddenly he seemed to stiffen. "Good God!" he muttered.

Anthony Ingalls grinned. "Yes, I quite agree. She *does* take one's breath away in that yellow confection she's wearing."

"What yellow confection?" North asked, still staring up through the glasses. "I should call it bronze . . . or rather, topaz."

Ingalls looked at his friend in some bafflement. "Where *are* you looking, old fellow?" he demanded.

There was a moment of silence, for North hadn't paid any heed to his friend's remark. Abstractedly, he lowered the glasses and stared straight ahead of him, his brow wrinkled. Ingalls observed this strange behavior for a moment and then reached over and removed the opera glasses from North's hand. Putting them to his eyes, he looked up at the box with renewed interest. "I'd certainly like to pass in the way of that yellow rose," he murmured. "I wonder who she is."

"It's her cousin from Lincolnshire, I believe," North said absently. "Linley, or Lindsay, if recollection serves."

"*Whose* cousin?" Ingalls asked curiously, lowering the opera glasses. "The dark one there?"

"Yes. Sarah Stanborough."

"Aha!" Ingalls said in sudden understanding. He lifted the glasses and turned his gaze to the box again. "So *that's* the unobtainable Sarah."

"I haven't laid eyes on her in months," North muttered, half to himself. "I'd heard she'd become almost a recluse." He took back the glasses and looked through them again.

"Yet there she sits, even more fascinating than ever. I wonder what's drawn her out."

"Look here, Jack," Ingalls asked in an interested amazement, "you don't mean to suggest that you're in *love* with the lady!"

North smiled coldly. "Love? Love is a sickness which afflicts only dolts and weaklings. I am merely . . . tantalized."

"Are you? After all these years?"

North favored his companion with a look of scorn. "Tony, my boy, I sometimes fear that you're too young for real intimacy with a man of my years. How can I explain this to a callow youth? She *refused* me, don't you see?" His eyes glittered icily. "I am not often refused, you know."

"I should think not," Ingalls quickly agreed. "The lady must be a fool."

"If she were a fool, I should not have asked her. No, she has all her wits about her, and yet she refused me. Hence the fascination."

"I see," murmured Tony, quite at a loss. They fell silent, each using the pause to glance up at the box again. "In any case, Jack, I must admit that I find the yellow rosebud more to my taste."

North shrugged. "I'm not surprised. It's another indication of your callow nature. Would you like to meet the rosebud?"

"Rather! Is it possible for you to arrange it?"

North smiled enigmatically across the theater at the all-unknowing occupants of the box. "As soon as the first act concludes, you shall meet your little tea rose. And I . . . my fascinating . . . er . . . topaz."

Chapter Six

THE MUSIC WAS GLORIOUS, the costumes splendid, and the scenery spectacular, but for Corianne the first act ran on much too long. As soon as the curtain fell, she leaped from her seat and requested her aunt's permission to leave the box. "Don't be silly, child," Lady Stanborough restrained her, "you can't run about alone. Besides, you haven't yet exchanged three words with Lady Howard or the members of her party."

So Corianne was forced to curb her impatience and trade pleasantries with the group in the adjoining box. Among them was a moon-faced, plump young man named Wilfred Shirley, whose first glance at Corianne reduced him to stuttering incoherency. In no time at all, she elicited from him an offer to escort her in a promenade about the corridors. With her aunt's permission, she flew to the door of the box where her new swain was to meet her. However, when she flung open the door, she found herself confronted, not by the fubsy Mr. Shirley, but by the very man she'd dreamed of meeting. "Lord *N-North*!" she gasped, stepping back in awe.

At the sound of the name, Sarah (who had just turned to Edward, seated at her left, and asked him if he'd enjoyed the music) felt a cold shudder run through her. Edward had leaned toward her to hear what she'd said, and he could almost *feel* the shiver and the sudden tension of her body. He looked up at the door with curiosity.

"How do you do? Miss Lindsay, is it not?" Lord North
was saying smoothly. "How delightful to see you in London
again."

Corianne colored with pleasure. "It is k-kind of you to
remember me, my lord," she said with becoming modesty.
"Won't you . . . er . . . come in?" She stepped aside, and
North entered, followed by his friend.

Wilfred Shirley, standing in the corridor, was bewildered
and confused, unsure of what was now expected of him.
"I say," he objected, catching Ingalls' arm, "she's supposed
to come walking with *me*!"

Ingalls raised his quizzing glass in a good imitation of
North's manner and looked Mr. Shirley over carefully.
"Some other time, my boy," he said in condescending dis-
missal and turned to enter the box.

"Not your place to dismiss me," young Shirley muttered,
angered into asserting himself. "Ought to tell me herself
if she's dismissing me." With unwonted courage, he followed Ingalls into the Stanborough box.

Meanwhile, inside, Corianne was announcing in barely
restrained glee the arrival of their lofty visitor. "Aunt Laurelia, look who's come to see us!"

"Why . . . it's *North*!" Lady Stanborough exclaimed with
pleasure, casting a sidelong glance of triumph at her daughter. "Where have you been hiding this age, my lord?" She
held out a hand to him. "In all sorts of iniquitous places,
I have no doubt."

"She's supposed to be taking a stroll with *me* ," Wilfred
Shirley mumbled to no one in particular.

North smiled at Lady Stanborough enigmatically, kissed
her fingers and presented his friend. "Pleasure to meet you,
ma'am," Anthony Ingalls said with a deep bow. "I hope
you and your sisters are enjoying the music."

Lady Stanborough giggled with pleasure, tapping Ingalls
affectionately on the wrist with her fan. "Did you hear that,
Lady Howard?" she chortled to her friend on the other side
of the barrier. "My *sisters* , indeed! You are a dreadful
flatterer, Mr. Ingalls. That young lady over there is my very
own daughter, Sarah. And this one is my niece, Corianne
Lindsay. And may I also present Squire Edward Middleton,

who is visiting London for a while?"

Bows and greetings were exchanged, and Lord North came to the front of the box to take a better look at the man rising from the seat beside Sarah. This left a bit of room for Wilfred Shirley to come closer to his target. "She's supposed to be taking a stroll with *me*," he repeated, a bit louder.

North surveyed Edward carefully through his quizzing glass. "Middleton, is it?" he asked, reaching out a hand. "You look deucedly familiar. Where have I seen you—?" He paused as a shock of recognition flashed across his mind. "Sarah, my dear, is he not . . . the *bumpkin*?"

"I see that your manners haven't improved with time, my lord," Sarah said coldly.

"I probably *am* a bumpkin, sir," Edward said pleasantly, "since I *am* from the country and feel at a decided disadvantage. *Have* we met before?"

Lord North snorted and looked from Edward to Sarah with brows raised. "You don't remember? Well, if Miss Stanborough has not seen fit to remind you, I shall also refrain."

Anthony Ingalls, having made his bow to all the ladies in both boxes, closed in on his target. "Miss Lindsay, I wonder if you would care to take a stroll in the corridor to exercise your limbs before the onslaught of the second act?" he asked in Corianne's ear.

"I heard that!" Wilfred cried furiously. "I heard! I s-say, Miss L-Lindsay, didn't you tell me that *I* was to escort you?"

"Go away, fellow," Ingalls said in a low voice, trying to urge the agitated young man from the box. "Can't you see the lady's occupied elsewhere?"

But Mr. Shirley was determined to make a fight of it. "Stop pushing!" he grunted, shoving back at Ingalls with all his strength. "She promised *me*—!"

The force of his exertion succeeded in causing Mr. Ingalls to totter backward and trip over a vacant chair. He and the chair tumbled to the floor with a noisy crash. Although no damage was done either to the chair or to himself, Ingalls flushed with fury and humiliation as Mr. Shirley crowed with impolite, ignoble, but very satisfactory triumph.

Lord North helped Ingalls to his feet, while Edward frowned at Corianne in disapproval. This was just the sort of scene the girl always seemed to inspire. Corianne, however, was enjoying herself hugely, hoping that her power to bring grown men to fisticuffs was making an impression on Lord North. "Oh, dear," she murmured guiltily as she glanced up at North with a mischievous twinkle, "I *did* promise Mr. Shirley! How dreadful that I forgot about him. I suppose I *should* stroll out with him, but I shouldn't like to disappoint your friend, either. You must help me, your lordship. What shall I do now?"

North glanced down at her and said smoothly, "The only course is to take them both. One on each arm."

Corianne, who had expected him to offer to take both their places, was trapped. "Very well, your lordship," she said with a pout, "if you think I should." And, taking each one of the combatants by the arm, she did as he bid. The trio left the box, but none of them was made happy by the compromise.

In the quiet that followed their exit, Lady Stanborough invited Lord North to take the seat vacated by Corianne, just at Sarah's right. After exchanging a few more words, Lord North turned to Sarah. Lady Stanborough moved her chair closer to the barrier between her box and Lady Howard's, and the two began to whisper. It was not hard for Sarah to guess the subject of their exchange.

"Have you come to London on business, Mr. Middleton?" Lord North asked, again scrutinizing Edward through his quizzing glass.

Edward, who had not resumed his seat, was wondering if his presence was interfering with what could be a tête-à-tête. "No, my lord," he answered, "I'm on a holiday, you might say." He turned to Sarah. "I wonder, ma'am, if you'd care for a glass of champagne before the second act begins."

"No, not at all," Sarah said quickly. "I'm not the least bit thirsty. Please don't trouble."

Edward was not deaf to the plea in her voice. But Lady Stanborough, who had quite the opposite intention for her daughter than her daughter wished, looked up at him at once. "*I* should like a glass, Mr. Middleton, if you don't mind. All that strenuous singing has left me parched."

Sarah bit her lip in chagrin, but Edward had no choice. He bowed and left.

North, fully aware of the byplay, smiled wickedly. "So, Miss Stanborough, you've been outmaneuvered. You *must* speak to me, like it or no. Tell me, my dear, is that fellow a new suitor?"

Sarah shuddered again. Would North never change? "I don't see that it is any concern of yours, my lord," she said quietly, "but I shall admit that I barely know the man. He is escorting Miss Lindsay, who has just arrived from Daynwood."

"I see. I didn't think so during our first encounter, but he's a pleasant-enough fellow, isn't he?"

"I couldn't say, my lord," Sarah responded, carefully noncommittal.

"I sincerely hope, Sarah, that your acquaintance with Mr. Middleton will not develop into intimacy."

Sarah looked at him coldly. "I don't know what you mean, sir."

"Don't play the innocent, my girl. With time and further acquaintance, the fellow may take more than a friendly interest in you. If that should happen, I advise you not to encourage him."

Sarah sighed in discouragement. She'd endured this sort of conversation with him so many times before. "Lord North," she began, *"please—"*

"I mean it, Sarah. I haven't changed. I'm still determined that no one but I will ever lead you to the altar."

She clenched her hands tightly and forced a smile. "What nonsense you speak, sir. Surely you realize that I'm well past the age for marrying. I'm quite content with matters just as they are."

Lord North leaned back against his seat and looked her over admiringly. "It's you who are speaking nonsense. To me you're one of those rare women who will remain desirable even when you reach advanced age."

"Thank you, my lord, but I think the dim light has obscured your vision."

He laughed and reached for her hand. "You're still evading me, aren't you? What can I do to earn a jot of encourage—?"

But Edward had returned. The sound of his step distracted Lord North enough to permit Sarah to snatch her hand from his grasp. Edward brought the two glasses of champagne to Lady Stanborough and her companion, and Lord North rose, whispered to Sarah that he would find a way to see her soon again, and took his leave.

Edward took his seat, glancing at Sarah in some concern. He'd seen her snatch her hand away from Lord North's hold, and the slight tremor of her fingers showed him that she was still agitated. He wondered what had passed between them. But, of course, the matter was not his affair. "A little while ago, Miss Stanborough, you were asking me what I thought of the music," he reminded her gently, hoping to take her mind from the troubles which were evidently besetting her.

She smiled at him gratefully. "Yes, I was. The singing is superb, don't you agree? What did you think of Madame Milani?"

"I'm far from expert on sopranos, I'm afraid. I found the music to be sometimes lovely and sometimes tedious." He grinned his disconcerting grin at her. "You see, I have only a *bumpkin's* taste."

Sarah colored. "I must apologize for Lord North. He can sometimes be . . . tiresome."

"Not at all. As a matter of fact, I found his remarks very interesting. Would I be *gauche*, Miss Stanborough, to inquire about where he'd met me before?"

"Not *gauche*, sir, but I would prefer not to answer. It would be a matter of extreme embarrassment to me to recall to your mind a scene which does me little credit."

"I can't believe you've *ever* done anything discreditable, ma'am. But I shall refrain from pressing you further. Besides, the curtain is about to go up."

He settled back into his chair. Then, suddenly, he remembered Corianne. "Confound it," he murmured, looking back at the door of the box, "what can be keeping Cory? Doesn't she know the curtain's up?"

Sarah didn't answer. Corianne was being thoughtless,

as usual, but it was unlikely that there was any reason to
feel alarm for the girl's safety. She glanced over at Edward's
face. He was looking at the stage, but his brow was knit
in troubled irritation. Corianne's hold on his emotions must
be very strong, Sarah thought, to cause him such concern.
Sarah felt her spirits sink even further. Poor Edward Middleton. How sad that he was burdened with a love that was
obviously hopeless.

After a few moments, the box door opened and Corianne
tiptoed in, smiled apologetically at her aunt and slipped into
her seat. Edward glanced at her disapprovingly, but she
didn't look in his direction. Her cheeks were flushed and
her eyes shining. She'd evidently enjoyed the intermission
more than the opera.

He sat back and turned his eyes to the stage, but the
opera failed to engage him as it had before. The intermission
had given him much to think about. First and foremost was
the fact that, even in London, the provincial Corianne attracted too much attention. He would have to find a way
to convince her to restrain her tendency toward flagrant
flirtations with casual acquaintances, but he was not at all
sure he would be successful. Secondly, he would like to
help the troubled Miss Stanborough. She was in some way
deeply involved with Lord North. He knew it was none of
his business, but he didn't like to see an admirable young
woman like Miss Stanborough lose her heart to such a man.
His first impression of the man was not at all favorable.
There was something about his lordship that set up Edward's
bristles . . . a coldness in the eyes and the look of the vol-
uptuary about the mouth. Edward glanced at Sarah surreptitiously. Her eyes were fixed on the stage, but her fingers
were plucking nervously at the thin scarf in her lap. Except
for that small movement, there was nothing in her upright
posture, the aristocratic tilt of her head, or the repose of
her features that revealed any inner turmoil. She was much
too fine, he thought, for a man like North.

Just then she turned her head and met his eye. He gave
her a small, awkward smile and abruptly looked away.
Sarah, too, turned her eyes back to the stage. But the little
smile he'd given her was oddly comforting. Even though
the conversation with Lord North had chilled her to the

bone, she suddenly realized that the evening had not been without its triumphs for her. There had been two. Not large triumphs, perhaps, but rather pleasing nevertheless. The first had occurred when she'd come down the stairs and had seen Edward's expression of astonished admiration. And then, during the intermission, she'd actually caused him to forget about Corianne, at least for a minute or two. And *that*, under the circumstances, was a triumph indeed.

Chapter Seven

THE EVENING AT the opera marked the beginning of an intoxicating whirl of activity for Corianne, for it was not only Anthony Ingalls who had admired her appearance that night. Several other young gentlemen in the audience had leveled their glasses in her direction. As a result, a number of Mamas of enterprising young sons found themselves knocking at Lady Stanborough's door with invitations in their reticules or their eager young sons in tow. And when Lady Howard let it slip that the girl was *very* well to pass (". . . and, my dear, how many of your *true* beauties are rich as well?"), the number of aspirants practically trampled over each other to reach her door.

They found themselves more often frustrated than not. As Wilfred Shirley remarked to his mother in disgust, "That damned nail Ingalls seems to have gotten the inside track." Tony Ingalls *did* seem to be running ahead of the pack, and he was quite puffed up with his success. But Corianne tactfully refrained from admitting to Mr. Ingalls the reason she so frequently accepted his invitations—that he was the one, of all her suitors, who was intimately acquainted with her Marquis, Lord North. Quite calculatingly, she permitted Mr. Ingalls to believe that she was a bit attracted to him. She confided the truth to no one but her friend Belinda, to whom she poured out her heart every few days in long, cross-hatched and emotional letters. The letter she wrote about a week after the night at the opera was typical of many. *I've seen Tony three afternoons and two evenings this Week*, she wrote, *and cannot help but Laugh at how readily he accepts the belief that I have developed a Tendre for him. He is quite Puffed up with his own Consequence. He grows to be a Dreadful Bore, even though his Appearance is top-of-the-trees, and he is very Knowing. But I must keep him Dangling, since he is the only link I have to J.N. So far, however, I have seen J.N. only once since the Opera. No matter how loudly and gaily I laughed that Evening, and no matter how many teasing Quips I tossed in his direction, J.N. took no Notice of me. I am beginning to realize that my task may not be as Easy as I first believed. I shall not Despair, however, for I have many Callers to keep me occupied, and dozens of Invitations for all sorts of Amusements. My Aunt says I am quite the Rage, and although I know you will think me Shockingly Boastful to repeat the remark to you, it is quite true.*

Corianne received only an occasional brief reply from Belinda, but understanding that the country girl would be unlikely to have as many fascinating adventures as she was having, she felt no resentment. Even when Belinda wrote back bluntly that *"you have indeed become Shockingly Boastful, my dear girl,"* Cory didn't mind.

The rapid pace of her activities soon wore down her aunt's energy. Lady Stanborough began to realize that she needed an evening or two a week at home—for rest and repair. On those occasions, she permitted Corianne to go out without her, provided she herself was acquainted with the young man who would serve as escort and that their destination—usually a properly chaperoned house-party, formal dinner or a visit to the theater—was approved in advance. Tony Ingalls always managed to win Lady Stanborough's approval, not only because of his flattering remarks to her but because his close acquaintance with Lord North was enough to ensure her favor.

Sarah, however, began to feel some concern about the lack of restriction placed on Corianne's activity. As Corianne began to spend more and more time with Mr. Ingalls, her concern grew. She had none of the confidence in the gentleman that her mother felt, and his friendship with Lord North did nothing to add to his standing in her eyes.

One morning, at about half-past eleven, Corianne came into the breakfast room looking weary-eyed and dissipated. She found Sarah sitting at the table drinking a cup of tea. "Did you, too, sleep late, Sarah?" she asked tiredly.

"I had my breakfast at eight. I only came in for a cup of tea. Shall I ask Tait to bring you some eggs?"

"Ugh, no. I couldn't eat a thing. Is the coffee hot?"

"I think so. Here, let me pour it for you. Did you have a pleasant evening?"

"Oh, yes, very. Mrs. Saxon maintains a very modish salon. I found her to be a true woman of the world. She had at least thirty guests. Lord North was there."

Sarah put down her cup, her brows knit worriedly. "*Mrs. Saxon*? I thought you were going to the rout at the Silvercombs'."

"Yes, we were. But Tony said it was a great bore, so we ran off to Mrs. Saxon's after staying at the Silvercombs' for less than an hour."

"You ran off with *Ingalls*? Cory, how *could* you?"

"Why shouldn't I? Tony was quite right—the party at the Silvercombs' *was* a bore."

"But . . . was anyone else with you when you left?"

"No. What difference does *that* make?"

Sarah shook her head in perturbation. "What do you suppose Lady Silvercomb must have *thought* when she saw you leave—unchaperoned—at so early an hour? Really, Cory, it was not at *all* the thing to do. Does Mama know any of this?"

Corianne stirred her coffee irritably. "No, I haven't seen Aunt Laurelia yet today."

"Well, when you do, I hope you will tell her."

"Very well, I will, but I don't see why you're making such a fuss."

Sarah stretched her arm across the table to squeeze Corianne's hand. "It's important for you to understand, love, that London is quite different from Lincolnshire. It is so large . . . and crowded with all sorts of people . . ."

"I don't know what you are hinting at, Sarah," Corianne

said impatiently. "What are you trying to say to me?"

"Only that . . . oh, how *shall* I say it? . . . Mrs. Saxon is, well, not quite the thing."

"Really? Do you mean she's disreputable? I don't believe it. Tony says her salons are most exclusive."

"I shouldn't take Mr. Ingalls word on these matters as being the most reliable," Sarah said drily, picking up her cup.

"I don't see why you say that," Corianne said with a pout. "Tony is a veritable Pink-of-the-Ton."

Sarah felt a wave of irritation, and she put down her cup so hastily that the liquid sloshed over the side, burning her fingers. "Your Tony," she said, unable to keep her disgust hidden, "is a *loose fish!*"

"A loose fish? Listen here, Sarah—!"

Sarah dried her fingers, but the pain made her wince. "No, Cory, I think *you* should listen." She rose from her chair and walked angrily to the door. "He's as ramshackle a fellow as you're likely to meet anywhere, and everyone knows it but you and Mama."

"I don't believe you!" Cory threw back at her, outraged. "You're only saying these things because . . ."

"Because?" Sarah asked, surprised at Corianne's sudden hesitation.

"Because you're *jealous!*"

"What?" Sarah couldn't help but smile at her cousin's childishness. "Oh, Cory, *really!*"

She pretended to be so Innocent, Corianne wrote later that day to Belinda, *but I wasn't fooled. I've seen Sarah sitting at Home, day after day, having Nowhere to go and not one Suitor to pay her a call. She* must *be Jealous. I can't Forgive her for trying to Malign poor Tony. And as for Mrs. Saxon being Disreputable, I think it is all a pack of Lies. Mrs. S. is very beautiful, even though she is quite old, and her clothes are Bang up to the Mark. It seemed to me that Lord North stood on quite Familiar terms with her, and if he finds her Acceptable, I don't see why I shouldn't. I don't think Mrs. S. is Disreputable at all. I'd wager that if Miss Prissyface Stanborough were ever Invited to one of the Salons, she'd jump at the Chance to attend like a Shot.*

* * *

Sarah had laughed off the insult Corianne had thrown at her, but the incident itself was no laughing matter. The younger girl was too innocent to realize the danger of associating with people of unsavory reputation. If Corianne was seen too often in the company of people of that sort, she might find herself being labelled "fast." That label, once it attached itself to a girl's name, was very difficult to erase.

Sarah had little confidence that Corianne would make a proper report of her activities to Lady Stanborough. Therefore, with extreme reluctance, she decided to tell her mother herself. Feeling guiltily akin to the slimy little tattletale who'd lived next door when she was a child, she entered her mother's dressing room to perform the distasteful task. "Has Cory told you where she went last evening, Mama?" she asked without roundaboutation.

Her mother was stretched out on a chaise near the window, her eyes covered with a lotion-soaked cloth. "She went to Lady Silvercomb's, I believe," Lady Stanborough answered. "Why?"

"I wish you will sit up, Mama. This is important."

"I can hear you, my love. My treatment is important, too, you know. Ten minutes a day of soaking one's eyelids with cucumber lotion works absolute wonders. It soothes away wrinkles, eliminates shadows and makes the skin feel *years* younger. You should try it, too."

"Never mind about the lotion, Mama. You have more important matters to think about. You must speak to Corianne."

Lady Stanborough didn't budge. "Well, go on. What is it?"

"She spent last evening at one of Mrs. Saxon's *salons*."

Lady Stanborough snatched off the cloth from her eyes and sat bolt upright. "*Mrs. Sax*—! You can't *mean* it!"

"But I *do* mean it. She told me so herself."

"But how can this be? She was to go to the Silvercombs'!"

"Your precious Tony Ingalls took her."

Lady Stanborough fell back against the chaise and put

a trembling hand to her brow. "Good heavens! Has the boy no *sense*?"

"It isn't *sense* he lacks. It's *character*."

Lady Stanborough moaned. "I *knew* I shouldn't let the girl come. I *knew* it. You young people are becoming much too difficult for me to handle."

"There's nothing difficult about this, Mama," Sarah suggested calmly. "Just tell Cory that she may not see Mr. Ingalls again."

"Not *see* him? *Ever*?" Lady Stanborough looked up at her daughter doubtfully. "That's a bit strong, isn't it? Why don't I just tell her that she mustn't ever go to Mrs. Saxon's again?"

"Yes, of course you must tell her *that*, but it seems to me that Tony Ingalls has proved himself to be completely untrustworthy. You cannot wish to permit him to escort Cory after this, can you?"

"No, I suppose not," her mother admitted. "But she seems to prefer him to the other young men who call." She sat up and sighed. "I shall have to make sure to go along with her in the evening from now on. What a nuisance. I shan't have a moment's peace."

"Don't look so dismayed, Mama. Perhaps Mr. Middleton will share the chore with you, if you ask. And I can attend some of the affairs—the ones where I could be certain that—" She caught herself up short.

"Certain that what?" her mother asked.

"Nothing."

Lady Stanborough snorted irritably. "I know what you were going to say. Those affairs where you could be certain that Lord North would not be in attendance. I don't know what's wrong with you, Sarah. You try my patience."

"I'm sorry, Mama," Sarah said simply. She had long since given up trying to explain to her mother her feelings about Lord North.

Lady Stanborough grunted sourly and lay back against the chaise again. "Between the two of you, I shall have an attack of the vapors. I *know* I shall."

"No, you won't, Mama. You'll do just as you ought, and everything will be fine." With those soothing words, she took the cloth from her mother's unresisting fingers, gently laid it over her eyes again and went quickly from the room.

Lady Stanborough kept her word. She spoke to Corianne firmly about the dangers of associating with people like Mrs. Saxon, and she chaperoned the girl regularly. When she became particularly worn out, she sent for the obliging Mr. Middleton. Sarah, much relieved, put the entire incident from her mind. She didn't realize that her mother often left her chaperonage early, leaving Corianne in the care of whatever gentleman was in favor at the moment. But a chance encounter a week later brought the matter back to her consciousness with a shock.

The encounter took place just outside Hookham's library. It was a particularly balmy October day, and Sarah, out for a stroll, had decided to stop in for a quick browse through the bookstore before returning home. In the doorway, she almost collided with a tall, lanky gentleman whose face was buried in his just-purchased copy of *The Gentleman's Magazine*. "*Really*, my dear sir—!" Sarah sputtered, her face having narrowly missed being bruised by the magazine.

The startled, guilt-ridden gentleman dropped his magazine in dismay and opened his mouth to apologize. "I'm *terribly* s— *Sarah*!"

"Lord *Fitz*! Good heavens, what are you doing in London?"

Lord Henry Fitzsimmons was the husband of Sarah's dearest friend, who, when last heard from, had written from the Fitzsimmons' estate in Norfolk that she'd been delivered of a pair of twin girls. This, in addition to two small sons under the age of five, gave Clara Fitzsimmons neither the time nor the energy to come to town. But Sarah was surprised to see Fitz here without her, for the two were usually an inseparable couple. Their fondness for each other was so great that they occasioned smiles from all onlookers. Fitz never referred to his wife by any other name than "my Clara." Yet here he was, alone.

Lord Fitz looked down at Sarah from his great height, his eyes twinkling with mischievous delight. "My Clara has

thrown me out. Well, not thrown me out, exactly, but . . . I'll
explain later. Arrived only today, you know. I was just on
my way to *call* on you! My Clara has given me all sorts
of messages for you. What a lucky chance to have run into
you like this!"

"*Blundered* into me, you mean," Sarah laughed. "What
do you *mean*, Fitz, by saying Clara's thrown you out? Did
you leave that poor woman to cope with four babies all by
herself?"

Lord Fitz rubbed his thick moustache guiltily. "Had to,
don't you see? Well, I didn't exactly *have* to, but my Clara
said it would be good for me to get away from crying babies
for a time."

Sarah giggled. Fitz still had not lost his way of equiv-
ocating whenever he made a statement.

"Said I was getting in the way," he continued. "Well,
not exactly getting in the way, perhaps, but she thought I
needed a bit of time for myself. Besides, I needed to spend
some time with my man of business. But if you ask me,
Sarah, I think she thought I was getting housebound. A
good woman, my Clara."

"Yes, she is indeed," Sarah said affectionately. "But it
is good to see you, Fitz, even if you *are* alone. Come and
walk along with me, and tell me all about the twins."

Lord Fitz happily obliged, for talking about his children
was his favorite pastime. He took Sarah's arm and, turning
with her in the direction of Stanborough House, they were
soon engrossed in his account of the remarkable progress
of the two most beautiful and clever baby girls in the world.
It was not surprising, therefore, that they failed to notice
Edward Middleton, who was hurrying down the street, approaching them from the opposite direction. As they were
about to pass each other, Edward recognized Sarah. "Good
day, Miss Stanborough," he said, lifting his beaver.

"Oh, Mr. Middleton, good day to *you*! Everyone in the
world seems to be out for a stroll today. May I present my
friend, Lord—"

"*Fitz!*" Edward chortled. "Fitz, as I live and breathe—!"

"Ned?" Lord Fitz asked in astonishment. "Is it really
you? I don't *believe* it!"

They pounded each other on the back in delight, while

Sarah watched them in amusement.

I thought you were fixed in Norfolk," Edward said when they'd sufficiently pommeled one another.

"And I thought you *hated* London."

Edward laughed. "I haven't the time to explain now, I'm afraid. I've been putting up at the Fenton, which is deucedly uncomfortable, so I've finally made an appointment with a rental agent to see about renting some rooms. I'm late now. I shall leave the explanations to Miss Stanborough, who is completely familiar with my situation. Stop by the Fenton later, old fellow. We have a great deal of catching-up to do."

They pounded each other's backs once more, and Edward ran off. Lord Fitz and Sarah continued their walk toward her home, Sarah telling Fitz about Edward's mission in London as guardian of his Lincolnshire neighbor, and Fitz telling her of his long-standing friendship with the Squire from Lincolnshire. They'd met at school, where they'd become inseparable friends, and although they'd seen each other only infrequently since, they'd kept in touch by the exchange of warm if only occasional letters. "He was to have been best man at my wedding," Fitz explained, "but his mother took ill just at that time and died a week afterward. Well, perhaps not a week, but shortly thereafter."

Sarah, who had been Clara's maid of honor, murmured, "Then I might have met him six years ago," without realizing she'd said the words aloud.

Fitz cast her a quick look. Was there something between Sarah and his friend? He would have a great deal to write to his Clara that evening. "Ned's the best of good fellows, and I can't tell you how glad I am that he's in town. Don't know why he had to run off to rent rooms . . . he can stay with *me*. Who is the young woman he's in charge of? A relation of yours?"

"Yes, my cousin. She's the daughter of my uncle, the Earl of Daynwood, whose lands, I understand, adjoin your friend's. Her name is Corianne Lindsay. If you have time to stop in, you'll meet her in a moment."

"Corianne Lindsay? A little blonde beauty with shockingly deep blue eyes?"

"What? Have you met her already? Really, Fitz, I shall

have to write to Clara to order you home. You are getting about much too quickly."

But Fitz was not listening to her quip. His brow knit, and his expression clouded over. "Yes," he said absently, "I met her last night."

Sarah looked at him sharply. "What is it, Fitz? Is there something troubling you?"

Fitz's step faltered, and he glanced over at Sarah in some embarrassment. "The girl is under Ned's guardianship, you say?"

"Yes, in a way. She is staying with *us*, you know. But Mr. Middleton is here to keep an eye on her—for her father's peace of mind."

"I see. I suppose, then, that I ought to tell you . . ."

"Tell me what, Fitz?"

"I don't know how to say it, really. Perhaps you'll think it quite repugnant that *I* was there . . . my first night away from my Clara, too. But you see, I'd gone to my club where I ran into North—"

Sarah whitened. She could almost anticipate what would follow.

"—and he insisted so tenaciously that I go with him . . . saying that everyone would think me henpecked and unmanly if I refused . . . so . . . I went."

"To Mrs. Saxon's?" Sarah asked frankly.

He raised his brows in surprise, and then he nodded glumly. "I felt like a fool and a cad all evening, and, believe me, I left within an hour despite all North's devilish ragging." He looked at her shamefacedly, his eyes almost pleading for her understanding.

Sarah smiled at him wanly and squeezed his hand. "I know," she said quietly. "Lord North can sometimes be . . . a problem. But, Fitz . . . were you going to say that *Corianne* was there?"

"Yes, she was. North introduced me. Can't believe that Lady Stanborough would think that's the proper place for a girl like that."

"I assure you, Fitz, that Mama knows nothing about it," Sarah confessed, deeply troubled.

A sudden change in the wind caused them to hurry their steps. They walked on for a moment in thoughtful silence.

"I suppose I ought to . . . well, perhaps not, but . . . do you think I should tell Ned?" Lord Fitz asked.

Sarah considered for a moment. The first time Cory had gone to Mrs. Saxon's *salon*, the girl had been ignorant of the significance. But *this* time, she'd gone with the full knowledge of the danger. The matter was therefore a great deal more serious than before. "No, Fitz. Thank you, but I think this is a subject which I'd better discuss with Mr. Middleton myself. And soon."

Chapter Eight

MARTIN, EDWARD'S HEAD GROOM, had been impressed into service as Edward's "man" for the London trip. He acted as valet, butler, groom, confidante and companion and still had not enough to do. It was therefore good news to him that the Squire was moving out of the Fenton. For Mr. Middleton had informed him that he was going to share a suite of rooms on Curzon Street with Lord Fitzsimmons. It was a large apartment which Lord Fitz kept for his convenience on trips to town. Martin was quite pleased—or as pleased as he could be away from his horses and the green hills of Lincolnshire. The past few weeks had been unbearably dull for both master and man. Mr. Middleton had no acquaintance in town except for the family at Stanborough House, and therefore there had been little to do. Lately, some invitations had begun to arrive for the Squire from some of the people he'd met while escorting Miss Corianne, but he'd turned down most of them unless he'd undertaken to accompany her. Now, however, with Lord Fitz to keep him company, Martin had little doubt that the pattern of their days would be much more active.

As he packed the clothes, Martin whistled happily, glancing occasionally across at the Squire who sat at the window reading the morning *Times*. "When shall I take out the carriage, sir?" he asked, eager to be gone from the staid Fenton. "In about an hour?"

"No, don't hurry, Martin," Middleton responded. "Fitz won't be home until later this afternoon. He's seeing his solicitor this morning."

There was a tap at the door. Martin opened it to find the hotel footman standing there, a look of restrained disapproval on his face. "There's a lydy downstairs says she wants to see Mr. Middleton," he said coldly.

"A lady?" Martin echoed in surprise.

"A lydy. Alone. Sittin' in the lobby waitin' for 'im."

Edward, puzzled, threw his paper aside. "Did she give a name?" he asked, coming to the door.

"No, sir, she didn't."

"I see. Well, tell her I'll be down directly."

He put on his coat quickly and went downstairs. Sarah was sitting primly on one of a number of Sheraton drawing-room chairs which lined the walls of the ornate lobby. She looked elegantly graceful in a plum-colored velvet pelisse and a fetching bonnet of natural straw trimmed with purple ribbons. A number of passers-by cast sidelong looks at her. Perhaps, like the footman, they disapproved of a young lady who permitted herself to make an appearance in a public room without escort. But Edward thought their glances were more likely of admiration than of censure. No one with an ounce of sense, he thought, would find anything to criticize in a creature who carried herself with such an air of serene composure.

But Sarah felt anything but composed. She had taken upon herself a most unpleasant mission, and she was not at all sure that she would be thanked for her pains. Nevertheless, she looked up at Edward with a smile to match his welcoming one, feeling comforted by the warmth of his expression. "I'm sorry to have disturbed you, Mr. Middleton," she said, rising, "but I have a matter of some urgency to bring to your attention. Is there . . . somewhere we can go . . . somewhere private . . . ?"

Edward hesitated. He could scarcely invite her to his room. "The only place I can think of is a small writing room just across the lobby that is usually deserted," he said. "Shall we try it?"

She nodded and preceded him across the lobby. Fortunately, the room was unoccupied. Edward led her to a chair placed before the writing table, the top of which was inlaid with squares of polished leather. He pulled a chair from another desk and set it across the table from her. While he did so, she looked around the room with approval. "This is a lovely hotel, is it not? I hope you are comfortable here, Mr. Middleton."

He grinned. "I suspect it was designed more for the comfort and pleasure of ladies than for the likes of me. The furniture is all too small. My feet hang over the end of the bed, you know. But I've been comfortable enough. However, I move away this afternoon. You've caught me in the nick of time, Miss Stanborough."

Sarah's heart seemed to stop. "Move away? Not . . . you're not going back to L-Lincolnshire?" she managed.

"Oh, no. I'm moving in with Fitz. He says his accommodations will be more to my liking. Since we intend to spend a good deal of time in each other's company, he says the new arrangement will be more convenient."

"What a good scheme," she said in relief. She looked at him closely. "I'm afraid that my mother and I have been thoughtless, Mr. Middleton. You must have been very lonely here. We should have made an effort to entertain you more frequently."

"Not at all. This trip was designed for Cory's entertainment, not mine, and I'm most grateful for all you're doing for her. I assume, however, that you didn't come here to inquire after *me*. Is something wrong with Cory?" His face clouded over with sudden anxiety. "She hasn't taken ill, has she?"

"No, no, her health is excellent. It's . . . something else entirely." She met his worried, questioning eyes and lowered hers in some embarrassment. "It's something I find a little awkward to discuss."

"Please, Miss Stanborough, don't stand on points with me," he urged. "I'd be thankful if you just came out with it . . . whatever it is."

A quick study of his face convinced her that a direct approach was the most suitable for so straightforward a man. "Well, then, sir, without roundaboutation, I must tell you that Corianne has taken to associating with people of . . . questionable reputation. Although these associations can lead to dangerous consequences in themselves, I don't mean to imply that Cory's behavior has ever been less than ladylike—"

"Good God!" Edward burst out, wincing. "I certainly *hope* not!"

"But even if she'd behaved in an *exemplary* fashion, the stain of such companionship is bound to rub off on her. I know I sound like a veritable prig, Mr. Middleton, but the gossips of London—and I assure you that there are many of those, even in the highest circles—are bound to learn of this before long, and they will sully her name beyond repair." Quickly she outlined the details of what she knew of Corianne's two visits to Mrs. Saxon's in Ingalls' company.

Edward stared at her for a long moment and then swore under his breath. "Damnation! I *knew*—" He checked himself and slapped an angry hand on the table. "I beg your pardon, Miss Stanborough, but where has your mother *been* all this time? Does she have no control over the girl?"

Sarah colored, bit her lip and lowered her head. "My mother is not very . . . I mean, she really is rather inexperienced in . . . that is—"

Edward, hardly hearing her, got up and began to pace about the small room with angry strides. "Of *course* she's inexperienced. This is just the sort of thing I warned Lord Lindsay about. Cory is too lively and impetuous to be left in the care of a woman who's never had to cope with the sort of problems that she can generate. I'm sure *your* conduct never gave your mother a moment's concern."

Sarah felt a sting of irritated pain. Was he implying that she was too dull and conventional ever to have flouted authority? He was so foolishly besotted over the spoiled, coquettish Corianne that he found even her *scrapes and excesses* to be merely a result of her overwhelming charm! "I will take that as a compliment," she couldn't help retorting coldly, "even though it suggests I lack your beloved charge's . . . er . . . *joie de vivre.*"

"*Joie de vivre!*" he repeated in disgust. "I don't see how you can call Cory's behavior the result of *joie de vivre*. My beloved charge, as you call her, is a spoiled little chit who should be given a good hiding and hauled back home!"

Sarah gazed at him with sudden compassion. The poor fellow was so completely immersed in his tormented feelings for the girl that he missed entirely the exposure Sarah had made of her own wounds. "Yes, you *can* haul her back home," she said thoughtfully, scarcely realizing that she spoke aloud, "so that she'll be properly shielded from temptation and will eventually marry *you*."

Edward stopped in his tracks, whitened, and stared at her. "*What* did you say?"

Sarah's hands flew to her mouth. "Oh, I'm *sorry*! I didn't mean . . . I *never* should have—!"

Edward dropped into his chair. "No, don't apologize. I appreciate a little frankness. What makes you think I want to marry Cory?"

"Don't you?"

"No, I don't."

Sarah shot him a challenging glance. "I thought you wanted to be frank. It's plain as pikestaff you're in love with her."

Edward, confounded, looked at her in alarm. "Is it so plain to everyone as all that?"

"Not to everyone. Not to anyone but me, as far as I know," Sarah said kindly.

"How did you—?"

She smiled. "It's in your eyes when you look at her. A sharp observer can usually tell."

"I see." He put his elbows on the table and propped his chin up with his hands, studying Sarah with new appreciation. "You're an unusual young lady, Miss Stanborough. And, I think, a wise one. But although your sharp observations may be correct, and I may love Cory as you say, I assure you I have no intentions of marrying her."

"No? Why not?"

"Why *not*? Surely you know the answer to that. In the first place, I'm too old for her. In the second place, we should not suit. In the third place, she wouldn't have me."

Sarah, with a wry twist in her smile, met his eye. "The first two objections would disappear in a moment, if you could change the third."

Edward gave a reluctant laugh. "You're probably right. But there's devilish little chance of changing the third."

"I don't know about that. You *may* be right, of course, but one can't be certain about these things. You *might* be able to win her if you went about it in the right way."

Edward cocked an eyebrow at her quizzically. "I won't say you don't interest me, Miss Stanborough, but even if you were right, what makes you think that a marriage between Cory and me is '*a consummation devoutly to be wished*'?"

Sarah was asking herself the same question. This man, so unusually open, honest and manly, so unspoiled by all the affectations and superficialities of the fashionable set, so untouched by greed and so untainted by the corruption of the upper classes—he was much too good for Corianne Lindsay. But Corianne Lindsay was the girl he wanted. Perhaps Sarah should help him to win his heart's desire. "You would make Corianne an excellent husband," she said flatly.

He blinked at her doubtfully. "Do you really believe that? I'm fifteen years her senior, you know."

"You're in your prime. That is the first thing you must remember if you want to win her, you know."

"It sounds to me, Miss Stanborough," he said, sitting back in his chair and studying her with amusement, "that you're about to embark on a matchmaking campaign. I don't think the role suits you."

"Don't you? Why not, sir?"

"You're much too young and pretty. You should be busy plotting matches in your *own* behalf."

"Never mind the flattery, sir. We are not discussing me."

"I never flatter, Miss Stanborough. But you're quite right. We were discussing Cory. I take it, then, that you think I *should* take her back to Daynwood, away from London temptation, and try to marry her myself?"

"No, that would be *fatal*! She'd never forgive you. You must stay here and enter the lists yourself."

"*What*? Stay *here*? I thought you *wanted* me to take her away from Ingalls and Mrs. Saxon and the like. Isn't that why you came?"

"No, not at all. I *came* to suggest that you undertake more complete supervision over her activities. But now I think that *I* shall do that, while you undertake your campaign to win her."

"But this is nonsense! What chance would I have against such youthful pattern-cards of elegance as Mr. Ingalls?"

"Leave that to me. All you must do is promise to be guided by my advice."

Edward shrugged. "It's an easy-enough promise. I'm certain I couldn't do better than to put myself in your hands. Very well, Miss Stanborough, you have my promise. What must I do?"

Sarah grinned wickedly. "You should have asked that question *before* you gave your word. You may be sorry when you hear my first instruction. You must find yourself a young lady to court."

"A young lady to—? I don't understand."

"You see," Sarah explained, "our first objective must be to change Corianne's habitual way of looking at you. She sees you as—"

"As an old uncle she can twist around her fingers," he supplied drily. "I'd quite like to know how you think you can change *that*."

"By making her think you've lost your heart to someone else. Cory has had your undivided affection for so long she takes it for granted. If she suddenly finds that affection withdrawn—and given to another lady—she is bound to feel—"

"A monumental indifference," Edward supplied sardonically.

"A monumental *jealousy*," Sarah insisted.

Edward rubbed his chin dubiously. "I don't know, Miss Stanborough. It seems to me that this entire scheme is—"

"You gave your word, Mr. Middleton."

He grimaced. "Yes, I did, didn't I! Very well, ma'am. Where am I to find this lady to court?"

"A good question. Her selection is very important. She must be attractive enough to make Cory bristle. Let me think a moment."

Edward watched her as she knit her brow in intense concentration. This entire plan had developed much too quickly for him. What was he letting himself in for? He'd had no idea that the quiet Miss Stanborough could be so managing a female. Into what mires of trouble and deception would this clear-eyed, innocent-seeming creature lead him?

"Betsy Orping! The very girl!" Sarah exclaimed suddenly.

"What?"

"My friend Elizabeth Orping. She told me she met you at the Denisons' dinner the other evening. She sat opposite you at the table and found you a charming companion. 'At home to a peg,' she confided to me."

"Orping? Oh, yes, I seem to remember. Butter-faced female with a high-pitched laugh?"

Sarah frowned at him. "How unkind. She said much more complimentary things about you. 'Ruggedly handsome,' that's how she described you."

"That *was* kind," Edward said, somewhat abashed, "but she won't do. Not at all. Cory would *never* believe—"

"You must *make* her believe it," Sarah said firmly.

"I have a better idea. A young lady of my acquaintance whom I think will suit much better."

"Really? That's splendid. Why didn't you say so? Who is she?"

"Her name is Sarah Stanborough—"

"*M-Me?*" She gaped at him, aghast. Her heart fluttered against her chest like a spider caught in its own web.

Edward smile broadly, its effect on her more devastating than ever. "Now *there's* a girl," he continued teasingly, unaware of the turmoil he was creating in the girl sitting so calmly across from him, "who's lovely as a sunset and has a laugh that comes lilting up from deep in her throat like the trill of an oboe."

Sarah's throat constricted tightly. "No, that's impossible," she said curtly. "I couldn't—"

"Why not, ma'am?" Edward insisted. "It's the perfect scheme. I could be on hand more often to help supervise Cory. And there would be no harm in my pretending with *you*, since you are fully apprised of the pretense. If I were to pursue some other female, I might lead her into believing that I had serious intentions. You, on the other hand, couldn't be misled."

"You could *tell* Miss Orping the truth beforehand," Sarah

suggested desperately. Feeling herself more and more attracted to Edward, she felt a premonitory warning that this increased intimacy would inevitably lead to heartbreak for her.

"Tell her that I want to use her this way? Somehow, I doubt if she would be pleased with that suggestion. She'd more likely call her butler to throw me out bodily."

"B-but . . . you see, I don't care to go out much, Mr. Middleton. I'm quite reclusive, you know."

"Yes, I've noticed that. I don't understand why, of course. But you can't remain so if you intend to supervise Cory."

"Oh, dear, that's *true*," Sarah admitted, sighing in discouragement.

Edward studied her face again. What was behind her peculiar reluctance for social intercourse? Did it have anything to do with Lord North? The only explanation that occurred to him was that she was in love with the fellow but knew he was a bounder. She'd evidently decided that avoiding him was her best course of action. "Would it be too distasteful to you to increase your social activity? Under my escort, you would be protected from . . . from any unwanted attentions . . . at least to a greater degree than is possible when you venture out alone."

"Yes, but . . ."

"However, I don't wish to press you. The entire scheme is quite rash anyway. I think my best course is simply to return Cory to her father at Daynwood. She will be safe, her reputation unsullied, you would be relieved of this unconscionable burden, and none of us will be in worse case than we were before we came."

Sarah looked down at her hands. "Except you. Corianne will hate you for it."

"That doesn't matter," Edward said ruefully. "There's not much difference between being a *favored* uncle and a *dis*favored one. Neither role is very satisfying."

For a moment they both sat still, each steeped in melancholy musings. Then Sarah squared her shoulders and declared resolutely, "No! You *won't* take her home. We're going to go through with it."

"Do you mean you are *willing*?" He looked at her

closely. "Are you quite certain? Perhaps you'd better take some time to think this over, Miss Stanborough."

She rose and held out her hand to him. "I'm quite certain. And now, Mr. Middleton, you may perform your first act as my new suitor and take me home."

He jumped up and grasped her hand. "Miss Stanborough, you are a rarity. Thank you. No matter what happens as a result of this crack-brained adventure we're embarking on, you will always have my admiration and gratitude. And now that I've made my speech, I am at your disposal."

He smiled his extraordinary smile at her, and her stomach seemed to flip over inside her. *I'll have to teach myself to control these reactions*, she told herself sternly. But aloud she simply said, "Then let's be off."

She took his arm, and they strolled in a leisurely fashion across the hotel lobby to the outer door. "One more thing, Mr. Middleton," she added as they stepped out into the bright October sunshine, "If you're going to become my new suitor, you'd better refrain from calling me Miss Stanborough in that formal style."

"Very well, Sarah," he said obediently. "Anything you say."

Chapter Nine

EDWARD DIDN'T MANAGE to move into Lord Fitz's rooms until late that evening, for his entire afternoon had been spent in executing a number of directives which Sarah had given him. First he'd been instructed to order a few dashingly modish coats from Nugee, the tailor preferred by the Dandy set (whose style Sarah felt would most impress Corianne). Then he'd found a florist from whom he'd ordered a beribboned nosegay to be delivered that evening to Stanborough House (where Sarah would arrange to leave it on a table near the doorway where Corianne would be bound to discover it), on which he attached a note, ostentatiously unsigned, bearing the message *To S.S. in Gratitude for a Memorable Afternoon.* Lastly, he had to write a note to Corianne herself (arranging for it to be delivered the following morning), in which he was to beg her to excuse him from their appointment to ride. (The plan was that he would appear the next morning at Stanborough House in his riding clothes and take *Sarah* riding instead.) Only after these chores had been attended to did he give Martin permission to load the carriage, and the two departed for Fitz's rooms.

Fitz had been waiting impatiently for his arrival. He gave Edward only a brief half-hour to survey his new surroundings and change into his evening clothes before bearing his friend off for an evening on the town. A lavish dinner at the home of his wife's grandmother (at which the conversation centered on the babies in Norfolk) was followed by a visit to Drury Lane where they laughed uproariously at a very foolish and slightly indecent farce, and they wound up at White's for an hour or two of cards.

Since Edward was not a member, he had not visited the famous gambling club before, although he'd noted it in passing on a stroll down St. James Street. One couldn't help but notice the building with the famous bow windows in which a number of gentlemen could always be seen ogling the ladies passing on the street below. Edward found the inside of the building to be pleasant, commodious and masculinely utilitarian. Fitz laughingly pointed out to him a balding fellow snoozing on a chair in a corner of a first-floor room. "That's Raggett, the proprietor," he whispered. "They say he waits up all night so that he can do the sweeping up of the gambling rooms himself. He's made an enormous fortune on those sweepings—well, not enormous, perhaps, but sizeable—for the number of gold coins the gamblers, in their drunken state, drop on the floor is remarkable."

Edward laughed and looked about him. There was gaming going on in all the surrounding rooms, some deep and some casual. The gaming rooms offered attractions of all kinds: basset, Faro, tables of EO and the newer *roulet*. And several smaller rooms held tables for all sorts of card games where the rules of play were set not by the house but by the players themselves. At Edward's insistence, Fitz took himself off to his favorite Faro table, leaving Edward to wander about at will.

Edward was not expert at cards, having spent his limited leisure time at home mostly at reading and chess, but picquet and whist were quite familiar to him. After watching a game of picquet between two elderly gentlemen, he was soon invited by the winner to try his hand. "Saw you come in with Fitzsimmons," the white-haired gentleman remarked. "Nice lad, that. I'm Carnaby Styles. Knew his father well."

Edward introduced himself and sat down. Lord Styles signaled for a fresh piquet deck and, with a brush of a finger against his white moustaches, he settled himself back against his chair for a new round of play. The stakes he set were modest, and Edward found himself enjoying the game.

Lord Styles was a good player, but Edward soon discovered that he was somewhat careless in his discards and began to draw ahead in the score.

Lord Styles was not accustomed to being bested. He began to play cautiously, and the score teetered back and forth excitingly. A small crowd began to gather, some of the onlookers placing side bets on the outcome far in excess of the sum wagered by the players themselves. The size of the crowd around the small card table aroused the curiosity of a pair of *roulet*-players who had just left their table. "I say, North, what's the attraction over there?" Ingalls asked his friend.

They pushed through the crowd. "Good lord, it's the *bumpkin!*" North chortled. An overindulgence in the club's excellent Madeira had weakened his already loose hold on good manners.

A murmur of disapproval ran through the crowd. Lord Styles and Edward both looked up, and Edward, to his chagrin, felt his color rise. Lord Styles frowned angrily, his white moustaches quivering at the ends. "Damned nail!" he muttered under his breath. "Don't let that sort of thing bother you, m'boy," he said bluntly to Edward. "Means to rattle you, that's all."

"Don't worry, sir, I'm not in the least rattled. In fact, I think I've made a quint."

Lord Styles chuckled. "Good fellow! That's the rubber. My hat's off to you, even if it costs me a rouleau." He paid his losses and patted Edward on the shoulder. "Damn good game, my boy. Enjoyed it heartily."

The crowd gave a round of applause while Edward rose to leave the table. But a hand on his back stayed him. "Don't go yet, Middleton," North said suavely. "How about trying your hand against a *real* player?"

"You flatter yourself, North," Lord Styles interjected coldly. "I've bested you on many a day. You needn't let us keep you, Middleton," he added, trying to help Edward out of what he feared would become a dangerous situation.

"Thank you, sir," Edward said to Lord Styles, "but I've no objection to accepting Lord North's challenge." He turned to North. "Lead us to a table, my lord."

Lord Styles got up from his chair. "If you're determined,

Middleton, to play with that . . . with North, you can sit here. I've had enough for tonight."

The crowd, which had begun to disperse, reformed. The feeling ran high that this would be a match worth watching. "What stakes were you playing for?" North asked, taking fresh picquet cards from a waiter's tray and dropping some coins in their place.

"It was merely a friendly bout," Edward said. "Five shilling a point."

"Paltry, sir, paltry," North said disparagingly. "A mere *country* wager."

Edward looked across at Lord North shrewdly. The stakes he'd named were quite adequate—he was not such a bumpkin that he didn't know that. North was trying to rattle him. His eyes glinted with amusement. Did his lordship believe that because he came from the country he was necessarily behindhand in wordly goods? "You may name the stakes yourself, my lord," he suggested calmly.

"Then shall we play for ten a point?"

The crowd murmured, but Edward merely smiled. "As you wish," he said.

"And fifty pounds the rubber, to sweeten the pot," North added slyly.

"I *say*!" Lord Styles objected. "That's too deep by half! What are you up to, North?"

But Edward smiled confidently at Lord Styles. "I don't mind, Lord Styles. You needn't concern yourself."

Styles subsided, but he couldn't help grunting to the gentlemen standing near him that North was pulling a rum trick on an innocent stranger.

Some time later, Fitz, having lost all he could afford to the Faro bank, came looking for his friend. Seeing the large crowd in the rear card room, he joined them curiously and discovered, to his complete amazement, that *his Ned* was at the center of the congregation. "What goes on here?" he whispered to an acquaintance.

"Some sort of blood match, I think," was the whispered response. "Piquet."

"I can see it's picquet," Fitz said irritably. "Who's winning?"

"Hard to say. A rubber apiece, so far."

"Shhhh!" hissed Lord Styles in front of them, turning around in annoyance. "Oh, Fitzsimmons. Glad to see you, lad. Think your friend's gotten himself in a bit of a hole. North's got 'im playing too deep."

When Styles had informed him of the stakes, Fitz frowned. He had no notion of the condition of his *friend*'s finances, but he knew that *North* had little need to worry over the size of the stakes. He bit his lip, fingered his thick moustache, and watched the game with anxious eyes.

Edward, however, had no such concern. After two rubbers, he had the measure of his opponent. North played well and daringly, but he often gambled on slim chances. Edward, therefore, took pains not to bet against the odds. Soon the advantage of his strategy began to show. The murmurs of the crowd grew louder as Edward began to pull ahead in the score. He capped the final game with a quint major, causing the entire crowd, even those who'd bet against him, to burst into applause.

Lord North shoved a pile of rouleaux across the table insolently and clumsily pushed himself to his feet. "If I hadn't drunk s' much, it would've been diff'rent," he mumbled in a surly tone. "I s'pose you play this stupid game all the time in . . . where *is* the rusticity you come from? . . . Lincolnshire?"

"We're much too busy in the country—yes, it's Lincolnshire—to spend time at cards," Edward came back promptly. "Of course, we play occasionally—when we have visitors from town. There's so little else you townsmen seem to know how to do."

The crowd laughed and surged in on Edward. Fitz clapped him enthusiastically on the shoulder, and Lord Styles pumped his hand. Lord North was joined only by Ingalls, and the two made a prompt exit from the club. But before North left the card room, he heard Lord Styles declare loudly that he was putting Middleton up for membership the first thing in the morning.

"That country *put* cost me more than five hundred pounds," Lord North muttered for the tenth time later that night, as he and his crony sat sprawled on two loveseats in his lordship's drawing room, to which they'd repaired after leaving the club. Boozy and depressed, they'd tossed aside their coats, loosened their neckcloths and ordered the butler to bring them a decanter of brandy. With a careless disregard for the damage they might do to the satin upholstery, they'd filled their brandy glasses and sprawled over the furniture, each one preoccupied with his own discontents. "Five hundred pounds in less than two hours. 'S a disgrace."

"Not such a disgrace," Ingalls remonstrated. "Not as bad as letting a silly chit like Corianne Lindsay keep one dangling like a marionette."

"'S a disgrace," North insisted. "I let th' fellow make a fool o' me."

"I wouldn't say that," Ingalls argued. "Just lost a game o' cards. Nothin' so very foolish about that. Everyone does it. But to let a snip of a female do it—"

"Lost to a *bumpkin*. Don't like losin' five hundred pounds to a bumpkin."

Ingalls nodded in agreement. "Don't like bein' *dangled* by a bumpkin, either. A female bumpkin."

North emptied the dregs of the decanter into his glass unsteadily. "Somethin' about that bumpkin I don't like. Don't like at all."

"Too high in the instep, that's what she is," Ingalls declared bitterly.

North blinked at him appreciatively. "That's it. Just what's been irritatin' me. Too high in the instep. You've put your finger on it. He's too high by half."

"Who?" inquired Ingalls.

"The bumpkin . . . Middleton. Who else?"

"Oh, yes, Middleton. Don't refine on it, old f'low. Everyone loses at cards sometimes."

"Too high in the instep, I say!" North roared.

"Yes, that she is. That's what I've been sayin'," Tony explained carefully.

"Must take 'im down a peg. That's what to do. Take 'im down a peg."

"Who, Corianne? What a good idea . . . take 'er down a peg. Don't know *why* the chit won't have me. Does she fancy herself too good for me? She *plays* with me . . . like a cat with a mouse."

Lord North tried to shake the cobwebs from his brain

by rapidly shaking his head from side to side. "I'm not talking about your silly little chit. Do you hear me, Tony? Talking about *Middleton*. Never *did* like that bumptious makebait . . . not from the first time I saw him. Owe him a lesson."

"Yes, of course. Middleton. Take 'im down a peg. Just the thing to do. And Corianne, too, if it comes to that."

North smiled. "Yes, why not? Both of 'em." He studied his empty glass for a moment and then turned it over to make sure it was empty. "We'll *break* 'em!" he declared, tossing his empty glass into a corner of the fireplace where it shivered into a thousand pieces. "Just like that!"

Tony Ingalls started. Did he mean the glasses or . . . ? Then he laughed and, following his host's example, tossed his glass, too. The crash sent a tinkling spray of splinters against the fire screen. "Just like that," said, chuckling uneasily.

Corianne had spent the evening under her aunt's chaperonage at a small dinner party held by Lady Ridgelea in honor of her daughter's betrothal. From Corianne's point of view, the evening had been a horror. The guests were, she decided, almost all in their dotage, the rooms were airless and stuffy, the food was insipid and the music boringly tame. The betrothed girl was made so much of that no one had eyes for anyone else. And worst of all, there were only two young men present who could be considered eligibles. One was the omnipresent Wilfred Shirley, whom she was coming to despise, and the other was a stranger named Clement Fenell, for whom the best that could be said was that he wasn't *quite* bald.

She made no objection at all when her aunt took her home at the shamelessly early hour of eleven. Even bed was to be preferred to that disastrous party. The two ladies entered the foyer of Stanborough House wearily, handed their cloaks to the butler and started for the stairs. But Lady Stanborough's eye was caught by a splash of color on the table near the door. "What's that, Tait? Flowers?"

"Delivered this evening, my lady. For Miss—"

"For *me*?" Corianne asked eagerly, running down the stairs again.

"No, ma'am. For Miss *Sarah*. I suppose she forgot to

take 'em upstairs with her."

Lady Stanborough's eyebrows rose delightedly. "For Miss *Sarah*? But *who*—?"

Tait shrugged. "I'm sure I couldn't say, ma'am. I believe there was a card . . ."

But her ladyship was already *reading* the card, with Corianne looking over her shoulder. "How irritating!" Lady Stanborough muttered. "It isn't signed."

"Why . . . that looks like . . ." Corianne sucked in her breath in a horrified gasp. "Like *Edward's* writing!"

"Edward *Middleton*?" Lady Stanborough blinked at Corianne while the information slowly percolated into her consciousness. "You don't mean it!" Her eyes began to gleam with a matchmaker's rapacity. "Edward Middleton! How very *interesting*!"

Corianne snatched the little card from her aunt's hand and stared at it. "No, it couldn't be. This is some sort of coincidence. I must be mistaken."

Lady Stanborough's eager smile faded. "Yes, I suppose it *is* too much to expect." And with deflated spirits, she went up the stairs to bed.

Corianne followed. For the first time since her arrival, she felt a surge of discontent. London could sometimes be a great bore. As she walked down the hallway to her bedroom, she shook her head in disbelief. "It *couldn't* be Edward," she said aloud. "Not in a hundred years."

Chapter Ten

CORIANNE WAS STILL abed when the note from Edward was brought in by a housemaid. Cory ordered the curtains opened, read the note uninterestedly, tossed it aside, ordered the curtains redrawn and flung herself into the pillows again, pulling the covers up to her neck. The maid was tiptoeing out of the room when Corianne sat up with an anguished cry. Ordering the curtains opened again, she stumbled out of bed and searched impatiently about for the paper she'd tossed aside. She found it on the floor and perused it again, this time with intense curiosity.

There was nothing much to be gleaned from the note. He'd only asked, in the most mundane style, to be excused this morning from their semi-weekly ride. Since she'd always found this ride to be rather a chore—for Edward always subjected her to a veritable cross-examination concerning her activities—one would think she would be relieved to be able to avoid it. Instead, however, she flounced angrily across the room to the window seat and threw herself upon it with petulant irritation. For she had a sudden and vivid recollection of the flowers—and the accompanying card—she'd seen the night before.

"Is there somethin' wrong, Miss?" the surprised housemaid asked.

"No, nothing. Why are you standing there gaping? Go on about your duties," Corianne muttered curtly.

The girl whisked herself out of the room while Corianne stared out of the window at a grey, ominous morning that exactly matched her mood. The note was crumpled in her right hand while she thoughtfully chewed at her left thumbnail. It was a strange coincidence. The note on the flowers had been written in a hand that looked like Edward's. And now this. It was not that she minded the cancellation of the ride but that the circumstances made her feel suddenly insecure. Edward had always been so reliable. His constant and protective affection had been hers since childhood . . . like the very ground beneath her feet. Perhaps that was why his note this morning made her feel as if she'd stumbled into a hole.

But she was being foolish. He probably had some business to take care of. Hadn't he said something about moving out of the Fenton? She'd scarcely paid attention when he'd informed her and Aunt Laurelia of his change of address, but *that* was probably what occupied him this morning. She'd no reason to upset herself. Although, she thought petulantly, he *could* have arranged to move at some hour other than the one he'd set aside for *her*.

And as for the flowers, *they* must have come from someone else. Edward was not the sort to make pretty gestures. He had never sent flowers to *her*. Even on her birthdays he'd given her only practical things—a saddle, or a pair of ivory combs, or a box of writing paper. He would *never* have sent flowers. She was foolish to have alarmed herself about it.

Besides, Edward would never look at a dry-as-dust female like Sarah . . . not in *that* way. Her friend Belinda always said that Edward would never look at another female while Corianne was around. She had never before thought about the prospect of Edward's taking himself a wife, but she thought about it now. It would not be terribly shocking, she supposed, if he should do so. He was, after all, what Aunt Laurelia—and Belinda, too—seemed to consider a "good catch." But the prospect depressed her unutterably. He was *her* Edward . . . hers! Her female instincts had always told her clearly that she held Edward Middleton's heart in the palm of her hand. She had grown up with that knowledge—it was a deeply ingrained part of herself. She couldn't lose it . . . it would shake her too deeply.

She ran to the mirror to look at herself. Was she becoming old and losing her looks? But the face in the mirror was dewy with youth. Her cheeks were still flushed with sleep, her tousled hair framed her face charmingly, and her eyes were still wide and darkly blue. No, she would not lose Edward to the older Sarah. If Sarah *did* have a beau at last, it was not Edward.

Of course, Edward might marry some day. She would not mind, *if* he did so *after* she was safely married to Lord North and had no further need of him. She wouldn't mind it then. But in the meantime, it was comforting to know that Edward was hers, always at hand and at her disposal.

He *was* at her disposal, wasn't he? She jumped up and ran to the little writing desk in the corner. Snatching up the pen, she wrote hastily, *Dear Edward, How can you Desert me when I've been Counting on you? Whatever it is that Occupies you this morning you must Postpone. I am quite Unhappy and must speak to you at Once. I shall be ready to ride at our Usual time. Don't Fail me. Your always affectionate Cory.*

She directed the note to the Fenton, hoping he was still there. She called the maid and ordered her to have the missive dispatched at once. Then she hurried into a morning gown. She would go down for an early breakfast. She was consumed with curiosity to learn who it was who'd sent the flowers.

Her aunt and her cousin were both at the breakfast table when she came into the room. She had barely greeted them when Laurelia chortled happily, "You were right last night, Cory dear. It *was* Mr. Middleton's hand that penned that card."

Corianne felt a curious wave of panic. *"R-Really?"* she asked, stupefied.

"Mama is making too much of nothing," Sarah said calmly, reaching for a biscuit.

Lady Stanborough jumped up from her chair in annoyance. "You are *impossible*, Sarah. I don't understand you. Do you *want* to be left on the shelf? If Middleton has shown an interest, you must *encourage* him. Don't you have any proper female instincts at *all*?"

"A little nosegay is not necessarily a sign of interest, Mama . . . at least not the kind of interest you mean," Sarah demurred. "He's a confirmed bachelor, isn't he, Cory?"

"Well, I . . . I . . ." Corianne looked bemusedly from one to the other. "I've always *thought* so. Edward never . . ." Her voice petered out in a pathetic little quaver.

"There, you see, Mama? Edward never pursues females." Sarah smiled brightly at her mother. "You refine on this tiny incident too much."

Lady Stanborough expelled a disgusted breath. "Don't you know that *every* man is a confirmed bachelor—until he finds a wife? I wash my hands of you, Sarah. I completely wash my hands of you." And she stalked out of the room.

Sarah was not the least discomposed by the little scene. She reached for the teapot and poured out a cupful which she placed before Corianne. "Sit down, Cory, and help yourself to a slice of ham and some biscuits. Everything is still warm."

"Th-Thank you, Sarah . . . but I'm . . . not v-very hungry." She turned and wandered bewilderedly out of the room.

But it only took her time enough to climb halfway up the stairs before her confidence returned. She'd been silly. She'd magnified the incident out of proportion. Edward had made a small, gentlemanly gesture—probably to thank Sarah for some kindness—and she, Cory, was interpreting it to signify a proposal of marriage! She was as foolish as Aunt Laurelia.

Besides, she'd sent him a note. If she knew anything of Edward, he was certain to come running. That would show them all! All she had to do was to get into her riding costume and wait.

It was shortly past eleven when Edward called. Corianne, who'd been watching at the sitting-room window, flew into the foyer before Tait had even taken his hat. "Edward, you *dear!* I *knew* you wouldn't fail me!" And she flung her arms around his neck triumphantly.

Edward was completely confounded. "Cory! What's wrong?" he asked in alarm.

"Nothing," Cory laughed. "I'm just so happy you managed to come in time for our ride."

"Our ride?" He looked at her askance. "Since *when* has our ride been so important to you? I've had the decided impression you found it rather a nuisance."

She stepped back, shocked. "A nuisance! How can you *say* such a thing!" She tugged at his arm. "Well, come on. I can hardly wait to get started."

Edward looked at her, baffled. "But . . . didn't you get my note? I won't be able to ride with you today."

"Yes, but . . . didn't you get *mine*?"

"You wrote me a note? No, I didn't—"

Cory looked up at him in dawning dismay. "Then . . . why are you *here*? And . . . wearing your—?"

The sound of a step on the stair caused them both to look up. Sarah was coming down, dressed in a riding dress designed to turn heads. It was of a dark green velvet, its skirt sweeping the stairs in long, graceful folds, and its jacket, tightly fitted to the body, emphasizing her slim waist. A cocky little green hat was set rakishly on her auburn hair, a white plume waving coyly from the side of the crown.

Corianne gasped, and her cheeks whitened. "Oh! Have you an appointment with . . . I mean, do you take . . . *her*?"

Poor Edward was quite stricken at Cory's expression. "Well, I had *meant* to . . . but Cory, tell me, why did you send for me? *Is* there something wrong?"

Cory drew herself up proudly. "Not exactly. I *had* intended to discuss something with you, but I'm sure it can wait. If you've already committed yourself to my cousin . . . in the one hour you reserve for *me* . . ." She turned away, her head proudly erect.

Edward cast a helpless look at Sarah, who stood waiting patiently on the stairs. "Listen here, Cory," he began placatingly, "if there's something on your mind, I'm certain that Miss Stanborough will excuse—" He looked up at Sarah for corroboration, but she shook her head warningly.

Cory turned. "What did you say?" she asked with a feeling that she might yet be victorious.

Edward shrugged helplessly. He had promised to be guided by Sarah's advice, but if Cory needed him . . . ! "I said," he repeated hesitantly, "that I'm certain Miss Stanborough—"

Sarah, disgusted at seeing him weakening, came smoothly

to the rescue. "Miss Stanborough will bring him back in plenty of time for you to have a *tête-à-tête* this afternoon," she said placidly, sailing down the stairs.

Cory almost stamped her foot in chagrin. Turning away angrily, she tossed her head and replied, "I am spoken for this afternoon. Mr. Denison comes to take me up in his new phaeton."

"If a ride in a phaeton takes precedence over your talk with your guardian," Sarah pointed out sensibly, "then the matter you wish to discuss cannot be so *very* urgent, can it?"

Cory wheeled about furiously. "It *is* urgent," she declared. "*Very* urgent."

"In that case," Sarah said firmly, taking Edward's arm, "you will be here when we return. Mr. Denison can call at another time, I'm sure. We won't be above a couple of hours, will we, Mr. Middleton?"

Edward was staring at Cory in profound astonishment. It was quite clear that she'd been testing her power over him, and the knowledge left him dumbfounded. Sarah's little stratagem had really *worked*! It was like a game. In matters of the heart, men were like innocent babes, but women played the game like champion chess masters at the chessboard.

"Mr. Middleton?" Sarah prodded. "Two hours, wouldn't you say?"

Edward shook himself out of his stupor. If love was a game, he could learn the strategy of it as well as any other. He smiled down at Sarah. "As long as you say," he answered with exaggerated gallantry. "And I must remind you, my dear Sarah, that you agreed to call me Edward."

"Edward," Sarah nodded, squeezing his arm in relief, "shall we go?"

Without a backward look, they sauntered to the door, leaving Corianne looking after them in tight-lipped mortification.

Despite the fact that it had begun to drizzle, Sarah and Edward agreed to go ahead with their ride. The bridle paths in the park, usually busily occupied at that hour of the morning, were pleasantly free of other equestrians, and they were able to let their horses gallop freely through the light rain. Edward found himself laughing out loud, partly because of the sheer pleasure of galloping at a speed he'd been unable to indulge in since he'd left Lincolnshire, and partly because of the excitement of realizing that Cory was not as far out of his reach as he'd believed. Sarah, keeping pace alongside him, lifted her face to the raindrops, shut her eyes and surrendered to the pure physical pleasure of the ride. When at last they slowed their pace, she opened her eyes to find him grinning at her admiringly. "You are a crackerjack horsewoman, too, Miss Stanborough. Are there no limits to your acomplishments?"

"*Sarah*, remember? I don't know what *other* accomplishments you refer to, sir, but I've been riding since the age of three. My father, you know, was as much of a *horseman* as his brother, my uncle Roland, is a *scholar*. Since my father had no son, he was determined that his daughter should have as good a bottom as any boy."

"It seems he succeeded. You are a source of constant amazement to me, you know. How did you surmise that Cory would be so affected by my pursuing *you*?"

"I didn't surmise. I *knew*."

"Well, then, how did you know?"

She shook her head in wonder at his artlessness. Even quite sensible men like Edward could be such dolts when they fell in love. She wouldn't even *try* to explain it to him. "Come help me down. I'd like to stretch my legs a bit before we ride back."

Edward flipped a leg over the saddle, slid down from his mount and walked over to her horse. "I will when you tell me. How did you know?"

She laughed down at him. "Because I'm a witch. How else?"

"If that's true," he teased, "then you can *fly* down from there without my help."

His eyes smiling up into hers caused the familiar little tremor in her stomach. "Come, sir," she pleaded, a bit breathlessly, holding out her arms, "*do* help me down."

"I suppose I'd better," he said, grinning, "or you may put a spell on me."

Completely engrossed in their foolish badinage, they

took no notice of the sounds of approaching hooves. Just as Edward lifted his arms, catching her at the waist as she slid from the saddle, a horseman thundered alongside and, with an intake of breath loud enough to be heard above the hoofbeats, pulled his horse to an abrupt stop. Startled, Edward kept Sarah pressed against him as they both turned their heads to look at the intruder. To Sarah's horror, she found herself staring into the icily menacing eyes of John Philip North.

Chapter Eleven

SARAH FELT THE blood freezing in her veins. Her mind whirled in an agony of fear. How *could* she, in her involvement with Edward's problems, have so completely forgotten North's existence? She'd merely devised a simple little scheme to bring Corianne to her senses, intending only to help Edward achieve his heart's desire . . . and believing that the *cost* of the subterfuge would be hers alone. Instead, she was causing a situation in which *Edward* might have to pay the cost. The threat in North's eyes was unmistakable. He would have Edward's *death*!

Her eyes never left North's face as Edward set her gently on her feet. Before she could bring herself to speak, North wheeled his horse around and thundered out of sight. But she'd seen, not only in the expression of his eyes but in his white-knuckeld grip on the reins and the cruel fury with which he'd spurred his animal, that his mood was explosively dangerous. She was certain he would find a way to force Edward into a duel. He'd done it before, with much less provocation.

"What is it, Sarah?" Edward asked anxiously, peering into her whitened face.

She merely shook her head and asked to be taken home. She would not speak of the encounter, and Edward didn't press her. They were both relieved, however, when they found, on their return to Stanborough House, that Corianne was not waiting for them. The first-floor rooms were mercifully deserted, and Edward followed Sarah into the drawing room, determined not to leave her alone in her obvious agitation.

Sarah's mind was whirling in a desperate attempt to find a way to undo what had happened. She had only one hope (and a faint one at that) to convince Lord North that there was nothing between Edward and herself. She had no idea how she was to accomplish that goal, but the first step must be to tell Edward that they could no longer pursue the little charade they'd begun. She had to explain . . . without really explaining . . . that they could not be seen together again.

"But why?" Edward asked in adamant objection after she'd made a lame explanation. "Everything was going so well! You said so yourself."

"Please don't ask . . . I can't explain," she mumbled almost incoherently.

But Edward persisted. "What has North to do with this?" he asked flatly. "You can't deny that seeing him today on the bridle path has upset you. Are you *afraid* of him, Sarah?"

She was truly at a loss as to how to explain. "Well, yes, in a way," she admitted slowly. "He tends to be . . . somewhat . . . possessive."

Edward studied her closely. It seemed to her that his eyes clouded with disappointment in her. "I see," he said in a voice tinged with disapproval. "You mean that there is some sort of . . . understanding between you."

"Understanding?" She looked away from him in hopeless frustration. His reaction was just what she'd expected. How could she explain . . . how could *anyone* believe that North's abnormal possessiveness had come about without any encouragement from her? "No, there's no understanding at all," she murmured, not really expecting him to believe her.

But he *wanted* to believe her. "Then what right has he to be possessive?" he asked reasonably.

Sarah shrugged helplessly. "No right at all. He's a very . . . strange man."

"So it would seem. But Sarah, you can't allow your life to be run by his strange whims, can you?"

She turned away and walked to the window. She stood staring out into the street where the rain was now falling in a depressingly heavy downpour. "You don't understand,

Edward," she said dully. "North can be quite . . . dangerous."

"Dangerous?" His voice sounded angrily impatient. "To whom? To *you*?" He came up behind her and turned her to face him. "Has he made some sort of *threat* to you?" he asked incredulously.

"No, not to me. To . . . *you*!"

"To *me*?" Edward gaped at her for a moment and then, surprisingly, burst out into a laugh. A *laugh*! He patted her gently on the cheek, smiled reassuringly at her and said carelessly, "You must let *me* worry about that, my dear." Dismissing the entire subject, he walked to the door. "Don't tease yourself any more about this, Sarah. I can quite easily take care of myself. I've been doing it for years." And with that he was gone.

Sarah didn't move for several minutes. Her throat was choked with unshed tears. She'd always dreamed of finding a man who would stand up to North—a man with the blunt honesty and courage to be himself . . . to follow his own path no matter what threatening obstacles blocked his way. And she'd found him at last. That careless laugh had made her almost tremble with delight . . . for a moment at least. Until she remembered two things—one, that he *wasn't* hers. And two, that he didn't understand the real menace of the threat that faced him.

She shivered. She must pull herself together, she told herself firmly, get out of her damp riding clothes and figure out a way out of this nightmare. She went slowly up to her bedroom, stripped off her clothing and pulled on a warm, woolen robe. She poked up the banked fire in her hearth and sat down on the rug before it. Hugging her knees to her chest, she stared into the flames abstractedly. Edward's face, with its transforming smile, seemed to be hovering between her and the amber glow of the fire. He was a rare man, indeed, and too fine and good for Corianne Lindsay. If *she* were younger, she would try to win him from that spoiled little chit.

But she was forgetting North. Even if she *could* win him (and she knew that Edward's devotion to Corianne was too deeply ingrained in him to make it possible, even if she were still in her salad days), North would stand in the way. If ever she'd seen murder in a man's eyes, she'd seen it today. She shut her eyes in terror, trying to drive out the memory of Lord North's look. How could she make Edward understand? North had never been bested in a duel. Edward's courage was not enough to stop North's bullet from reaching its mark.

She had to find a way to keep North from challenging Edward. And she could think of only one way: North must be convinced that Edward was nothing to her. But how? Would it suffice to return to her seclusion? Even if she never again appeared in public in Edward's company, would North forget the incident in the park?

Perhaps he would, but Sarah doubted it. Besides, Edward had declared his intention of continuing to call on her. She could scarcely prevent his coming to call, especially while Corianne remained under this roof. North would be bound to learn that Edward was a frequent visitor at Stanborough House. No, nothing would be gained by seclusion.

Could she go to North and tell him in so many words that Edward was nothing to her? Would he believe her, especially when she, in her heart, knew the words to be a lie?

However, she *could* explain that Edward was in love with Corianne—*that* might make a difference. But would North believe that? Anyone observing Corianne's indifference would be sceptical . . .

But if she could *prove* it . . . if everyone knew that Corianne and Edward were *betrothed* . . . ! That was *it*! Sarah jumped to her feet and began to pace about the room in nervous excitement. If only she could arrange for Corianne and Edward to become betrothed! Lord North would have no reason for putting Edward out of the way if he were safely betrothed to another. All Sarah had to do was to convince Corianne of Edward's desirability. And she had to do it *soon*.

She sat down on her bed thoughtfully. *Could* she do it? Remembering Corianne's obvious jealousy this morning, she felt a wave of hope. She'd already made an enormous stride in the right direction. The scheme had worked perfectly, so far. Sarah had no doubt that Corianne would come to accept Edward someday, if she and Edward could follow her plan. But it would take time, and there *was* no time.

Sarah very much feared that North would act soon.

Somehow, Corianne would have to be pushed *headlong* into a quick change of heart. Sarah would have to concoct a scheme so dramatic, so shattering to Corianne's complacent acceptance of Edward's constant devotion, that the girl would fall into his arms. But how on earth was this to be contrived?

Sarah's breath caught in her throat. There *was* a way . . . a way so shocking that she blushed to her ears just *thinking* about it. It was daring . . . and completely shameless . . . but it *might* work.

Yes, it might work, but how could she propose such a brazen scheme to Edward? Every instinct rebelled against it. no, she just wouldn't tell him. She'd simply thrust it upon him at the proper time.

There remained but one decision to make; she had to decide just *when* that proper time would come. It had to be soon, for even now Lord North might be making plans of his own. If she tried, she might be able to arrange matters for tomorrow evening. But no . . . by tomorrow, Corianne might well have recovered from the attack of humiliation and jealous rage which had overcome her this morning. Sarah could not afford to permit Corianne's tumultuous feelings to ebb. If the desperate game of hearts was to succeed, *tonight* would be the time for Sarah to play her trump card.

John Philip North, the Marquis of Revesne, had not appeared in public all day. He'd missed an appointment at the boxing club, had failed to make his usual afternoon stop at White's, and had not shown his face at the coffee house where he'd agreed to meet Tony Ingalls. Ingalls was much put out by North's failure to keep the appointment—he'd counted on some much-needed assistance from his lordship. In pique, Ingalls took himself round to Revesne House in Cavendish Square and demanded of the butler to see Lord North immediately. When the butler objected, saying that Lord North was not receiving, Ingalls brushed by him unceremoniously and made his way to the library. There he found North seated at a long table, carefully cleaning one of a pair of ivory-handled duelling pistols.

Ingalls stopped in the doorway in surprised alarm. "Good Lord, Jack," he gasped, "what are you doing *that* for?"

The butler came chugging up behind him. "Shall I remove the gentleman, your lordship?" he asked, his chagrin showing behind the butlerish imperturbability.

North made a dismissing motion of his hand to the butler. "Never mind, Neames. You may go." He flicked his eyes over Ingalls briefly and continued to attend to the pistol. Sighting down the barrel, which he pointed at Ingalls, he asked coldly, "Didn't Neames make it clear that I was not receiving?"

"Will you point that thing in another direction?" Ingalls muttered peevishly, entering the room with a show of bravado. "I should think you'd greet me with a little less antagonism, old man. After all, you *did* fail me, you know. Kept me waiting at the Smyrna for almost an hour."

"There were more important matters on my mind," Lord North replied indifferently.

"You're not planning another duel, are you?" Ingalls licked his lips worriedly. He had performed as second for his lordship on two occasions, both of which had caused him extreme discomfort because of the necessity of dispatching the wounded opponents and dealing with the magistrates.

"I'll inform you of the matter when I'm quite ready. In the meantime, be a good fellow and take yourself off," North urged in a voice from which all emotion had been expunged.

Ingalls was not easily put off. "But I've a serious matter to discuss with you," he insisted. "I must have some advice."

North was unmoved. "Another time, Tony. Another time."

"I can't wait for another time. I shall be seeing her *tonight*."

North put down the pistol and gave his friend a look of annoyance. "Is this to be another outpouring of despair concerning your lady-love? Can there be *anything* pertaining to that subject which I haven't already heard a dozen times?"

Ingalls dropped into a chair. "But the situation grows

crucial! My creditors are beginning to hound me, my tailor refuses to extend any more credit, my family threatens to force me into a lengthy ruralization, and—"

North held up a restraining hand. "Spare me, my boy. I will agree that your troubles are mounting."

"But they can all be avoided . . . if only I could announce my betrothal to the rich and beautiful Miss Lindsay."

North shrugged. "Then announce it."

"How can I announce it, if the girl hasn't *agreed* to it?"

"Well, Tony, be reasonable. If the chit won't have you, it's no good whining over it."

"I don't know if she'll have me or not. I never get the chance to *ask* her. She's almost never left alone with me these days. And if I *do* manage to a minute with her, she plays this little game . . ."

North laughed unkindly. "Yes . . . they can avoid a confrontation while flirting quite outrageously, can't they?"

Ingalls nodded bitterly. "She's marvelous at skirting the subject. Don't know *how* she became so skilled. After all, she's only a country coquette."

Lord North resumed his work on the pistol. "I sympathize with your problem, Tony, but I don't see what *I* can do about it."

"There are two things you can do," the younger man said promptly. "One is that you can come to the Maitlands' ball tonight and distract the aunt long enough for me to get the girl alone. And two, you can advise me on how to pin her down."

North ceased his polishing and looked keenly at Ingalls. "Your little what's-her-name will attend the ball with *Lady Stanborough*? Not with her *guardian*?"

"You mean Middleton? I don't know. She'll be there with one or the other. They don't permit her to go out under *my* escort of late."

Lord North's eyes glittered interestedly. "One or the other, eh? But you don't know which?"

Ingalls merely shrugged and slumped in his chair.

"But it *will* be one or the other? You're sure of that? Very well, Tony, I'll be there. I hope she comes under Middleton's escort. I've a *very* strong desire to see him again."

The coldness of his tone was a warning signal to Ingalls. "You're not still smarting under that card-game defeat, are you?" he asked curiously.

North's lips tightened. "The card game has nothing to do with it."

"Then, what—?"

"Don't trouble your mind about it now, Tony. Let it suffice if I say that I shall be glad to detain Mr. Middleton while you accost your little game-pullet."

Ingalls didn't like the sound of this. "But what if it's the *aunt* who's to escort her?"

"I shall be disappointed," Lord North muttered.

"But you'll still manage to detain her, won't you?" Ingalls pleaded, his suit to win the fair Corianne uppermost in his mind.

"I've already agreed to it, have I not?" was the icy response.

Tony smiled in gratitude. "Thank you, Jack! I *knew* you'd come through. *Now* if you can only advise me on how to make the most of my time alone with Corianne—"

"My advice," North said, returning to his pistol-care, his interest in Tony's affairs fading quickly, "is simply to refrain from idle talk. In fact, I would refrain from conversation completely. Take her in your arms and overwhelm her. A frontal assault. She'll surrender in short order."

Ingalls looked doubtful. "Do you *mean* it? Isn't she a bit too young? She might become frightened and cry out."

"Don't be a mooncalf," North said, waving him out. The entire subject bored him. "It's the sort of behavior they all crave, young or old, although they'd rather die than admit it. Try it and see."

Ingalls rose to go. "Yes, I suppose you're right. I can't do any worse with her than I already have. See you tonight then. The Maitlands. About ten."

As he went to the door, he chuckled to himself. "A frontal assault, eh? That's good. Very good."

But North didn't look up from his work on the pistol. It had to be in gleaming readiness. With any luck, it would be put into use on the morrow.

Chapter Twelve

LADY STANBOROUGH HAD looked forward to attending the Maitlands' ball, but by the time evening approached she'd almost changed her mind. She'd developed a slight case of the sniffles, and the late-October weather had turned unpleasant. Although ordinarily she would have loved to attend what promised to be one of the greatest crushes of the season (for George and Henrietta Maitland were celebrating their twenty-fifth wedding anniversary in high style), Laurelia was on the verge of deciding that she would be wise to miss the event. "I might contract an inflammation of the chest, and *then* where would we be?" she asked her daughter plaintively, pulling her bedclothes up ot her neck. She had taken to her bed at the first sneeze and had sent for Sarah at once.

Sarah studied her mother worriedly. A crucial cornerstone of her plan for the evening was her mother's attendance at the ball. "You don't *look* ill, Mama," she said comfortingly. "Are you certain you shouldn't go? I was *counting* on you."

"Counting on me? For what purpose?" her mother asked, confused.

"I can't explain it to you now. But it's *terribly* important for you to take Corianne to the ball tonight."

"But why? We can ask Mr. Middleton to escort her. I'm certain that he'd have no objection—"

"That's just it, Mama. He's coming *here* . . . to . . . er . . . to see me," Sarah said, unable to keep from blushing.

Laurelia Stanborough blinked at her daughter in considerable surprise. "What? Again? Didn't you ride with him this very afternoon?"

Sarah merely nodded.

Her mother's expression changed as she gazed at Sarah with slow-dawning delight. "Oh, my *dearest* girl! Oh, my own *darling!*" She sat up in bed and threw the covers off. "Do you mean—? Are you . . . at *last*—?" And she pressed her hands to her breasts in joy.

Sarah urged her to lie back against the pillows. "Now, Mama, please! Don't refine on this—"

"Not *refine* on it?" Lady Stanborough demanded, pushing Sarah's hands aside and jumping out of bed. "What *else* can it mean when you want us out of the house so that you can talk to Mr. Middleton alone? Oh, Sarah, how wonderful that he can be asking . . . so *quickly* . . . !"

Sarah put a weary hand to her forehead. "No, *no*, Mama, you *mustn't* think . . . ! It's not *that*, really! I'll explain it all to you one day," she said urgently, trying to restrain her mother's transports.

But Lady Stanborough would not be restrained. "Oh, my *dear*!" she sighed, embracing her daughter, misty-eyed. "The *Squire*! Such an *impressive* man! Not as rich as North, of course . . . and no titles, which is really too bad. But I understand his lands are *extensive*! And *everyone* agrees that he's so pleasant and clever . . . and attractive, too! Oh, *Sarah*!" Moved almost to tears, she sniffed into the large handkerchief which she had already in hand. "I'm so h-h-happy!"

Sarah sighed in discouragement. "Mama, you are jumping to the most unwarranted conclusions," she insisted, but she knew she spoke to no purpose. Here was yet another idea which had taken hold of her mother's mind and would be almost impossible to dislodge. "At least you won't *repeat* any of this, will you?" Sarah begged.

"Of *course* not!" Lady Stanborough declared in offended dignity. "What do you take me for? I'm not some Hans Town housewife, bragging to the nobodies about my daughter's 'catch.' As soon as you've accepted him, I shall make an announcement with the proper formality. And now go away, for I must make myself ready for the ball."

"Are you *going*, then?"

"Yes, of course. You've put me in the most *energetic* mood, my dear. I feel completely reborn."

"Then, Mama, there is one thing you *must* do for me tonight," Sarah said, forcing herself to concentrate on her primary objective. "Something rather difficult . . ."

"Anything you ask, my love," her mother said effusively, "anything at all. Even my sniffle shall not keep me from—"

Sarah interrupted the outpouring by planting a light kiss on her mother's cheek. "Thank you, dearest. But you must listen carefully, because this is crucial to . . . well, to a plan I've concocted. You must bring Corianne home at the stroke of twelve. Even if she objects violently and insists on remaining."

"The stroke of *twelve*?" Lady Stanborough regarded her daughter with utter stupefaction. "Do you mean like *Cinderella*? *Why*?"

"That is something *else* I can't explain just yet. Will you do it?"

Her mother frowned impatiently. "Really, Sarah, you can sometimes be the *strangest* creature. *How* can I manage to tear her away at eleven-thirty if she insists on remaining?"

"Tell her your cold has become worse. She *cannot* refuse you *then*, can she?"

"No, I suppose not. But what if she says that someone *else* will take her home?"

Sarah took her mother by the shoulders and said forcefully, "No, Mama, you mustn't let her! Under no circumstances must you let her remain past eleven-thirty. She *must* be home by twelve, is that clear?"

"Clear? It's the greatest muddle I've ever *heard*! But I shall do it, if I must."

"Thank you, Mama. I shall be eternally grateful to you."

"I only wish I understood what this has to do with Mr. Middleton's proposal of marriage," Lady Stanborough muttered irritably.

"There isn't going to *be* any propo—" Sarah began. But

her mother wasn't listening. She had the most uncanny way of turning her mind away from whatever information contradicted an idea she had fixed on. It would be of no use whatever to argue with her. Sarah, with a sigh, gave up the struggle and left the room.

The preparations for the evening were soon under way in three bedrooms of the house. Sarah had little to do to prepare for her plan except to write a note to Edward. *Dear Sir*, she wrote, her embarrassment at the entire situation making her wording unwontedly formal, *I have need to discuss with you a matter of utmost urgency. Please call upon me at eleven tonight. Although the hour is an awkward one, it is* imperative *that you appear at that time precisely. The matter is of great importance to both you and C.L. I place all my reliance on your consent. Most sincerely yours, S.S.*

Lady Stanborough's preparations were more complicated. Her sniffles were growing worse with every passing moment, and she looked at herself in the mirror in dismay. When Madame Marie Antoinette Honore Dabbs entered to dress her hair, the strong-willed maid put her hands on her hips angrily. "Y'r ladyship ain't going out in this weather with that cold!" she said firmly.

"But I must, Madame," Lady Stanborough told her bravely. "Do what you can to cover my red nose. But what you can do with these rheumy eyes I just don't know."

When Madame was finally convinced that her ladyship would not change her mind, she shrugged in true Gallic style and put her considerable talents to work. In a few hours she managed to make Lady Stanborough passably presentable.

As for Corianne, *she* had no difficulty with her appearance. It was her *mood* which needed bolstering. She had spent the entire afternoon pouting in her bedroom. Edward's defection had shaken her badly. She'd paced about in chagrin, written a half-dozen letters to Belinda and thrown them all away, railed against his disloyalty and thoughtlessness, decided to go home, decided to stay but send *him* home, and wept into her pillow in a frenzy of self-pity. But when the room darkened in the late afternoon and she began to think about the evening (intending to send a message to her aunt to go without her), she remembered a chance re- mark Tony Ingalls had made. Tony had said that Lord North might be in his company at the Maitlands' ball.

Lord North was the reason she'd come to London, and Corianne had not yet been able to capture his attention. Edward's behavior was unimportant when compared with North's. Studying herself in the mirror, Corianne's confi- dence began to reassert itself. She would put Edward out of her mind . . . for the time being. North was bigger game. She had to concentrate on *him*.

She washed her face and sent for her abigail. She chose to wear her favorite gown, a Dutch-blue lustring cut low across the shoulders and tantalizingly covered with an ov- erdress of silver gauze. Madame Marie found time to dress the girl's hair in a very becoming Grecian style tied with silver cord. Then Corianne stepped into a pair of silver slippers, put on the diamond earrings she'd inherited from her mother, and pulled on a pair of long white gloves which covered her arms up to and over her elbows. These touches of elegance made her feel exhilaratingly worldly. Her mood climbed, and she began again to believe that she could do anything . . . accomplish anything . . . and win anyone. North tonight. Edward tomorrow.

Lady Stanborough and Corianne were at last ready to depart, and Sarah, bidding them goodnight at the foot of the stairs, complimented them profusely. Corianne, not having forgotten her earlier chagrin, merely tossed her head and walked disdainfully out to the carriage. Sarah whispered to her mother a last-minute reminder to have Corianne back by midnight; Lady Stanborough grunted in compliance, blew into her handkerchief and left.

With a sigh of relief that the first phase of her plan had been accomplished, Sarah turned her attention to her *own* appearance. It was important to look her best, for Corianne's confidence had to be shaken to the core, and *that* would not be accomplished by a "rival" who looked like a dowd. Madame Marie was again called upon and again did her work well. When Sarah looked at herself in the glass, she was pleasantly surprised. Her appearance was just what she'd wished. Her dress, though simply styled, was of a soft, lilac-colored camlet that clung to her body in flattering lines, making her look tall and slender. And Madame had dressed her hair to fall, loosely casual, about her shoulders. The English dresser had achieved the perfect French aura of . . . well . . . romantic restraint. Her appearance exactly suited her purposes. For the first time since the meeting with Lord North that afternoon, she breathed a sigh of relief.

But the relief was only momentary. By ten-thirty, Sarah was pacing about the drawing room, her tension mounting painfully. At ten-forty-five, the door knocker sounded, inexplicable and urgent. Sarah felt a stab of despair as the butler admitted a red-eyed and wheezing Lady Stanborough! *"Mama!"* Sarah cried. "What—?"

"Don't look at me like that, Sarah," her mother said with asperity, "for I'm not up to it. My head aches, and my eyes burn, and I shall undoubtedly develop a severe inflammation. I'm going to bed."

"I'm sorry, Mama. Of *course* you must go to bed. But, where's Cory?" Sarah was trying desperately to keep her extreme perturbation from showing in her voice.

"I've taken care of everything, so you needn't worry. I gave young Ingalls the strictest instructions to deliver her by twelve," her mother assured her. "Where's your Mr. Middleton?"

"He'll be here shortly. Let me help you upstairs and into bed."

"No, no, I shall manage. You stay right here and proceed with your doings. Don't mind me. I shall have Madame prepare a tisane for me. I shall have no need of you at all. But Sarah, as soon as Middleton leaves, you *must* come up with the news. I'm sure I shan't be asleep, but even if I am, you must promise to wake me. Nothing can be more beneficial to my health than word that you're betrothed."

Sarah was too upset to remonstrate. Lady Stanborough took herself up to bed, and Sarah resumed her pacing. Things were going wrong already, and she had no power to correct them. Corianne would no doubt come home *hours* late. Could she manage to keep Edward sitting here all that time? What a troublesome state of affairs!

At ten-fifty-five, Sarah dismissed the butler. "Go to bed,

Tait," she ordered. "I shall wait up to admit Miss Corianne myself."

Tait frowned. "Don't see why you *should*, Miss Sarah. I always—"

"I know you do, Tait. But please indulge me tonight. I want you to ignore the sound of the knocker for the rest of the night."

The butler reluctantly withdrew, and Sarah sat down to calm herself and wait. Edward arrived on the stroke of eleven, looking worried. But his brow cleared as he noted Sarah's appearance. "You couldn't look so beautifully serene," he said in relief, "if something were seriously amiss."

Sarah smiled wryly. "If I look serene, my dear sir, then I wear a false face indeed. My heart is jumping up and down in my throat quite alarmingly."

"Is it? *Is* anything amiss?" Edward asked, following her into the drawing room.

"Nothing . . . and everything," she answered enigmatically. "Sit down, Edward. I have a great deal to tell you, and I don't know how to say it or how much time I shall be given to make myself clear.

At the Maitlands' ball, Tony Ingalls was feeling as elated as his friend North was feeling irritable. For North, the sight of Corianne under the chaperonage of her aunt had been a source of considerable disappointment. In fact, he'd been so chagrined at the absence of his quarry, Middleton, that he'd gone out on the Maitlands' terrace (in spite of the rain and a rather frigid wind) and expelled a number of vulgar epithets into the night air.

But Tony was having better luck. Lady Stanborough had left him in charge of Corianne. With the assurance of North's help, he had every confidence that at last his campaign to win her hand would succeed. North, having eased his anger during his moments out-of-doors, and having nothing better to do for the next two hours (an appointment with a certain lady-bird had been arranged for half-past midnight), was ready to render his friend his promised assistance.

While the dancing was proceeding full tilt in the ballroom on the first floor, Ingalls and North persuaded Corianne to

accompany them to the upper floor to see the famous Rom-
ney portrait of Lord Maitland's mother. Tony led the un-
suspecting girl into the library. North, who'd been walking
alongside the pair, winked at Ingalls behind Corianne's
back, closed the door behind them and took a place nearby
to guard the door against any intruder who might wish to
enter.

Inside, Corianne turned a started face to the door which
had closed behind her. "What's happened to Lord North?"
she inquired, suddenly uncomfortable.

"He'll be back in a moment," Ingalls said with a dis-
arming smile. "There's the portrait, just behind you over
the fireplace."

Corianne turned, walked over to the fireplace and studied
the painting. "She was very lovely, wasn't she?" she said
admiringly.

Following his instructions, Ingalls didn't waste time in
idle chatter. "Not nearly as lovely as you," he said effusively, coming close and pulling her to him abruptly.

"Mr. *Ingalls*!" Corianne gasped in horrified shock.
"What are you *doing*?"

But Tony ignored her gasp. He clutched her tightly with
one arm while he grasped the back of her head with his free
hand and pulled her face to his. "You're the loveliest girl
I've ever known," he murmured, his lips against her
cheek.

"Let me *go*!" Corianne cried, pushing against him with
all her strength. But the vile creature only grinned and
pressed his mouth to hers. Corianne could hardly breathe.
She waved her arms helplessly about, but he was conscious
only of his power over her, the softness of her body against
his and the smell of the scent she'd dabbed behind her ears.
Again and again he kissed her, murmuring incoherent little
endearments, barely permitting her to catch her breath.
Desperately, she stretched out her hands to the mantelpiece
behind him. Her fingers reached a large porcelain vase. She
clutched it with both her hands and, trembling with fury,
she lifted it as high as she could and let it crash down upon
his head.

Ingalls dropped to the floor like a stone, completely
unconscious. Corianne stared at him in horror for a moment

and then flew to the door. Throwing it open, she found Lord North standing there. "Oh, my lord!" she cried, casting herself into his arms. "I've *killed* him!"

"What?" Lord North looked over her shoulder into the room where Tony lay motionless amid the debris of the broken vase. "Good God!" he exclaimed. "What on earth have you *done*, you silly widgeon?"

"He . . . He . . . *attacked* me!" Corianne said, trembling from head to toe and beginning to sob.

North extricated himself from her embrace. "Stay right there. Don't move," he ordered. "And stop sniveling. You don't want to attract a crowd, do you?" He strode over to Tony's prostrate body and knelt beside him. He turned his friend's face toward him and, to his relief, Tony groaned. "So you're *not* dead," he said drily.

"Wha' happened?" Tony asked stupidly. A large lump was growing at the top of his crown, and a small trickle of blood was making its way down his face.

"Nothing. You botched it. The girl floored you."

"Floored me? How?"

"With a vase, obviously. Are you all right? Can you stand?"

Tony lifted his head, wincing in pain. "Yes, I . . . think so."

Corianne, standing miserably in the doorway, gave a tearful cry of relief. "He's *not* d-dead . . ." she said in a choked whisper.

Ingalls threw her a look of bitter accusation. "No thanks to you," he said, putting a hand to his aching head.

Corianne came into the room with a gingerly step. "It's your own f-fault," she declared, quivering. "You must have gone mad!" With a trembling underlip, she turned to Lord North, who was surveying them both with an air of extreme disgust. "I want to g-go home," she said pathetically.

"Very well," Ingalls said, allowing North to help him to his feet. "If you'll wait until this dizziness passes, I'll take you."

"You?" Cory squealed in alarm. *"Never!* I shall never permit myself to be alone with you again!"

"But Cory . . . !" He wobbled unsteadily toward her. "I promised your aunt—

She backed away from him nervously. "I don't *care*! I won't go with you!"

North intervened, taking Ingalls aside and speaking to him with quiet authority. "The girl's right, Tony. You've botched it. And forcing her to go with you now will only make things worse. You look a sight, anyway. Why don't you clean yourself up and slip out of here quietly? Get a night's rest. Tomorrow will be soon enough to find a way to smooth over this disaster."

Tony nodded in gloomy acquiescence. "All right. Will you take her home?"

North shrugged. "I suppose I shall have to."

In his carriage, Corianne grew calmer. She had been appalled by Ingalls' unprecedented behavior, but the incident was over now with no permanent harm done. Her mind quickly moved to more immediate matters; there was an opportunity right at hand. Here in his carriage, she was alone with Frozen North for the first time! It was the best opportunity yet for her to make a mark on him. She glanced at his immobile face opposite her. He looked frozen indeed. "Are you qu-quite angry with m-me, my lord?" she asked with charming shyness.

"Angry?" His voice was completely indifferent. "Why *should* I be? Your affairs of the heart have nothing to do with me."

"That was *not* an affair of the heart!" Cory declared pugnaciously. "I have no such . . . er . . . *relationship* with Mr. Ingalls."

"Oh?" his lordship inquired coolly. "Then why did you lead him on?"

"Did he say I led him on?" she asked, outraged. "If he did, he's shamming it shamefully. I *never* did so."

Lord North raised an eyebrow. "Didn't you? I have eyes, you know. Do you think you can run sly with *me*, my dear?"

This was the sort of conversation Corianne truly enjoyed. It centered on herself, had a touch of flirtatiousness about it, and it could lead to all sorts of promising outcomes. "I didn't know you *ever* took notice of me, my lord," she said coyly.

He smiled at her disdainfully. "How can I *not* have

noticed you? You've thrust yourself under my nose at every opportunity."

Cory drew herself up in mock offense. "How *can* you say such rude things to me? It's quite unkind of you, sir."

"Yes, it is. I'm not much known for my kindness."

"Yet you *can* be kind, I know. You're being kind by taking me home like this," she suggested, smiling at him enticingly.

"Save your flirtatiousness for the younger men, Miss Lindsay," he said coldly, completely dampening her spirit. "I'm not attracted to the coquetry of children."

Corianne, abashed, withdrew to the corner of her seat. The silence in the coach grew oppressive, and she was conscious of the fact that her best chance to impress him was dissipating rapidly. "Can you tell me the time, my lord?" she asked desperately, in a weak attempt to stir conversation up again.

He took a watch from his waistcoat pocket and examined it. "Almost eleven-thirty," he said with a slight yawn.

Sarah had been trying for the past half-hour to explain to Edward the plan she had in mind. But she feared he might object to it . . . or, worse, storm out of the house in disgust. This fear affected her normally sharp mental processes and the clarity of her expression. She resorted, instead, to a kind of circumlocution by which she hoped she could make her plan clear to him without actually saying the words. "Do you see, Edward," she asked for the third time, "that a quick and dramatic act might be the very way to push Corianne over the brink?"

Edward was eyeing her with bemused tolerance. "No, I'm afraid I don't see. You have thus far only presented me with a number of incoherencies which make no sense to me at all."

Sarah gave a nervous little laugh. "Yes, I know. But you *do* understand that I have a plan to make Corianne see the light . . . and we are to execute that plan tonight?"

"Yes, I understand that much. But I told you this afternoon that there was no need for hurry. What you haven't made clear is why you've brought me here in the dead of night for something we'd agreed earlier was not a pressing problem."

She took a turn about the room, wringing her hands in agitation. "It is a more pressing problem than you realize," she said earnestly.

"I can see *one* thing, Sarah," Edward said grinning, a grin which had its usual devastating effect on her insides. "I was quite wrong about your being serene. As a matter of fact, you are being rather charmingly distracted. I only wish I knew why."

"I'm *trying* to explain, Edward. Really I am. It's just so . . . difficult . . ."

Edward came up to her and put his hands on her shoulders in an attempt to calm her. "I wish you could feel free to come to the point. I promise I won't eat you. There's nothing you can say, you know, which would affect my respect and admiration for you."

"I wish I could be sure of that," she muttered under her breath.

"What did you say?" he asked.

At that moment, however, she heard a carriage draw to a stop outside. "Oh, good *God*!" she cried in trepidation. "They're *here*! And I haven't even *begun* to explain—!"

"Explain *what*? *Who's* here?" Edward asked, utterly confused.

"Never mind that now. There's no time! Just come here and sit down beside me!" Grasping his hand, she pulled him to the sofa and pushed him down, seating herself beside him. The sofa stood directly opposite the doorway of the drawing room. The door had been left open, and anyone passing it on the way to the stairs would be bound to see them. "There, that's it," Sarah muttered distractedly. "Now, put your arms around me . . . *quickly*!"

"What?" Edward asked, astounded.

She lifted his arms and placed them firmly around her waist. "Now, Edward, try not to be too shocked. I want you to . . . *kiss* me!"

Edward gaped at her. "You can't mean—!"

"Yes, I *do*!" She threw her arms around his neck and lifted her face to his. "Kiss me, Edward . . . as if you *really mean it*!" she demanded and closed her eyes.

Chapter Thirteen

EDWARD WAS ONLY HUMAN, after all. Sarah's face was close to his, tilted up with unwittingly enticing charm. The glow of the firelight and the few candles which lit the room gave her skin an amber warmth. The lashes of her closed eyes brushed against her cheeks with a faint tremor, and her lips were moist and inviting. So . . . in spite of a feeling of complete bewilderment, Edward did as he was bid. He kissed her.

She shivered in his arms. Without thought, he tightened the slack hold he'd had on her waist. The movement seemed to comfort her, for he could feel her relax against him. The touch of her lips on his was intoxicating. The bewilderment that had troubled his mind suddenly swirled away, as a dream does when one is abruptly awakened. He was aware only of a sensation of surprised pleasure . . . and a desire that this moment should not end.

Her arms tightened around his neck. "Don't move," she murmured, not taking her lips from his.

"No, never," he answered foolishly, pressing her to him hungrily, as if to prove by action as well as word that he intended never to let her go.

Outside, on the stone steps leading to the front door, Corianne was detaining Lord North. "You see, my lord? There is a light in the drawing room." She fluttered her lashes appealingly. "You must come in and explain things to my aunt. I'm much too upset to be able to talk about it."

"You're an artful little creature, aren't you, Miss Lind-say?" his lordship queried sardonically. "You know quite well that your aunt has taken her cold up to bed an hour ago."

"Then it must be Sarah," Corianne persisted menda-ciously. "You can explain it all to *her*." She knew that Sarah never waited up for her. It was the only pretense she could find, however, for prolonging her *tête-à-tête*.

Lord North looked at her with sudden interest. "Sarah? Does she always wait up for you?"

Corianne couldn't meet his eyes. "Most of the time," she said sweetly, looking down at her shoes. The words were said in flagrant disregard of the truth and the twinges of her conscience.

"Then lead the way, my dear," North said with a sudden smile.

With a feeling of triumph, Corianne opened the door and led him into the foyer. The fact that Tait, the butler, was nowhere in evidence was another bit of luck, she thought. She had no wish to share these opportune moments with anyone but Lord North himself. She led him down the hall toward the drawing room. When they came up to the door-way, however, they both froze in their tracks, struck com-pletely dumb by the scene being enacted across the room.

There was nothing artificial or tentative in the embrace they found themselves witnessing. The two people on the sofa were so tightly entwined they seemed almost to have melted into one being. They appeared to be completely un-aware of anything or anyone else in the world. North could barely stand the sight of them! The way the soft skirt of her gown had fallen over his leg, the way her hair hung down from her back-tilted head and brushed against his arms, the way the position of his broad shoulders seemed to be shielding her from any outside attack—all these things were instantly maddening to Lord North. A low growl sounded in his throat and, with a shake of his head, he threw off his stupor and burst into the room. *"Damnation,"* he raged, "I'll kill him *tonight*!"

At the very first sound of his voice, Sarah started as if she'd been shot. She lifted her head, turned, saw the face she dreaded and cried out in panic. Corianne, still in the doorway, could now identify the man who'd been embracing her cousin. *"Edward!"* she shrieked, appalled. "Edward, how *could* you?"

For a moment after Sarah had pulled away from him, Edward didn't move. He sat staring at her as if he'd never seen her before. But her terrified expression drew his attention to Lord North, who was advancing on him with murder in his eyes. With only his instinct for self-preservation guiding him, Edward jumped up and swung his fist as hard as he could at the enraged Marquis' chin. The sound of the impact was dreadful, causing both Sarah and Corianne to scream.

North, thrown off balance by the blow, tottered backward and fell heavily against a table. Momentarily dazed, he leaned against it to steady himself. Corianne flew to his side, almost hysterical. "Oh, my God! Are you hurt? Edward, have you gone *mad*?"

Edward, his own brain muddled with a dozen confusing emotions, had no patience for hysteria now. "Cory, go up to bed. This is not your affair."

"Look! He's *bleeding*!" Cory cried in alarm, ignoring her guardian's orders.

And indeed there *was* a small drop of blood trickling down from the corner of his lordship's mouth. North lifted his hand to his face and then looked at his blood-stained fingers in some surprise. He smiled at Edward menacingly. "Well, bumpkin, you seem to have drawn first blood."

"Cory," Edward repeated firmly, "I've told you to go up to bed."

"No, I won't! Don't treat me like a child! You're not my father, you know," she said furiously. "Lord North is *my guest*, and—"

"Do what you're told, Miss Lindsay," North interjected coldly. "You're decidedly in the way here."

Corianne gasped and looked from Edward to North with eyes filling with tears. She felt as if she'd been slapped. Sarah took a step forward, as if she were about to comfort the girl, but a slight gesture from Edward stayed her. With a little sob, Corianne wheeled about and ran out of the room, pulling the door closed behind her with a noisy slam.

There was a long moment of silence during which the three remaining in the room studied each other warily. Lord North removed a lace-edged handkerchief from his pocket and dabbed at the blood on his chin. The blow to his face and Middleton's altercation with Corianne had given him time to collect his wits and recover his equilibrium. He realized that his intention to choke the life out of Middleton could not be accomplished here in Stanborough House before the eyes of witnesses—not if he wished to escape the consequences. He had to curb his rage. However, the damnable bumpkin *had* provided him with ample cause to issue a challenge, and *that*, after all, had been the very object of his participation in this evening's escapades. So things were not progressing so very badly after all.

He was the first to break the silence. "So . . . I find you, for the second time in one day, in each other's arms. I *thought*, Sarah, my dear, that you'd told me this fellow means nothing to you. How do you account for this astonishing behavior?"

Sarah looked at him fearfully. "You don't underst—"

"Damn it, North," Edward interrupted angrily, "I don't see why she should account to you at *all*! This entire matter doesn't concern you."

"Ah, but it does, bumpkin. It does."

Edward gritted his teeth. "I begin to find that epithet a trifle wearing, my lord. I suggest that you address me by *name* in future."

North sneered. "Really? And how do you mean to compell me?"

"I'm quite prepared to draw second blood," Edward replied promptly. "Shall we take off our coats?"

North waved his handkerchief disparagingly. "Fisticuffs? My dear sir, how unutterably vulgar. This is a matter to be settled like *gentlemen* . . . on a field of honor."

"A field of honor?" asked Edward, puzzled. "Are you speaking of a *duel*?"

"By all means. I've long been anticipating such a meeting."

Edward raised his brows. "A duel? I had no idea that such nonsense was still . . . *wait* a minute! I seem to remember being challenged like this once bef—"

Sarah drew in her breath and put her face in her hands.

"Good *Lord*," Edward muttered, looking from North to Sarah, "I'd completely forgotten! Cory's come-out. That scene in the sitting room. That was *you*!"

Sarah made a helpless little gesture with her hand and turned away in shamefaced agony.

"Yes," North said regretfully, "I should have gone through with it *then*. I underestimated you, bumpkin. If I'd followed my first instinct, I'd not have to endure this *present* annoyance."

"You mean you were *serious* then?" Edward asked in disbelief.

"And I'm serious now. Well, bumpkin, when shall I advise my second to call on you?"

"Any time you wish, my lord," Edward responded.

"No!" Sarah whirled around. "Jack, are you *insane*? How long—? What good can come of it?"

North smiled wryly. "Some good, apparently, has come of it already. You haven't called me Jack in years."

Edward was taken aback by the intimacy of this interchange. There was *something* between those two, despite Sarah's denials. He felt a startling and painful constriction of the chest. What *was* it that had occurred between them? Had they been lovers? Were they lovers *still*? Edward almost winced at the possibility.

Meanwhile, Sarah had gone up to North and clutched at his lapels. *"Please!"* she was pleading, white-faced with terror. *"Listen* to me! What you saw when you came in was just a trick . . . a *game*! There is *nothing*—!"

Edward couldn't bear to listen. He came up behind her and wrenched her away, grasping her by the shoulders and almost shaking her. *"Don't,* Sarah! There's no *need* for this . . . humiliation. I told you . . . I can well take care of myself."

Sarah looked at him in utter despair. "Oh, Edward, you don't *know*—!"

"That's right, bumpkin. You *don't* know," North agreed. "She's trying to warn you that your days are numbered."

"I wouldn't be too sure of that, my lord, if I were you," Edward answered confidently.

North laughed. With an abrupt motion of his right hand,

he whipped from an inner pocket of his coat a small, silver pistol.

"Jack!" Sarah cried out in horror.

"I only want him to be prepared for what awaits him," North said with a leer. "Keep your eyes on that candle, bumpkin. The one on the table behind the sofa." He turned, strode to the corner of the room farthest from the candle he'd indicated, raised his arm, aimed and fired. The sound of the shot was deafening. The candle was instantly snuffed out. When the smoke cleared, they could see that the wick was gone, but the candle had not been nicked. And the bullet had lodged itself neatly into the wall behind.

Sarah moaned and swayed unsteadily on her feet. Edward moved instantly to her side. "It's all right," he said quietly, leading her to a chair. "Don't let these theatrics frighten you."

North laughed again. "Go ahead, bumpkin, make the most of your time. For soon it will be *your* light that's snuffed out." He sauntered to the door. "Regarding the matter of the visit from my second . . . will tomorrow suit you?"

Edward bowed mockingly. "I am at your lordship's disposal."

Sarah made a choking sound deep in her throat. North paused in the doorway and returned Edward's bow. "Good night, then. May you sleep well."

They could hear his sneering laugh as his footsteps echoed down the hall. *"Put out the light and then put out the light,"* he quoted threateningly as he let himself out of the house.

The sound of the outer doorway coincided with the alarmed cluckings of every member of the household who'd been awakened by the noise of the shot. They began to congregate on the stairs, in the hallways and at the door of the drawing room. Edward glanced at Sarah. The girl was sitting in the chair, staring unseeingly ahead of her, unmindful of the hubbub. Leaving her undisturbed, Edward went out to the hallway and closed the door behind him. He instructed the butler to send everyone back to bed. "Nothing's happened, I assure you," he said earnestly. "Nothing is at all amiss. Lord North was only demonstrating the efficacy of a new pistol. It went off by accident."

Only Lady Stanborough would not be put off. "Let me see for myself," she demanded, coming down the stairs in her bare feet and marching firmly to the drawing-room door.

Edward opened the door for her. "There, you see? Everything's fine."

Lady Stanborough looked up at him suspiciously. "Is it? Then why does Sarah look so pale?"

"I was just about to ask her. I was told, Lady Stanborough, that you are somewhat indisposed. Why don't you return to bed and let me talk to Sarah?"

"Haven't you talked to her *yet*? I don't know what's wrong with you young people." She cocked her head and squinted up at him provocatively. "*My* husband would have had me on his *lap* by this time. Well, go *on*, fellow. Don't stand about here gaping." She turned and pattered up the stairs.

Edward didn't trouble himself over her confusing remarks. He waited until she'd disappeared from view, and then he returned to the drawing room. Sarah had not moved from her chair. Edward looked down at her kindly. "If it's this blasted duel which has upset you, ma'am," he said reassuringly, "I beg you not to tease yourself over it."

Sarah shuddered and frowned up at him with a sudden outburst of impatience. "Not *tease* myself? He'll *kill* you, don't you understand?"

"It seems to me, my dear, that you and North *both* underestimate me. I can use a gun, too, you know. We bumpkins do a great deal more shooting than most Londoners are wont to do. You needn't worry about me." He paused and looked down at her thoughtfully. "Unless," he added, "it is not *I* who is causing your apprehension."

"What?" She blinked up at him. "I don't know what you mean."

"I mean that it occurs to me that it is *North* you're concerned about, not I. Isn't that it? There *is* something between you, isn't there?"

She stared at him for a moment and then turned away in annoyance. "Don't be a fool," she said dully.

"I think," Edward said slowly, "that I've been a fool all along. You've been *using* me ... like a pawn ... in this game you're playing with that . . . cad."

"Edward!" She turned back to him with eyes widened in pain and bafflement. "You *can't* believe that! You must *know* I only wanted you and Corianne to be . . . happy . . ."

"So I thought. But you must admit that this evening . . . the way you inveigled me here at the precise house when North made an appearance . . . and how he found us in—how can I put it?—in a compromising position—?"

"Edward!"

"And the intimacy of your conversation with him—"

"Please! You're quite *wrong*—!"

"Am I? Tell me the truth, Sarah. When you suggested the plan to make Cory jealous, when you embraced me there on the sofa . . . during *all* of this—weren't you pursuing your *own* objectives, not mine?"

She couldn't have guessed, a few minutes earlier, that she could ever in her life feel more miserable. But now something inside her chest seemed to crack wide open. "Can you really b-believe," she asked, trembling, "that I would knowingly expose you to a . . . d-duel? That I would r-risk your *life* for . . . for . . . ?"

Edward, looking down at her, was smitten with doubt. The face turned up to him, so full of sincerity and wide-eyed anguish, was hardly the face of a duplicitous *intrigante*. "I don't know *what* to think," he said with a sigh.

For Sarah, it was the last straw. She pulled herself out of the chair and turned her back to him. "I . . . can't speak of this any longer," she said wretchedly. "Please go, Edward."

"Yes, you're right. There's been quite enough said in this room tonight."

"More than enough," she agreed, turning to watch him leave. He walked slowly to the door. There he turned back and put out a hand. "I . . . ." But he went no further. Expelling his breath hopelessly, he dropped his arm, turned and left.

Sarah shut her eyes in anguish. She might never see him again. With a tremor that shook her from head to toe, she dropped down on her knees before the chair, cradling her head in her arms on the seat. "Oh, my *God*!" she wailed in despair. "What have I *done*?"

Chapter Fourteen

STANBOROUGH HOUSE WAS a dismal place the next day. Corianne refused to come out of her room. Sarah moved about. the house in a daze. And Lady Stanborough, who would normally have given vent to her feelings without troubling herself about the pain she would be inflicting on her daughter, this time maintained a tense silence. "I've never *seen* such a look on Sarah's face before," she confided morosely to Madame Marie. "It makes me want to weep. Put me back to bed, Madame. My sniffles may be better, but my spirit is decidedly out of curl." She burrowed, a tiny, pathetic creature, among the many pillows piled against her headboard and let Madame Marie tuck a comforter around her. "Do you think Middleton failed to come up to scratch? Is *that* what's upsetting her so?"

"I'm sure I couldn't say, my lady," Madame Marie answered with asperity, "but if that's wot hurt her, I'd like to scratch 'is eyes out! Miss Sarah is too *bonne* for him, if ye asks me. Men! Don't *savez* when they're well off, they don't."

"Yes," her ladyship agreed. "Pack of fools, the lot of 'em. But I had no *idea* that Sarah'd so completely lost her heart."

"I had a notion she'd taken to the Squire from the start,"

Madame Marie confessed, plumping up her ladyship's pillows as if she were pommeling all the hard-hearted men in the world for their cruelty to females. "Fussed with her hair a bit more'n usual, y'know. And she stopped wearin' that silly cap. I ain't never . . . *jamais* . . . seen her so taken wi' a gent."

"Oh, dear," Lady Stanborough said tremulously, her eyes filling. "My poor lamb!" Two large tears spilled down her cheeks. "My poor little lamb. I suppose she'll *never* marry now."

But Sarah herself had no time for tears. She was determined to find a way to prevent the duel from taking place, for if it did, she was certain it would end in tragedy. Early in the day, she'd sent a note to Lord Fitzsimmons to come round, and as the day wore on she watched the street from the drawing-room window in growing impatience. At last, shortly before three, he arrived, looking almost as pale and worried as she. "I know what you want to say to me," he told her at once. "At least, I'm not *exactly* certain, but if you're going to complain about the duel, there's no use jawing at *me*. He won't listen to me."

"Edward's told you, then? About the duel?" Sarah asked tensely.

Fitz nodded. "I'm to be his second."

"When—?"

"Tomorrow morning."

Sarah dropped into a chair with a groan. "My *God*, Fitz, there must be *something*—"

Fitz shrugged helplessly and sat down opposite her. "I talked myself blue! All *night*! All he said was that I'm unduly worried . . . that he can handle a pistol with the best of 'em."

"*Can* he?"

"Perhaps. How can I be sure?"

"Don't you *know*?" Sarah asked impatiently. "I thought you've been friends for years."

"I've never been *shooting* with him. I can't be expected to know everything about the fellow. I don't even know what they're *fighting* about! As near as I can make out, it's because North insists on calling him a *bumpkin*!"

"Never mind. It doesn't matter anyway," Sarah said hopelessly. "Even if he *can* shoot, it won't save him. They'll only kill *each other*."

"Do you think I haven't thought of that? However, Ned says he won't kill North. His plan is to aim for the right shoulder . . . put old Jack off his aim, y'see."

Sarah gave Fitz a disdainful glare. "He'll never have time."

Fitz lowered his chin on his hand glumly. "I know."

For the rest of the afternoon, Sarah prayed for a miracle, but by evening it was clear that no miracle would occur. There was only one thing left to do, and no matter how much her instincts rebelled against it, she had to do it. She sent for Madame Marie. "I want you to come with me for a short ride, Madame. I have to pay a visit to a . . . a gentleman—"

"Miss Sarah, no! *Non!* It ain't proper. Besides, I'm sure that if ye was to send the Squire a little *billet*, he'd come round like a shot."

"The Squire?" Sarah asked, frowning. "What makes you think I'm going to see the Squire?"

"Well, *ain't* ye?" the dresser asked, nonplussed.

"No. It's . . . something else. And it wouldn't do to have him come here. I must go to *him*. Are you going to stand there and argue with me, Madame, or will you help me?"

"I'll help you, o' course, but—"

"Very well, then. Get your cloak and meet me downstairs in ten minutes."

The coachman was stony-faced when they drew up before the Revesne house, but Madame Marie was horrified. "You ain't going in *there*!" she whispered, grasping Sarah's arm as the girl was about to climb down from the carriage.

"Why not, Madame?" Sarah asked her curiously. "Do you know this house?"

"Everyone knows it," Madame declared in a hissing undervoice. "All sorts o' *cher amis* goes in there. Common gossip. I won't *have* ye—!"

"Hush, Madame. You're not helping to steady my nerves with this kind of talk. I *must* go, don't you see?"

"No, I don't. I can't let ye go in there *toute seule*."

"But you'll be with me," Sarah assured her. "You can save me if I get into trouble."

Madame Marie considered for a moment and then nodded. "All right. But just let 'im lay a hand on ye . . . and we'll see wot we'll see!"

The two women walked quickly to the door. After they'd knocked and had to stand waiting for so long that they both began to feel uncomfortable, the door was opened by North's butler, a man almost impervious to shock. But a pair of unescorted *ladies* was not a sight he often saw on his doorstep. He permitted an air of disapproval to show on his face. "Is his lordship expecting you?" he asked depressingly.

In order to counteract a wild urge to run away, Sarah steeled herself with all the courage she possessed. "Step aside, please," she said boldly. "You've kept us standing in the wind quite long enough." She grasped Madame's hand and, pulling her behind, stepped past the butler with head high.

"Who shall I tell his lordship is calling, ma'am?" the butler asked, aware from Sarah's manner that this was undoubtedly a lady of quality.

"I shall ask the questions." Sarah was amazed at her own temerity. "Where is his lordship?"

The butler was nonplussed. He knew quality when he saw it, and he didn't like to offend a lady of her obvious station. "In the library, ma'am," he said, a bit more politely. "If I might have your name, I'll be happy to tell his lordship you're here."

"Never mind. Just show me to the library, please."

"But his lordship is—"

"Y' heard what my Miss just asked ye, y'lump! Hop to it!" Madame Marie ordered sharply.

The butler balked. It was one thing to take orders from a lady, but *this* skinny baggage was quite another story. "Now see here, my good woman—" he began.

"Please don't brangle," Sarah stopped him. "I'm in a great hurry. This is a matter of utmost urgency. Please take me to his lordship." She held out a gold coin. "I assure you he won't be angry with you for it."

On that assurance, and with the gold coin in his hand, the butler nodded. "He's got a visitor with him, you know," he remarked as he led them down the hall. "He may not like—"

"A visitor?" Madame Marie cast an alarmed glance at Sarah. "Not a *female*!"

"It's a medical gentleman," the butler offered in reassurance.

"Is his lordship *sick*?" Sarah asked, a spark of hope igniting in her breast.

"No, ma'am, but he might not wish to be interrupted."

"He will not mind the interruption," Sarah said with more confidence than she felt.

When they arrived at the library door, she pointed to a chair just beyond it. "Sit there, please, Madame. I shan't be long."

"Very well, Miss. Just sing out if ye need me," Madame Marie said, giving the butler a disdainful glance and sitting stiffly on the edge of the chair.

The butler opened the door. "Your pardon, m'lord, but there's a lady here—"

"Damn you, Neames, I told you I didn't want to be inter—"

"It's most urgent, my lord," Sarah said, presenting herself on the threshold.

"Good Lord! *Sarah!*" Lord North jumped up from the table at which he'd been sitting. A man in a black coat, who'd been sitting opposite him, also got to his feet. Sarah looked carefully about the room. It was dimly lit by a fire in the fireplace and a branch of candles on the table. In the candles' light, a frightening object on the table drew Sarah's eyes at once—a wooden case containing a pair of evil-looking, ivory-handled duelling pistols.

As North came round the table to Sarah, the stranger— a short, ruddy, large-bellied man with a head of dark, unruly hair—observed her with unmistakable interest. She returned his stare coolly. North came up and seized her hand. "What a delightful surprise! I regret that you've caught me in my shirt-sleeves."

Sarah brushed aside his concern with a dismissive wave of her hand. "That's quite all right, my lord." With a nod toward the stranger, she added, "I'm sorry to have intruded."

"May I present Dr. Crowell? He's to preside over tomorrow's affair. We've completed our business, haven't we, Doctor?"

The doctor bowed. "We have indeed. I beg you to excuse me, ma'am."

"Not yet," Sarah said, hope again springing up in its eternal way. "Do *you* approve of this business, Doctor? Surely a man in your profession cannot condone—even support—such activities. Can't you persuade his lordship to forget this dreadful affair?"

"I never interfere in these matters of honor, ma'am," the doctor said in an oily, unctuous tone that was at the same time offensively patronizing. "I only see that the rules are followed and that the wounded are cared for. It is not my place to make judgments other than those in my province."

Her last hope dashed, Sarah turned away from him and said scornfully, "Perhaps the magistrates may make judgments about *you* one day."

"The magistrates are paid well to overlook duelling, I'm afraid," the doctor said with irritating complacency.

"Well, go along, Crowell," North said, urging him to the door. "Neames will show you out."

Neames held the door as the doctor bowed himself out. "'Til tomorrow morning, then," the doctor said pleasantly as the door closed on him.

As soon as they were alone, Lord North came up behind her. "Let me take your cloak," he said, putting his hands on her shoulders, "although you've come for naught. I know your errand, but you can tell Middleton that even *your* good offices will not save him."

Sarah pulled out of his hold and whirled around to face him. "Edward did *not* send me, if that's what you're implying. He appears to be as stupidly eager for this . . . this *encounter* as you are!"

"Then I'm mistaken," his lordship acknowledged. "But not mistaken about the reason for your visit, I think."

She lowered her eyes. "No. You are not mistaken."

"Then let me have your cloak, my dear. We may as well be comfortable while you speak your piece."

She let him take her cloak, which he placed over the back of a chair. "I can't believe you will continue to be so unreasonable, Jack," she said softly. "You have no cause to fight this duel, you know."

His mouth tightened. "No *cause*, ma'am? I found you in each other's *arms*!"

"I tried to explain it to you last night. It was nothing but a trick . . . a trick for Corianne's benefit!" She came up to him and looked into his face earnestly. "There's nothing between Edward and me except friendship. It's Corianne he loves. Has done for *years*! I only tried to *help* him."

North looked down at her with brows upraised disdainfully. "How, my dear, would *your* embracing him assist him with Miss Lindsay?"

"Don't you see it? Corianne is a spoiled child, so completely sure of his affection that she takes it for granted. I thought she might be shaken out of her indifference if she believed he loved another."

"How generous of you!" North said scornfully.

"Generous? What do you mean?"

"To have permitted Middleton to use you for so selfless a reason as that."

Sarah reddened and turned away. "I suppose . . . it was . . . generous," she said awkwardly.

North came up close behind her and said contemptuously, "I hope you will forgive me, my dear, if I tell you that I don't believe a word of this. Although I will admit that you've invented an ingenious explanation. It shows a remarkably fanciful imagination. What talent! You should write novels, my love."

"It's all true! Every word!" she said urgently, turning to face him again. "Edward has eyes for no one but Corianne."

"That is the weakest point of your entire tale. Do you think for one moment that I believe Middleton could prefer that chit to you?"

"You flatter me, my lord. You cannot have taken a good look at Corianne. And you are remembering me as I was, not as I am."

He took her chin in his hand. "You haven't changed as much as you pretend." He studied her closely. "So . . . Edward prefers that child to you, does he? And how about yourself?"

She lowered her eyes. "Myself, my lord?"

"Yes. Are you trying to make me believe that you have no interest in *him* beyond the friendly? I saw your face as you looked down at him in the park, you know."

"You are unduly jealous," Sarah declared as firmly as a trembling voice and a fast-beating heart permitted. "You give significance to glances and smiles and other trivialities that have no meaning."

"Don't take me for a fool, my dear," he said, dropping his hand from her face. "It's a grave mistake to underestimate me."

"It's an even more grave mistake, my lord, for you not to believe what I tell you. To go through with that ridiculous duel."

"Your concern for this man is quite excessive, is it not? How can I believe in your indifference to him when you plead for him like this?" North asked sardonically.

"My concern is not only for him. It is also for *you*!"

"You need have no concern for me. I shall have no difficulty at all in killing the bumpkin."

"I don't doubt it. But such a killing would find society outraged. They would all be against you. Yes, even *you*, my lord, will find it hard to escape the consequences. At best, you will be ostracized by everyone who counts. At worst, you will have to flee the country for years."

He regarded her curiously, walked across to the fireplace and leaned on the mantel. "Are you trying to pretend you *care* about the consequences to me? I would have thought you'd *rejoice*."

She met his eye bravely. "How little you know me, my lord."

"You haven't *allowed* me to know you. After all these years of your holding me at a distance, I can't believe *now* in this sudden change in your feelings."

"You know nothing of my feelings . . . then or now."

His eyes kindled interestedly. "Are you suggesting, my dear, that you've always been 'concerned' for me? This is not the first time I've fought a duel over you. Why have you waited until now to show this concern?"

"I never believed, until now, that you would *kill* ."

His brows knit suspiciously. "Are you expecting me to swallow this tale that all these years, you—?"

"Would you believe me, Jack, if I agreed to marry you? If you still want me to, of course."

Slowly, his eyes never leaving her face, he crossed the room to her again. "Do you love that bumpkin as much as *that* ?" he asked with a vicious sneer.

She gasped and whitened. Were her feelings so transparent that even the lure of marriage—a marriage he'd sought for so many years—had failed to deceive him? She'd failed . . . failed completely. And they were all doomed. With a little cry from deep in her throat, she ran to the chair where he'd placed her cloak and snatched up the garment. There was nothing more to be done here.

But his hand caught her arm. He had no intention of letting her go now. He hadn't dreamed she would go so far to stop the duel as to offer herself to him in marriage. He'd desired that marriage for years. If it was indeed within his grasp, he would not let the chance disappear so easily.

Could she be telling him the truth? he wondered. Had she fallen in love with that clod Middleton, or had she cared for *him* secretly all these years? Both possibilities seemed equally unlikely. It was hard to imagine that she, a woman who'd refused a number of likely candidates beside himself, could have succumbed to a nobody like Middleton. *On the other hand* , he asked himself, *if she cared for me, why would she have hidden the fact for so long* ? Women, however, could be very strange. He was aware that she'd not liked the way he'd handled matters when he'd courted her. He'd been, in her view, too demanding and arrogant. Perhaps her pride had made her hide her feelings. She *was* a female of great pride.

It was her pride that most made him want her. Her breeding, her grace, her slender, unobtrusive beauty all made her the perfect choice to be the Marchioness of Revesne, but it was her pride he liked best. He was attracted to her, he admitted, but in truth he cared nothing for love in the romantic sense. For his sexual desires, he had many outlets . . . but for marriage, it was only Sarah who would satisfy him. He would always want a life apart from a wife,

but Sarah was the sort who would have the good sense—
and the pride—to let him go his own way. And her pride
would keep her from complaining in public—or private—
about his excesses. It would be that pride which would keep
the name of Revesne unsullied by scandal.

So what did it really matter *why* she had come to him?
Even if she *had*, for some inexplicable reason, lost her head
over Edward Middleton, it didn't matter. So long as she
agreed to wed him, she might cry in her pillow at night
over whomever she wished.

"Let me go, my lord," she was saying in a choked voice.
"I see it is no use to say anything more."

He held her arm tighter. "Did you mean it? *Will* you
marry me?"

"What?" She turned to him in surprise. "But you said
that you . . . didn't believe me . . ."

"I want to believe you. And you *know* I want you for
my wife."

"Enough to cancel the duel?" she asked frankly.

He grasped her waist with both hands and pulled her to
him. "It would be a small price to pay. Have we a bargain,
then?"

Stiff and tense in his embrace, she nodded slowly.

"Then look at me, Sarah. We must have a kiss to seal
our troth."

Obediently, she turned her face to his. But she couldn't
look at him. She shut her eyes and tried to keep her feeling
of revulsion from welling up in her throat.

The sound of the door made them both jump apart.
"*Pardonnez-moi*, Miss Sarah," said Madame Marie, stick-
ing her head in the doorway, "but ye've been here a longish
time. Are ye all right?"

Sarah almost sighed in relief. "We're just finished, Madame. I'm coming."

North helped her on with her cloak. "You've escaped
me for now," he muttered in her ear, "but there will be
other times."

Sarah held out her hand to him. "Good night, my lord.
You *will* send a letter to Mr. Middleton tonight, to inform
him that there is to be no duel, won't you?"

"As you wish," he agreed, taking her hand. "And you

will, of course, have your mother put a notice of our betrothal in the *Times*?"

Madame Marie drew in her breath. Sarah tossed her a
warning look. "Of course," she said to Lord North.

He lifted her hand to his lips. "You've made me the
happiest of men, my dear," he said, the note of self-satisfaction in his voice sounding like a death knell in her ears.

Chapter Fifteen

EDWARD HAD GONE to bed before the message was delivered, so it was Fitz into whose hand the letter was placed. The footman who delivered it informed him importantly that it was from Lord North and that no answer was required.

Although the hour was very late, Fitz had not even undressed. He'd known that his feelings of agitation would prevent him from even closing his eyes, so he'd spent the evening pacing about his drawing room. But he was weary to the bone, he was agonized about the forthcoming duel which was to take place at dawn and to which he was forced to be a party, and he was miserably lonely for his wife and babies. He'd spent the entire evening wondering, first, how Edward could possibly sleep so peacefully, and, second, how he'd even permitted his wife to let him leave his happy Norfolk home and family.

With the letter in his hand, he dropped into an armchair, loosened his neckcloth and stared at the letter's seal. What could Lord North possibly have written at this late hour? If there were some detail concerning the arrangements which he wanted to change, shouldn't he have asked Mr. Ingalls, his second, to call on Fitz himself? Of course, the letter might be a request for a postponement. That could be a hopeful occurrence which would give Fitz and Sarah another chance to work something out . . . But they'd done everything they could think of already. Besides, he didn't think he could *bear* another day of this tension.

It was too much to hope that North had decided to withdraw. No, that likelihood was too remote, for North had never been known to pull back from an engagement on the field of "honor."

Well, he thought wearily, letting his head fall back against the back of the chair and closing his eyes, *I'd better waken Ned and show this to him.* But he hated to do it. It was almost one o'clock, and Ned would have to rise and get full possession of all his faculties in little more than three hours' time. The fellow needed his sleep. On the other hand, the letter might be important. Fitz was tempted to break the seal and read the letter for himself, but he couldn't permit himself to do so. He'd better get himself out of his chair and wake poor Ned right away . . .

The next thing he knew, however, was that someone was shaking him. "Wake up, Fitz," Edward was saying. "It's after four."

"Mmmff." Fitz blinked, shook himself and stretched out his arms. He opened his eyes to find Edward bending over him, fully dressed for the out-of-doors. The candles had guttered out, the fire had died down to a dim glow, and the room was almost completely dark. Good heavens, he'd fallen asleep in his chair! "Must've dozed off," he mumbled apologetically.

Edward grinned at him. "You certainly did, and in your evening clothes, too. But it's just as well, for we've no time for you to change. Just wash your face, and we'll be off."

"What? In *evening* clothes?"

"I'm afraid so, old fellow. I don't want to be late and give North the chance to claim victory by default."

Fitz got up clumsily. "Right. Be with you in a minute. Well, perhaps not a minute, exactly . . ." And he stumbled off to his bedroom.

Edward paced about the room. He was not nervous, but impatient. It was not that he looked forward to this morning's work, but that he wanted to get it over with. When he took his second turn about the room, he noticed a letter, with the seal still unbroken, on the floor near Fitz's chair. He picked it up. In the dim light of the glowing embers, he could just make out his name scrawled across the front. He went over to the window and pulled the drapes aside, but it was darker outside than in. Hastily, he crossed to the mantel and fumbled for a match. He lit two candles and scanned the letter quickly. With a furious growl, he read it again from the top, this time more slowly. But the second reading only angered him more, and he crumpled the paper in his hand.

Fitz emerged from his bedroom with his hat and cloak. "Well, I'm ready," he said unhappily. "I suppose we may as well get started."

"Never mind," Edward told him irritably. "It's all off. You are free to go to bed and get some sleep."

"*Off*? It's *off*? How do you—?"

"He's written to me," Edward said, tossing the crumpled note into the fireplace.

"Oh, Lord! The *letter*! I clean forgot! Did he postpone—?"

"Reneged altogether, the blasted cur!" Edward muttered in disgust.

"*Reneged? North?* I don't *believe* it!" Fitz chortled delightedly, tossing his hat in the air and catching it behind him with a little dancing step. "What a marvelous bit of *luck*!"

"Luck!" exclaimed Edward furiously. "It wasn't luck. I could wring her neck!"

"*Her* neck? Whose?"

"Your friend Sarah's. *She's* at the bottom of this."

"I don't know what you're talking about, Ned, but if this is *her* doing, you ought to get down on your knees and thank her."

"Is that so? Listen here, Fitz, I've told you both—over and over again—that I can handle North. But both of you persist in believing that I'm incapable of taking care of my own affairs. Well, I won't be able to prove myself now, but if you think I'll *thank* either one of you for that, you may think again!"

He strode to the door, more enraged than Fitz had ever seen him. "If you want to know how I feel," Edward stormed as he quit the room, "I find your confidence in me far short of admirable!"

Fitz stared after him for a moment, chewing his moustache in bafflement, and then looked at the spot where Edward had tossed the letter. The crumpled paper had struck the grate and bounced out onto the hearth. This time, Fitz permitted his curiosity to overcome his conscience, and he picked up the paper and smoothed it out. *To Mr. Edward Middleton, Esquire, my dear Sir:* he read, *I find that I must extend an apology to you and ask you to permit me to withdraw my challenge. Miss Stanborough has explained to me that I seriously misconstrued certain events which occurred yesterday and that my action in issuing the challenge was ill-considered. Now that I understand the circumstances, I quite concur with her in this opinion. In fact, since Miss Stanborough and I have agreed to announce our betrothal, a quarrel with you at this time would be inappropriate. Therefore, I have taken the liberty of informing my second and Dr. Crowell that the matter between us has been cleared, with honor on both sides, and that tomorrow's meeting will not take place. With best wishes, I remain yours, etc., John Philip North, Marquis of Revesne.*

Fitz would have sworn a few minutes earlier that anything which prevented the duel would please him enormously, but this letter left him feeling puzzled and irritated. No wonder Ned had been angry. "Honor on both sides," indeed! His lordship's arrogance was truly vexing. Who was *he* to decide so insolently on when and where to duel, when *not* to duel, and where the honor lay? North merely snapped his fingers and expected everyone to dance to his tune.

And what was the meaning of the sentence about a betrothal to Sarah? Was the girl demented? Didn't she realize the excesses of North's character? Fitz sighed in disappointment. He'd hoped that she and *Ned* might make a match of it. He'd been sure that she'd shown signs of a *tendre* toward his friend. If only Fitz could discuss all this with his Clara. *She* would understand it better than he ever could. Clara would probably say that Sarah had sacrificed herself—

Good *God*! Could *that* be the explanation? Yesterday, Sarah had been almost beside herself with worry. Had she taken this drastic measure to save Edward? And if so, should she be permitted to go ahead with her scheme? Was there anything that he, Fitz, should *do* about it? "Oh, my Clara," he muttered under his breath, "where are you when I need you so?"

Before he could ruminate further, he heard Edward stride past the drawing-room door. "Good heavens, man," he called out, "where are you going?"

"I told you. To wring Sarah's neck!" came the terse reply.

"What? *Now?* It's half-past *four!*"

There was a moment of silence, and then Edward came sheepishly into the room. He met his friend's eye and broke into a grin. "I forgot," he said and dropped into a chair. He would wait. It would only take six hours.

Lady Stanborough dropped her biscuit into her coffee cup in astonishment. "*North?*" she squealed. "*North?* But I thought it was the *Squire* who—!"

"You only imagined that, Mama," Sarah explained with a strained smile, reaching across the breakfast table and patting her mother's hand. "Edward and I are only friends. I thought you'd be *delighted* at my news."

"I *am*. I'm all atwitter. It's just . . . so unexpected! It's wonderful, of course . . . if I could only . . . grasp it."

"Poor Mama. I'm sorry to have shocked you so. Just give yourself time to let the news sink in. Once it does, I know you'll be overjoyed."

"I *am* overjoyed. Oh, Sarah, what a *match*! Only *think* of his wearing the willow for you all these years! I've always said it, haven't I? I always knew—"

"Yes, you did, Mama. You were quite right," Sarah said, lifting her cup to her lips. She hoped that a good swig of hot coffee would melt the lump in her throat. It certainly would not do to burst into tears at this supposedly joyous moment.

"Wait until people hear!" her mother said ecstatically, the significance of Sarah's news beginning to dawn on her. "The whole of London will be *agog*!"

"Why?" asked Corianne, who walked into the breakfast room during Lady Stanborough's effusion. "What's happened?"

"Oh, Corianne," chirped her aunt excitedly, "*you* shall

be the very *first* to hear! Sarah is to become the *Marchioness of Revesne*! Lord North has finally convinced her to become his *wife*!"

Corianne's expression of interested expectation did not change for a few seconds. Then she paled, wavered slightly back and forth, her eyelids trembled shut, and she slid to the floor in a swoon.

It had not been a very good morning for Corianne even *before* she'd heard Sarah's news. She had not recovered her spirits from the blows to her self-esteem of the two previous days, and the morning had brought a letter from Belinda which had given her additional pain. Belinda's tone had been ecstatic, but Corianne had not been able, in her wounded state of mind, to take Belinda's news in good part. *You are not to believe*, Belinda had written, *that I don't miss you dreadfully, Cory, for I do, but your absence has had some delightful results. Now that you are gone, three of the young men whom you "carried in your pocket" have found themselves able to look elsewhere. Sidney Gleggins has become enamored of Alice Burgess, and they are to announce in the spring. (Yes, the same Alice Burgess whom we've so often described as an awkward goose, but she has blossomed out amazingly since Sidney began to court her and now is thought of as a pretty and graceful creature!) And your once-devoted Sir George Farrow seems to be on the verge of offering for, of all people, the feather-headed Trixie Merideth. At every gathering they sit with their heads together, Trixie giggling throughout like a veritable zany. But the best news of all is that* yours truly *has managed to convince a certain Thomas Moresby that she is desirable above all other human creatures—even you!—and he has actually spoken to Father! We are to be married in May, and you must be sure to come home in time, for I must have you beside me as my maid—or matron?—of honor!*

Corianne knew that she ought to be happy for her friend, but it did not add to her wounded self-esteem to realize that, even in Lincolnshire, she was not as devastating to men as she'd been before. To her credit, she scolded herself severely for her lack of generosity, she composed herself as best she could, and she assumed a cheerful demeanor for her entrance into the breakfast room. But the news that Sarah had snatched North away from under her nose had been the last straw. Thwarted beyond her endurance, she simply fainted.

Sarah administered hartshorn, and Corianne came round. She insisted that it was nothing, but Lady Stanborough ordered her to bed. A doctor was immediately summoned. He, too, told Lady Stanborough that nothing was wrong with the girl. "Probably burning the candle at both ends," he diagnosed, and he prescribed nothing more drastic than a day or two of rest.

Sarah was trying to decide whether Edward should be informed when the man himself knocked at the door. It was just after ten, a rather early hour for a call, and Tait's announcement of Mr. Middleton's arrival took Sarah by surprise. *He has a sixth sense when it comes to Cory's welfare*, she thought with a pang of envy as she went downstairs to greet him.

But, of course, it had not been for Corianne's benefit that Edward had come. It had been Sarah herself who had been troubling his thoughts since four that morning. Fitz had kept him company for a while, but Edward had made his friend go to bed when the clock struck five. Since that time, he'd reviewed everything he knew about Sarah Stanborough in a troubled attempt to understand what she'd done. He knew that his speculations were not as clear as they should have been, for the recollection of their embrace kept interfering with his normally analytical thought processes. He had to admit that the incident had shaken him badly. The lustrousness of her face as she'd held it up to be kissed, the sweetness of her lips on his, the sensation of holding her in his arms had been as exhilarating as it had been unexpected. He was far from a green boy, but he could remember no caress which had so disquieted him.

He tried to push the memory aside. He was in love with Cory, wasn't he? And for the first time in all these years of unspoken attachment, he was actively pursuing her. He'd felt a sense of disloyalty in even *remembering* his feelings for Sarah during that embrace. So he'd forced himself, instead, to recollect the details of the quarrel he'd had with Sarah at the end of that disastrous evening.

The recollection of the quarrel did little to clarify his thinking. He was deeply ashamed of himself for his part in that exchange. He'd accused Sarah of *using* him to pursue her own ends, but later reflection had convinced him that he'd acted out of an unjustified and unexplainable jealousy. How *could* he have challenged her basic and unmistakable honesty? And what right had he to be jealous at all? Never in his life before had he behaved like such a cad. He owed her a most humble apology.

But she owed him an apology as well. She'd had no right to interfere with the consummation of the duel. She, like Fitz, had too little faith in his capabilities, and that fact infuriated him. He would have liked to duel with the despicable North just for the opportunity to *prove* himself to Sarah! If she'd sold herself to that blackguard just to prevent the duel, it was a sacrifice that he, Edward, could not permit.

If the duel was her reason . . . the "if" was the key word. Why *had* she taken such a drastic step? How could Edward guess her real motivation? There were certainly signs, last night, that she and North had some connection. But Fitz had told him that it was common gossip that North had been pursuing her for *years* without success. She'd refused him until now. Edward could well understand that refusal. A girl with Sarah's sweetness and sensitivity could not be drawn to a sybaritic scoundrel like North! *Could* she?

There was nothing for it but to ask. If she'd taken this step in his own behalf, Edward had to stop her. He'd come to this decision before eight. He'd spent the next two hours wandering about in the streets. At ten, unable to wait any longer, he'd made his appearance on her doorstep.

Sarah greeted him matter-of-factly and told him about Cory's indisposition. She noticed that he listened with a rather surprising air of abstraction. Nevertheless, she hastily assured him that the doctor had found nothing wrong. "I'm convinced that the doctor would have no objection to your going up to see her for yourself," she urged with a kind but withdrawn politeness. "She's not asleep."

"No, thank you. If the doctor says she's well, I see no reason . . . that is, I've come on a more pressing matter. May I talk to you in private, ma'am?"

The tension in his face gave Sarah a clue to his purpose

in coming, and she had no wish to pursue the discussion. "I'm rather tired, sir," she said, matching his strained formality with her own. "I wish you will excuse me for the time being."

His mouth tightened. "I've been waiting since four o'clock this morning to talk to you, Sarah," he burst out angrily, "and I won't wait any longer. Is this room occupied?" Without waiting for an answer, he took her by the elbow and drew her into the breakfast room just beyond where they'd been standing. "I'd like to know the meaning of this, ma'am," he demanded, waving the crumpled letter before her eyes.

While she scanned the letter, he shut the door. When he came back, she thrust the paper back into his hand. "It seems to me to be quite clear," she said, walking around the table to the window and staring out of it with unseeing eyes.

"It's clear that you found it necessary to go to North to plead in my behalf, and *that*, ma'am, is an act I find humiliating and . . . unacceptable."

"I'm afraid you'll *have* to accept it, Edward, for it is already done."

He came up behind her. "It can be *undone*!" he exclaimed urgently. "Tell him you will *not* marry him after all."

"I will tell him no such thing," she said implacably.

"But why not? Please, Sarah, *listen* to me. If the duel drove you to take this step, I *beg* you to believe that you need not feel alarm about it. I promise you that I am quite capable of—"

"I don't wish to discuss that blasted duel!" Sarah cut in. "The incident that prompted North to challenge you has been explained, and . . . the matter is *finished*!"

"Not for me." He took her gently by the shoulders and turned her to face him. "I can't permit you to go ahead with this marriage. Surely you don't *wish* for it!"

"But I *do*," she declared staunchly.

He stared at her. "I don't believe it!"

"Why don't you? You said yourself, the other night, that I . . . I . . . arranged that misbegotten little plot for my own purposes."

"But I didn't mean it! Forgive me for what I said the

other night, Sarah. I don't know *what* . . . ! I must have lost my head."

"There is nothing to forgive. You were quite right."

"Are you saying that you *did* plot to lure North here to discover us embracing?" he asked in disbelief.

She couldn't meet his eyes. She looked down at her clenched hands. "Perhaps not, but—"

"Of course not! Why *should* you have done such a thing? There was no need . . . Fitz says he's been asking you for years to wed him. And you've been refusing him for years, isn't that so?"

"Yes, but—"

"Stop this nonsense, Sarah! Look at me! It *was* the duel that made you accept him. Admit it!"

She drew a deep breath and looked up at him levelly. "Perhaps the duel brought matters to a head," she lied, "but I would have accepted him sooner or later."

"Sarah!" The look of shocked pain in his eyes was almost more than she could bear. "You can't mean what you're saying. The fellow's a . . . a . . ."

"Please, Edward, don't. I can't permit you to speak badly of him . . . not to me."

"But the man's completely *unworthy* of you. Are you expecting me to believe that you *love* him?"

"Why should you *not* believe it?"

Nonplussed, he floundered for an answer. "He's not . . . not at *all* your sort of man. Do you think, in the past few days, that I've learned nothing of your character? Do you think I haven't seen your innate quietness, your deep reserve, your dislike of society's extravagances? Can a man be in your company for more than an hour without recognizing your gentleness, your kindness . . . so many qualities of sweet good nature? How can you claim to love someone who is so completely your antithesis?"

Sarah was overwhelmed by this flood of words. Her throat burned with tears she couldn't shed. She turned back to the window, unable either to look at him or to speak. After a while, hoping she could control her voice, she attempted to answer him. "What has *l-love* to do with *character*?" she asked quietly. "Does one fall in love only with one's *likeness*?"

"Perhaps not," he answered, "but one *doesn't* fall in love with someone one can't respect."

"Are you so sure of that?" she asked, turning on him. "What about *your* love for Corianne?"

He took a step backward, struck speechless. He'd always admitted to himself that his feeling for Corianne was illogical at best. The differences in their ages and tastes were great enough to make his love seem as ludicrous as Sarah's for North. He had no answer for her.

They stared at each other for a long time, pale and shaken. At last, Edward broke the silence. "You *do* love him, then," he said dully.

She turned back to the window, her silence an assent.

"Then I suppose there's nothing more to be said. I . . . I wish you happy, ma'am."

"And I you," she responded in a choked voice. Her resolute bravado quite worn down, she lacked the courage to turn and look at him.

Chapter Sixteen

CORIANNE REMAINED IN bed for two days. Except for a visit from Edward and sympathetic attention from her aunt and cousin, she saw no one. Her depressed condition was explained to callers as excessive fatigue, and since such conditions were commonplace among the young ladies of the social set, her brief hiatus from her usual activities caused few raised eyebrows.

In the many hours she spent alone, Corianne had plenty of time to think about what had happened to her, and what was to become of her. Edward had suggested wistfully during his visit to her bedside that they return to Lincolnshire without further ado, but Cory insisted that she wished to remain until the two months which they'd originally planned on should have elapsed. She had half the allotted time left. What should she do to make the most of the month?

Her plan to attach Lord North had obviously failed. Tony Ingalls had not shown himself at Stanborough House since the night she'd knocked him down. Young Denison had inexplicably stopped calling. (She suspected that his mother had heard she was "fast," and had put her foot down.) The only suitor she could count on—and this was the very symbol of how far she had fallen!—was Wilfred Shirley. What made matters worse, she could neither understand nor explain why she'd failed so dismally. As far as she could see in her mirror, she was still the most beautiful girl in the Marriage Mart. Through all her tribulations, she had not developed a single spot to mar her complexion, she had not become gaunt or, worse, gained a pound, she had not lost the rich gold color of her hair nor the deep blue of her eyes. What had gone wrong?

More puzzling was the fact that the two most important men in her life—North and Edward—had turned to Sarah. What on earth did they see in *her*? When Sarah came in to sit with her at her bedside, Cory studied her with care. Sarah was really quite advanced in age (for Cory was well aware that a woman who was still unmarried at twenty-seven was beyond hope), although her years had not yet left telltale marks like wrinkles around the mouth and grey strands in the hair. Sarah's face was well-modelled, and her skin was smooth. And her carriage had a graceful dignity—Cory granted her that. But she was always so pale—and more so now than ever—and her eyes underlined with dark shadows. Her smile was wan, her hair (always tied back so severely) showed no special highlights, and her dress was drab. How could this colorless creature have kept a man like Lord North dangling after her for years? And how could she have won Edward's attention away from Cory herself, after Cory had had him in the palm of her hand since she was a little tot?

Sarah sat in a rocker near the bed, reading to Cory from *The Mirror of Fashion* magazine as Cory scrutinized her. She had to admit that Sarah's voice was low and mellifluous. Cory supposed that a man might admire the sound of it, but surely that couldn't be *all*! What was her secret?

Two days of scrutiny and cogitation, however, did not reveal the answer to Corianne, and she gave up trying to understand. She decided that it was something she herself would learn with age. In the meantime, she would make use of something *she* possessed that Sarah lacked—youth. And she did *not* intend to waste any more of it in bed. She had a month of her London adventure left. All was not lost.

Even without encouragement, Corianne's innate, youthful instincts would have shaken off depression and bounced back into normal optimism, but this natural recovery of her self-confidence was aided by two observations the girl made during her time in bed. The first was that Edward seemed to have recovered from his interest in Sarah. He came to the house only to see Cory, and as soon as he left her bedside, he left the house. (Of course, with the announcement of Sarah's betrothal, it was clear that he could no longer pursue Sarah as a suitor, but it seemed to Cory that he could, if he wished, still spend a little time in her company. The fact that he didn't do so was proof to Cory that he'd lost interest in the older woman.)

The second observation was that Lord North spent only a minimal amount of time with his betrothed. For example, he'd been invited to dinner the night before, but he'd left the house as soon as the meal was over. Cory had not gone down to the table, but she'd watched from her window and seen him leave. She could see no sign that Sarah and North had made a love-match. Perhaps, she speculated with rapidly rising spirits, the marriage arranged between them was to be only *de covenance*. A marriage of convenience was not uncommon. And it would explain much that was puzzling to Cory.

Was there, then, still a chance for her to accomplish what she'd originally set out to do? If she could still win North, she would not mind if her swains back in Lincolnshire deserted her. They were, after all, just a pack of silly boys—very much like Wilfred Shirley. With newly recovered self-confidence, she reasoned that all she needed was another chance to be in the company of Lord North alone. She didn't know how that could be accomplished, but she decided the best course to take would be to return to the social swing and watch carefully for her opportunities.

Lady Stanborough, too, was deeply involved in making plans. Her only daughter was betrothed at last, and she intended to celebrate the occasion by holding a ball which would set the *ton* on its ear. The problem was that Sarah would not agree. The most she would concede to her mother's desire for celebration was a small party for their closest friends. The subject was argued for hours. Finally, a compromise was agreed upon: a buffet dinner party for no more than fifty. But Lady Stanborough did not capitulate until Sarah reluctantly agreed to the addition of music and dancing.

When they actually drew up the guest list, Lady Stanborough found fifty to be a woefully inadequate number, and with instant tears managed to convince Sarah to expand the list to sixty-six. By the time she'd written the invitations, however, Lady Stanborough sent out an additional dozen cards. And without breathing a word to her stubbornly unsociable offspring, she sent an invitation to the Prince. She had no real expectation that he would attend, but since his highness was acquainted with the prospective bridegroom, she might dare to hope.

Leaving herself only a few weeks in which to prepare, her ladyship was soon involved in a flurry of activity. An expanded kitchen staff was already in the midst of preparations, seamstresses' fingers were flying over newly cut silks and gauzes, housemaids were polishing and dusting every corner of the house, musicians were in rehearsal, extra plate and cutlery were being delivered periodically, and an air of excitement infected every inhabitant of the household. Except the prospective bride.

Sarah tried admirably to throw herself into the spirit of the festivities. She listened to her mother's numerous plans with attention, tried to help solve the many problems which such preparations generate with calm good sense, permitted herself to be fitted into her new gown as frequently as an over-fastidious modiste required, and submitted to the effusive congratulations of her mother's friends with good grace. But anyone with an observant eye might have seen the strain behind her smile, the slight tremble of her fingers when her hands were at rest, the appearance of gaunt shadows in her cheeks, and a haunted look in her eyes when she believed no one was looking at her.

Fitz was one of the observers who noticed these changes. And he had strong suspicions of the cause. After a morning call at Stanborough House, he returned to his rooms in a troubled state of mind. Finding Edward in the drawing room, occupied with nothing more urgent than his perusal of the *Times*, he decided to voice his concern. "I say, Ned," he ventured, "have you had a good look at Sarah in recent days? I don't think she's looking at all well."

Edward glanced up at him with raised brows. "Isn't she?"

"I think she's lost weight. Looks peaked to me."

"Do you think she's ill?"

Fitz shrugged. "I've asked her. She says she's fine. I think it's the upcoming wedding. Giving her the dismals, if you ask me."

Edward hesitated, grunted and turned back to his paper.

Fitz dropped into a chair and glared at his friend lugubriously. "Don't see why you're pokering up, old man. I thought you were a *friend* of the lady. Don't you feel any concern?"

"I don't see that it's any affair of mine," Edward muttered, not looking up.

"Then you should *make* it your affair," Fitz said bluntly. "She got herself *into* this coil to save you!"

Edward lowered the newspaper with an exasperated sigh. "Confound it, Fitz, whatever gave you *that* idea?" he demanded.

"You did yourself. Isn't that what you concluded when you received North's letter cancelling the duel?"

"Yes, but I was quite wrong."

"Wrong? You *were*? How do you know?"

"The lady told me so herself."

Fitz sat back and gaped at Edward. "Are you telling me that Sarah *wishes* for this match?"

"That's what she led me to believe," Edward said with finality, hoping to silence Fitz on a subject which he found utterly depressing. He raised his paper and pretended to read, but in reality he couldn't concentrate on it.

Fitz refused to believe that Sarah could care for a man of North's stripe. "Well, I suppose she *had* to tell you that," he mused. "What else could she say under the circumstances? If she told you otherwise, you'd have insisted on fighting the fellow."

"Do you think I didn't think of that?" Edward asked, throwing aside his newspaper in disgust. "I asked her . . . *begged* her to reconsider. I told her the fellow was beneath her. I assured her repeatedly that there was nothing to fear from the duel. She had an answer that silenced all my objections."

"Oh? And what was that?"

"That she loved him."

Fitz looked at his friend searchingly. "She *said* that? In so many *words*?"

"You needn't look so aghast. I know it's difficult to understand," Edward said glumly, "but women are *attracted* to these . . . bounders."

Fitz fingered his moustache dubiously. "My Clara would never—"

"Your Clara is undoubtedly a nonpareil among women," Edward said with an indulgent smile at his friend.

"Yes, she is. But Sarah's not unlike her, you know. Best of friends, the two of 'em." He refrained from adding that he'd noticed signs on several occasions that it was *Edward*, not North, who attracted Sarah. "Strange creatures, females," he sighed. "Even the best of 'em."

Edward's smile became wry, and he reached for his newspaper again. "Not much stranger than we are. I think it's *love* that's strange. No logic in it at all."

Fitz slouched down in his chair and stretched his long legs out in front of him. Staring at the tip of his boots, he thought morosely of the truth of Edward's words. Love was indeed strange—especially if Sarah prefered the dastardly North to his friend Ned. If Sarah were truly in love with Frozen North, it didn't seem to agree with her at all. He wondered what his Clara would make of all this. Perhaps he ought to write her to come down. If she could be persuaded to leave her babies with the nurses for a few days, *she* might be the very person to set things straight.

Lady Clara Fitzsimmons had already received a card from Lady Stanborough for Sarah's betrothal ball and was considering if she could contrive to attend when the letter from her husband arrived. Although his masculine density had caused him to omit a thousand details she would have liked to learn, and although his equivocations about the value of his observations left her confused, Clara gleaned enough from the letter to realize that her friend was in deep trouble. She sent a message to her mother, who lived nearby in Aylsham, to come at once. And she began to throw various garments into a trunk.

"Have you gone mad?" her mother asked as soon as she arrived. "You can't go down to London now! The twins aren't yet weened! You've put on at least half-a-stone of excess weight, too. I'd vow you haven't a gown in that trunk that fits you properly. And, besides—"

"Enough!" Lady Fitz laughed, holding up her hands. "What sort of unnatural mother are you? And unnatural grandmother, too, for that matter. Don't you *want* to take charge of your grandchildren for a week or two?"

"You know I do, but—"

"But me no buts. I have a wet nurse for the twins, in addition to Miss Delane, and a governess for the boys, and a lovely, kind-hearted, *complimentary* Mama to oversee everything. So I'm going off without a qualm. Without a single qualm." She looked at her mother with one eyebrow cocked. "Do I really look as if I've gained half-a-stone?"

Lady Fitz did not write to her husband to announce that she was coming, but she appeared, bag and baggage, at the door to his London apartments two days later. Fitz and Edward were sitting in the drawing room, bent over a chessboard, when they heard her in the foyer. It was Edward's man, Martin, who'd answered the knock and, not having seen her ladyship before, had the temerity to ask who she was.

"Stand aside, man," she ordered impatiently. "I'm Lady Fitzsimmons. Don't gape like a sea-animal! Just take my luggage inside."

"Clara?" Fitz shouted, jumping up so precipitously that he upset the chessboard. "Clara, is that *you*?"

The figure who loomed up in the drawing-room doorway was indeed she. In two strides, Fitz crossed the room and enveloped her in a wildly enthusiastic embrace. Edward, who'd leaped to his feet as soon as she'd appeared, stood watching their animated greeting with a grin. While she explained to her spouse how she'd managed to leave her offspring, Edward took the opportunity to look at Fitz's Clara. She was not at all what he'd expected. In the first place, she was no little honey-vine to cling to a fellow's arm. Almost as tall as her husband, she was built on very sturdy lines and not at all likely to cling to *anyone*. Lady

Fitz was not what one would call a beauty—her face, covered with freckles, was broad and full in the cheeks and marked by a decidedly strong nose and a head of strikingly red hair. But her face was one which no observer would easily forget—the sparkle of her dark eyes and the ready smile making her instantly likeable.

"Come and meet Ned," Fitz said as soon as the pertinent facts of her visit had been explained to him. "I've wanted you two to become acquainted for years."

"So *you're* the famous Ned," Lady Fitz said warmly, grasping his proffered hand and shaking it vigorously. "Fitz always said I would like you on sight, and I do."

"Thank you, Lady Fitz," Edward grinned. "I can see now why your husband speaks of no one else."

"What a bore he must be, to be sure," she laughed.

"Not at all. It's only that, until this moment, when he spoke of his magnificent Clara, I could scarcely believe him. But it's all clear now."

Fitz chortled delightedly. "See, Clara, I *told* you he was a rare specimen."

"Yes," Clara agreed, beaming. "We must all three sit down and have a good coz. I want to know all about you, Ned."

"I shall be delighted to tell you whatever you like, Lady Fitz, but I think that, for now, I must see about removing to the Fenton. You surely will want to settle in."

"Remove to the Fenton?" Clara asked in surprise. "Whatever for?"

"That's where I'd been staying before I moved in with Fitz," Edward explained. "It was quite satisfactory."

"But why is it necessary at all? We've plenty of room here, haven't we, Fitz?"

"Of course. No need to go, old fellow."

"But . . ." Edward felt himself redden slightly.

"If you're thinking that there are only two bedrooms," Lady Fitz said bluntly, "you needn't worry. Fitz and I will share his. We do it all the time."

"Do you indeed?" Edward couldn't help grinning. "What a . . . *comfortable* couple you are, to be sure."

"He means," Fitz explained reprovingly to his wife, "that you are a shocking little baggage to admit such a thing."

"I meant no such thing," Edward denied with a guffaw. "I only hope, when *I* marry, that *my* wife will be equally outspoken. And equally amenable to shared bedrooms."

"Then it's settled," Clara said cheerfully, taking a seat on the sofa beside her husband. "You'll stay just as you were. Now, come sit down and tell me all."

Despite the fact that Lady Fitz enjoyed the afternoon with her husband and his friend enormously, she didn't forget the object of her visit. That very evening, she ordered Fitz to drive her to Stanborough House and to find himself something to do without her for an hour or two. She was admitted by Tait, whose surprise at seeing her was so great he almost gasped. "Lady *Fitzsimmons!* I . . . we . . . weren't told that you were in town!"

Lady Fitz winked at him. "Where's Miss Sarah?" she whispered. "I want to surprise her."

"In the library, my lady," the butler answered, lowering his voice conspiratorially. "She'll be so delighted! You'll find her alone, for Lady Stanborough and Miss Corianne have gone to a play."

Lady Fitz opened the library door softly. Her friend was seated in a chair before the fire, a book open in her lap. But she was not reading. Her eyes were fixed unhappily on the flames.

"A fine state of affairs for a girl about to be married!" Lady Fitz said aloud. "What are you doing at home all alone?"

Sarah turned toward the voice. "Clara!" she cried, jumping up and holding out her arms. "Oh, *Clara!*"

Lady Fitz ran to embrace her. "Why do you look so shocked?" she asked Sarah affectionately. "You didn't think I would permit you to celebrate your betrothal without me, did you?"

Sarah smiled, opened her mouth to express her joy, took one look at the warmly beaming, freckled face of her best friend and burst into tears.

Chapter Seventeen

"THE POOR CHILD," Lady Fitz confided later to her husband, "is utterly miserable. She's worn to the bone trying to show a happy face to the world, for she's not at all the sort who's adept at pretense and insincerity."

"Then why doesn't she break with North and have done?" Fitz asked impatiently.

"Would *you* if you'd given your word?"

Fitz hesitated. "Well, yes . . . well, no . . . I don't know. It's different for a man, you know. A *man's* work is his honor."

His wife threw him a look of scorn. "Do you mean to imply," she asked in high dudgeon, "that a woman has no honor? How dare you, Fitz!"

He threw up his hands in defense. "Don't rip up at me, my love. I meant no offense. I only meant that Sarah *must* find a way out of this, honor or no honor. Doesn't she realize how difficult married life can be even in the best of circumstances?"

Lady Fitz snorted. "I could take you to task for *that* remark, too, if I had a mind to distract myself from the subject at hand. But you can rest assured that I told her of the difficulties of married life. I spoke at length and quite frankly about the necessity for affection between a couple bound together with such intimacy as marriage requires. But she said she's quite given up the expectation for marital happiness."

"What nonsense. What did she mean? If she breaks with North, she can have *every* expectation—"

"No, my dear, she can't. She said that North had made her a virtual prisoner even *before* she'd agreed to marry him. Frightened off a *number* of suitors with his threats and his duels, did you know that?"

"No! Is that *possible*?"

"I suppose it is, with a man of his reputation as a duelist."

"What a poltroon the fellow is!" Fitz declared angrily. "I almost wish Sarah *had* let Edward duel with him. In fact, I'd like to have a shot at the fellow myself."

"It's no good shooting at him if he shoots you first, you know. Sarah is quite right about that."

"Well, we can't let her go through with this!" Fitz said, quite unequivocal for once.

"I don't see what else we can do. Sarah says she won't be in worse case as his wife than she'd been as the object of his attentions."

"Do you really believe that?" her husband asked incredulously.

"No, of course I don't. But I think she believes, because she's so dreadfully unhappy over someone else, that she cannot feel much worse."

"Someone *else*?" He looked at his wife eagerly. "Is it *Ned*? Did she admit it to you?"

Lady Fitz nodded sourly. "I don't see why you're so pleased about it, Fitz. Your friend Ned doesn't care for *her*. He has his eye on another female entirely."

"Ned? Interested in another female? Humbug! At least, I *think* it's humbug. Isn't it? What makes you think—?"

"Sarah told me. Didn't Ned ever confide in you about it?"

"Never said a word to me, blast him. Who *is* she?"

Clara shrugged. "Can't remember her name. A romantic sort of appellation. Daralynne . . . Marianne . . . Hermione . . ."

"You can't mean *Corianne*!"

"Yes, that was the name."

"But . . . she's his *ward*! Well, not exactly his ward, of course, but . . . she's a mere *child*!"

Clara made a *moue* of disgust. "When did *that* ever stop a man? Besides, Sarah says the girl's twenty. You can't call a female of twenty a member of the infantry, you know."

"I suppose not . . . but I wouldn't have thought that *Ned*—"

"No," his wife agreed glumly, "I wouldn't have thought so either."

"What a hobble! What can we do about it, love?"

"I don't think there's a thing we *can* do. Except to stand by . . . to help pick up the pieces."

The much spoken of fête at Stanborough House—now less than three weeks away—was intended to mark the official beginning of Sarah's betrothal to Lord North. In the meantime, North called dutifully on his betrothed every day, to take her riding or to join the family for dinner. But since the announcement was not to be made formally until the party, Sarah did not yet have to accompany him on the round of social events which were *de rigueur* for a newly betrothed couple. All that would come after the announcement. As the days before the betrothal party sped by, Sarah became more and more strained. Even the constant and soothing companionship of her best friend was not enough to ease the tension of her nerves or the pain in her chest.

The days sped by tensely for Corianne, too. With the fateful night fast approaching, Corianne was growing almost desperate. She had not had the opportunity to meet Lord North at any of the events she'd attended. And on the occasions when he'd called at Stanborough House, she'd never managed to win a moment alone in his company. As a result, her temper was growing short and her patience wearing thin.

One evening, a mere fortnight before the betrothal party, she agreed to accompany Wilfred Shirley to a large ball being held by his mother. Wilfred had told her proudly that more than two hundred would be in attendance. Corianne hoped that, among so many, Lord North might be discovered in the throng.

To her intense disappointment, the object of her desires

was nowhere in sight. To make matters worse, Wilfred Shirley followed her about all evening long, rarely permitting her even to *converse* with anyone else. He demanded, in his position as son of the hostess, to have the opening dance with her, as well as two more country dances and the right to escort her to supper. By the time the lavish meal was over, her tolerance had given out. The fellow was a self-satisfied, muffin-faced fribble, and she had to grit her teeth to keep herself from making waspish remarks to set him down.

It was at this moment—just when Corianne's irritation with him was at its peak—that the poor fellow decided to declare his affections for her. Urging her, despite her obvious reluctance, into the music room just behind the hall where supper had been served, he grasped her hands and fell to his knees beside her. "Miss L-Lindsay . . ." he stammered, "C-Corianne . . . you must kn-know—"

"Wilfred, what *are* you doing?" she asked impatiently.

He was startled at her tone. "What? Why, I'm . . . I'm . . ."

"Oh, do get up! Someone might come in and see us."

"No, it's all right. Everyone's gone upstairs for the dancing. P-Please let me tell you—"

Corianne tried to pull her hands from his grasp. "Wilfred, please! I want to go upstairs, too. I've promised this dance to Clement—"

"No!" Wilfred insisted stubbornly. "Not until I've finished. You *must* hear me out!"

"Whatever *for*?" she asked callously. "You're only making a cake of yourself, you know."

"But you . . . how can you *say* that? I want to ask you to . . . to *m-marry* me!"

Corianne looked down at him superciliously. "So I surmised from your position. Get up, Wilfred. I think it's time to take me home."

"Take you *home*? *Now*? But I'm down on my *knees*! I haven't even *begun*! All the sentiments I planned to . . . ! How can you be so *unfeeling*?"

"Well, I'll stand here and hear you out, if you insist, Wilfred, but it will be the greatest waste of time. I won't accept you, you know."

"Why not? You've done with Ingalls, haven't you?"

"Yes, I have, but—"

"There's no one *else*, is there?"

Cory smiled enigmatically. "That, my dear Mr. Shirley, is none of your affair."

Wilfred reddened and got to his feet. "You're t-toying with me, Corianne, and I won't have it! You needn't put on your puffed-up airs with me. Mama says that, pretty as you are, you're only a country belle . . . and that you should consider yourself fortunate that a gentleman of my station and income is offering himself—"

This was more than Corianne could stand. "Did she say that indeed?" she asked with venomous coldness. "Then you may tell her that *this* is what I think of my so-called good fortune!" She put both of her hands against his chest and furiously pushed him backward. Wilfred, completely unprepared, tottered back a couple of steps and fell down heavily on his rear. He let forth a pained bellow, but Corianne merely turned on her heel and started to march from the room. She hadn't gone two steps, however, when she found herself facing a gentleman just entering. It was Lord North.

He looked, with eyebrows raised, from the angrily flushed girl to the young man sprawled on the floor. "Well, Miss Lindsay, you seem to have done it again. What weapon did you use *this* time? I see no signs of a broken vase."

"I didn't need a vase," the girl declared proudly. "The strength of my arms was quite enough."

"You don't say!" His lordship lifted his quizzing glass and stared through it at Wilfred disdainfully. "What a collection of inept young men you seem to attract, my dear."

"Seems to m-me, my lord," Wilfred sputtered angrily, getting clumsily to his feet and brushing off his britches, "that you are a b-bit inept yourself to intrude upon a p-private discussion."

"The *discussion* was long over by the time his lordship entered," Corianne put in at once. "And even if it weren't, I'd have been grateful for his intervention." She smiled up at North. "Will you be good enough to see me home, my lord?" she asked with becoming shyness, her pulse racing at the prospect of the fruition of her dreams.

His lordship bowed in acquiescence. "Delighted, Miss Lindsay," he said drily.

Wilfred Shirley looked from one to the other with sulky belligerence. "I wish you well of her, my lord," he said bitterly. "And as for you, Miss Lindsay, I will simply s-say that I shan't forget this n-night's work."

Wilfred Shirley left them, limping out of the room with as much dignity as the pain in his hip and the wound to his self-esteem permitted. Corianne bit her lip to keep back her delighted giggle as she took Lord North's profferred arm and went with him out of the house. Later, in his carriage, she snuggled into the velvet seat with eager anticipation. Lord North was eyeing her with unmistakable admiration. *How ironical*, she thought. Because of the foolishness of Wilfred Shirley, North had taken notice of her at last.

"Does this sort of thing happen to you often, Miss Lindsay?" his lordship asked languidly.

The boredom of his tone did not discourage Corianne, for the gleam in his eye belied it. "Much more often than I like," she said with a coy, downward glance meant to suggest a becoming modesty.

"You *are* a vixen," he murmured, looking her over speculatively. "Someone should pull you down from your high ropes. You need a good shaking."

"Do I?" the girl asked tantalizingly. "Have you someone in mind to administer it?"

"Perhaps." He let his eye roam slowly from her face to her graceful neck, over the youthful but rounded breasts swelling beneath the folds of her cloak, along the curved line of her hips and thighs to the tiny ankles which showed briefly below the hem of her gown. She was a tasty plum, there was no denying it, and she had made it abundantly clear that she was ripe for his picking. But how could he pick her without upsetting the careful plans he'd laid for the ordering of his life? This girl was no lightskirt, to be used and discarded at will. She had a titled father, a family and a place in society. The repercussions could be more than embarrassing.

In addition, his friend Tony Ingalls still burned to wed her. The fellow talked of little else, despite the dismal failure of his last attempt. North had been unable to discourage him in his wish to pursue what appeared to be a hopeless quest. Ingalls had even won from North a promise to assist, although neither he nor Ingalls had an inkling of a scheme for turning the girl from her stubborn refusal to see Ingalls again.

But North was nothing if not resourceful . . . especially at finding ways to fulfill his desires. Even as his eyes made their admiring inventory of Corianne's bodily charms, an idea took shape in his mind. The more he thought about it, the more satisfactory a scheme it seemed and the more simple to execute. He needed only to persuade the girl to make a runaway trip with him to Gretna. That certainly should not be hard. While it was true that she would probably prefer a properly ostentatious wedding, he would convince her that, since he'd have to play the jilt, a runaway wedding was the only way. He could easily have his way with her on the trip north . . . *but the husband she would find waiting at the end of the ride would not be he, but Ingalls!*

It was perfect. He smiled across at the girl who sat watching him with such breathless, provocative innocence. He'd have not the slightest difficulty in persuading her to go. And once she'd spent a night in his company, she'd have no choice but to follow his plan. For she would be a ruined creature. He would simply refuse to wed her, and she would have no choice but to take Ingalls.

And if Tony objected to a blemished wife, North had no doubt he'd soon see the wisdom of the scheme. The girl would have him no other way. If Tony really wanted her— and her fortune alone was enough to induce Ingalls to overlook any overly nice scruples he might have—Tony would have to go along. The best part was that neither Tony nor Corianne would be able to reveal a word to anyone— not if they wanted to keep their reputations intact. Thus North would face no danger of exposure. It was truly a foolproof scheme.

He folded his arms across his chest in self-satisfaction. "Come here, child," he ordered, smiling at the girl challengingly.

"I'm not a child," Cory responded promptly, putting up her chin.

He fixed his eye on her meaningfully. "Come and sit here beside me," he said again. There was no time like the present to set his plan in motion.

Corianne did as he bid. When she'd slipped into place next to him, he pulled her into his arms and tilted her face up to his. "Now, my girl," he said softly, "let's see how you behave when you're kissed by a man who's not inept."

Chapter Eighteen

CORIANNE WAS ECSTATIC. North wanted to marry her! Only a couple of days had passed since he'd kissed her in his coach, and already he'd asked her to run away with him to Gretna Green . . . and already she'd accepted. His impatience to set the date made her head swim. He wanted her to leave with him the very next day! She had only to send word to him that she was ready, and in less than twelve hours they would be on their way!

But she had not yet been able to bring herself to send him that word. A nagging feeling of guilt nibbled away at the edges of her happiness. Could she permit herself—and North, too—to deal such a blow to her cousin Sarah? Sarah had been a bit of a nuisance in the matter of Lady Saxon's soirées, but she'd never meant to deal Cory any harm. She was a good sort, really, and had always treated Cory with the greatest kindness. Was it right for Cory to return that kindness with such a blow as this?

However, it was ridiculous to suppose that Sarah's emotions were *nearly* as strongly bound up with North as were her own. What could Sarah know of the pain of unrequited passion such as she, Cory, had suffered for North for so long? And what could Sarah know of the joy of blissful romance such as she was feeling at this moment? Sarah was not the kind of woman who was capable of experiencing the heights and depths of romantic emotions. Sarah was so self-contained and calm, not in the least endowed with the heightened sensibilities that Cory possessed in such full measure. Therefore, Sarah's pain would not be so very great when she'd learn that she'd lost North.

Besides, Cory was convinced that the nuptials arranged between Sarah and Lord North had been a matter of convenience, not love. North had never loved Sarah—that much was clear. Perhaps they had both agreed to marry because they thought they would never fall in love. But North was in love *now*, and he mustn't be permitted to waste away in a loveless marriage now that he'd learned true happiness! It was Cory's *duty* to be strong for them both.

Her father and Edward would not approve of an elopement, she knew, but she found the prospect romantic beyond words. It would have been easier, she supposed, to have done everything in the proper way—to announce the betrothal in the *Times* and to have a huge wedding with her father on hand to give her away and her friends in envious attendance—but North had explained that such arrangements would be impossible. "Besides," he'd said, "I do not care to wait for months to claim you as my own."

Corianne had quivered with elation at those words. She could hardly believe that this impatient lover was the same cool and remote aristocrat the polite world had dubbed Frozen North. She'd melted him—just as she'd told her friend Belinda she would! She yearned to write and tell Belinda her news, but North had given her the strictest instructions to say *nothing* to *anyone* until they'd returned from Gretna, safely wedded.

That was the most difficult part of the entire matter. Her triumph in winning the most unattainable bachelor in London lost a large part of its luster by being kept secret. Such a triumph could scarcely be enjoyed until people *spoke* of it, admired her publicly and envied her in private. She could hardly wait until the subject of her marriage was an *on-dit*, rocking the polite world with the aftershock.

What a joy it would be when they returned from Scotland! She would be the Marchioness of Revesne. She would wear a diamond coronet and hold exclusive soirées at Revesne House, receiving royalty with aplomb and moving among the most elite society with glowing indifference to their admiration. Her gowns would be copied by the fashionable, her remarks repeated by the sycophantic, and her success envied by all. She could hardly wait.

Yes, the sooner they set off for Gretna, the sooner she would return to enjoy her triumph. She sent North word that she would be ready at the appointed hour, and she immediately set about packing into a bandbox all the items necessary for a journey to the north.

For his part, Lord North was less than ecstatic about the adventure. In truth, it was beginning to seem more trouble than it was worth. The girl was too erratic and volatile to be counted on to keep her head. She might cause him all sorts of difficulties when she learned the truth. And Tony Ingalls had not been at all pleased with the idea. His first reaction had been to stalk out of North's house in a violent taking.

However, Ingalls soon had returned. He'd found, on his arrival at his own apartments, that a number of dunning letters awaited his attention and that two creditors were perched on his doorstep. As much as he disliked the thought of taking a tarnished and discarded woman to be his wife, a bit of calm reflection showed him that the only price he'd have to pay to acquire this rich and beautiful girl for his own would be to swallow his pride. Ingalls might always resent his friend North's machinations to have the girl first, but the fact remained that Corianne would not wed him otherwise. *Better this way than not at all*, he consoled himself, and he returned to North's house in a more conciliatory frame of mind.

North, who had been about to cancel the entire plan, permitted Tony to persuade him to reconsider. Then the two sat down, glasses of brandy in hand, to discuss the details of the scheme. North was to pick up the girl on the following morning. They would travel on the Old North Road until dark, when they would reach the Three Forks Inn, a few miles north of Wolverhampton. (Lord North had done business with the innkeeper of the Three Forks several times before and knew that his discretion could be relied upon—for a price.) There the two travellers would spend the night. The next morning, after Lord North had informed Corianne that he intended to go no farther and that there would be no marriage between them, Tony Ingalls would make his appearance. He would console the no-doubt-hysterical girl with gentle declarations of sympathy and affection, and he would offer himself as a replacement for the miscreant bridegroom. Ingalls and Corianne would then proceed to Gretna, while Lord North would return to London in plenty of time to ready himself for the forthcoming betrothal celebration at Stanborough House.

Tony had to admit that the plan was ingenious. He downed his remaining brandy in a gulp and got up to pace about the room. "The scheme is apparently quite flawless," he admitted after he'd mulled over all the details.

"So I told you," North said immodestly. "And when you've come dashing to the girl's rescue, and she falls gratefully into your arms, you'll want to thank me, my boy."

Tony looked at him with knit brows. "Yes, she *will* find me a rescuing hero, won't she?"

"She's *bound* to, you know. She will have become damaged goods. She'll be so grateful to you for offering for her, you'll be able to rest on your laurels for the rest of your life."

Tony couldn't help but smile at the picture in his mind of Corianne's gratitude. "Yes," he mused, "that's the best part of the scheme."

"Indeed it is. The more dastardly the girl finds *me*, the more heroic *you* will appear."

Tony nodded and offered his hand to his friend. "I *am* grateful to you, Jack. I know quite well she wouldn't have accepted me any other way. I'm not a valuable commodity on the Marriage Mart—I'm well aware of that. Everyone knows that I'm always in Dun Territory and that my reputation is unsavory. But Cory, at least, will think I'm commendable. You've concocted a masterly scheme, old man, and I'll willingly play along." He walked to the door thoughtfully and paused on the threshold. "But—do you know, Jack?—at last I realize . . . you really *are* dastardly."

The heavy grey sky and the cold November wind that shook her windows the next morning did nothing to dampen Corianne's spirits as she closed her bandbox and gave the final touches to her toilette. The weather might make it more difficult than she'd expected to convince her aunt that she was going to take a turn with Wilfred Shirley in his carriage, but she was sure she could manage it. She had already bribed one of the footmen to come in half-an-hour to carry her bandbox out the back door and down the street where North would be waiting in an unmarked, rented carriage. There was nothing else to do but wait.

She knew that down the hall Sarah was having yet another fitting of her ball gown. Poor cousin Sarah—how would she take the news that she was to be jilted? Corianne suddenly felt very sorry for her. Since Sarah was already so old, she was unlikely to find another suitor and would undoubtedly remain a bitter old maid for the rest of her life. Cory was smitten again with a twinge of nagging guilt. Sarah had always been kind to her—it was too bad that Cory would have to be the one to hurt her.

In a way, it was cruel of North not to warn Sarah that he'd changed his mind. If Sarah had some premonition . . . some warning . . . she could at least steel herself against the shock and turmoil that was bound to ensue when the news became widely known that she'd been jilted. Perhaps Cory ought to warn her. Of course, North had insisted repeatedly that Cory must not breathe a *word* of their plans. It would not do to have anyone learn of their elopement—she could understand that. Edward might hear of it and would be sure to follow them. So secrecy was essential. But if she left Sarah a note . . . and arranged to delay its delivery until tomorrow, when it would be far too late for anyone to catch up with them . . . she might still be able to soften the blow to Sarah and ease her own conscience.

She ran to the writing table and hastily penned a note. Carefully, she folded and refolded it and dropped a large blob of candle wax along the fold to seal it. Then she opened the door to find someone she could trust to deliver it at the proper time. The door to the upstairs sitting room—where Sarah was having her fitting—opened, and out came Madame Marie. "Oh, *Madame*, you're the very person I want," Cory called out. "Will you come in here for a minute?"

Madame Marie scurried down the hall. "I have on'y a *petite moment*, Miss Cory," the dresser told her. "The train on Miss Sarah's gown . . . they're havin' trouble wi' the way it falls. I *tol'* her ladyship to find a French *modiste*."

"Yes, but I won't keep you. I only want to ask you a favor. Will you keep this note hidden for a day, and give it to Miss Sarah *tomorrow*? It's a kind of . . . of joke, you see. And part of the fun is that it must be delivered *tomorrow morning* and not a moment sooner."

"O' course, Miss, if ye like. But I hope ye'll *pardonnez moi* if I asks ye why y'can't deliver it yerself."

Cory blinked. She should have taken more time to think this through, she realized. "Oh . . . well, you see . . . if it came from me, it would . . . er . . . give the joke away," she said lamely. She was struck with misgivings. Perhaps she shouldn't have done this at all. "On second thought, I suppose I can deliver it myself," she said hastily, reaching out to take the paper back again.

Madame Marie regarded the young girl closely. "That's all right, Miss Cory. I don't mind holdin' it for you, nor deliverin' it neither. Though it sounds like a lot o' foolishness to me."

"That's all it is, Madame. A lot of foolishness. But you won't forget, will you?"

"No, Miss," the dresser said, tucking the note into her apron pocket and turning to go down the hall. "I won't forget."

Cory watched her go, biting her underlip worriedly. But the sound of the large clock at the foot of the stairs, striking the half-hour, came up to her and drove all else from her mind. It was time to go!

Madame Marie might not have given the note another thought had she not visited the kitchen a short while later to talk to her crony, the cook. Cook was clucking over "the sinful extravagance of the gentry," for someone had given Jayce, the laziest footman on the staff, a solid gold sovereign just for delivering a little bandbox to a carriage down the street.

"Who was so beetle-headed as to do *that*?" Madame inquired, shaking her head in disapproval.

"I wasn't told," Cook said in disgust, "but I ha'e a good notion."

Madame Marie had a good notion as well. She left the

kitchen, her brow furrowed thoughtfully. Why would Miss
Cory give Jayce a gold sovereign to carry a little bandbox
down the street when he would certainly have done it just
for the asking? The answer was obvious—the girl wanted
to spirit something out of the house *secretly*. But why? And
what? And did it have anything to do with the note that lay,
at this moment, right in her pocket?

It might all be only part of the joke Miss Cory spoke of,
but the maid didn't like the feel of it . . . not one bit. She
went to her room, removed the paper from her pocket and
studied it carefully. The wax seal was overly thick, and
although it was hastily and sloppily applied, it gave an air
of significance and mystery to the letter. Madame Marie
was uncomfortable about this entire business. It had the
distinct smell of trouble.

The entire house smelled of trouble, in Madame Marie's
view. She was with Miss Sarah when her betrothal had been
arranged, and she knew quite well that Miss Sarah was not
happy about it. Madame had her own ideas of why this was
so, and although she'd kept her peace, she sincerely wished
she could do something to stop the forthcoming nuptials.
It was not her place, of course, to make judgments about
the way her employers ran their lives, but she saw what she
saw, and she knew what she knew. And one of the things
she knew was that all this trouble started when Miss Cory
came to stay. In less than two months, a pleasant, cheerful
and self-assured Miss Sarah had become a pale, nervous
and unhappy being. And if Miss Cory was plotting anything
to give Miss Sarah additional grief, Madame Marie would
like nothing better than to stop her in her tracks.

Madame had been *entrusted* with the note, and she did
not like to betray a trust, but if Miss Cory had not been
telling the truth about the contents—and she was sure the
girl had lied—it might be better to turn the paper over to
Miss Sarah as soon as possible.

If she gave the letter to Miss Sarah now, the worst result
would be that she'd have spoiled some "joke." And she'd
have to face Miss Cory's displeasure. When Miss Cory was
displeased, she could make everyone miserable with her
sullens or her tantrums, but Madame Marie didn't intend
to worry herself over *that*. It would be worth any unpleas-

antness if, as she suspected, there was something more in this letter than what met the eye. *"Allons!"* she muttered firmly, marching to the door. "I'll give Miss Sarah this here *billet doux* right now . . . and take whatever comes like a *Comtesse* facin' *la guillotine*."

She quickly climbed the stairs and made her way to Miss Sarah's bedroom. "It's a note from Miss Cory," she explained, handing the letter to Sarah hesitantly. "She said I wasn't to give it to ye 'til tomorrow, but there's somethin' funny goin' on . . . so I thought . . ."

"Something *funny*?" Sarah asked, looking at the letter in complete bafflement. "What do you mean?"

The dresser shrugged. "I ain't certain, Miss Sarah . . . but Miss Cory's been acting strangely this *matin*. That's why I thought y'd better read it."

"Well, it *is* addressed to me," Sarah said, looking at the missive dubiously, "but if she said I wasn't to read it until tomorrow . . ." She looked up at Madame with a suggestion. "Why don't I just *ask* her about it?"

"She ain't home. She's gone off for a ride with Mr. Shirley."

"What? In *this* weather?" Sarah's brows knit as she looked down at the paper once more. "That *is* strange, Madame. Especially since she declared only a few days ago that she never intended to see Mr. Shirley again."

Without further hesitation, Sarah broke the seal. Her eyes flew over the contents, and she gasped and whitened. "The little *idiot*!" she said to herself, reading the letter again. Then she looked up at Madame Marie with unseeing eyes. "My pelisse . . . I'll need my pelisse. And . . . the carriage. Have them bring it round at once, will you, Madame? At once."

"But . . . it's real nasty and damp outside, Miss Sarah. And it looks like it'll come down rain . . . or even snow . . . any time now. Where're ye *goin'*?" Madame was alarmed. If she'd ever seen trouble in a person's face, she'd seen it now.

"Going?" Sarah echoed abstractedly. She looked up, her eyes focussing slowly on Madame's face. She blinked bewilderedly and sank slowly back against her chair. "I . . . I just don't *know*!" she murmured in baffled dismay.

Chapter Nineteen

THE SNOW THAT Madame Marie had predicted did not materialize. Instead, a dense fog crept in and cloaked the city in its thick invisibility. It caused Sarah to stumble against a curbstone when she alighted from her carriage in front of the building on Curzon Street where Fitz had his apartments. She had come to see Clara. She felt that she desperately needed her friend's counsel. Fog or no fog, she could not remain safely at home today.

She knew she *had* to stop Cory somehow, but she had no idea as to how to go about it. The *proper* thing to do, she realized, would be to enlist Edward's help, but the danger of a duel still loomed over the situation, and that prospect terrified her. In addition, she didn't want to hurt him. If only she and Clara could think of a way to rescue Cory without enlisting Edward's assistance, they might, with luck, keep him from ever learning anything about it.

Fortunately, Edward was not at home. "He's gone on his usual morning gallop through the park," Fitz told her, ushering her into the drawing room where his wife sat at the writing table penning a letter to her mother.

"Gone *riding*?" Sarah asked Fitz in some surprise. "But . . . the fog . . ."

"Ned would answer *that*," Clara said, looking up from her letter in amusement, "by saying that it's a mere nothing. The fellow declares that city life would be completely unendurable if he couldn't spend *some* part of each day in the open air. He never fails to take his daily—" At this point, Clara noted that her friend was even paler than usual. "Good heavens, Sarah, is anything amiss?" she asked, rising from her chair.

Sarah nodded. "Read this," she said tensely, handing her note to Clara.

Clara perused the letter quickly and raised her eyebrows. "What a foolish, impulsive creature that child is, to be sure!" was her brief comment.

"Is *that* all you have to say?" Sarah queried, astonished.

"What else *can* I say? We already *know* that North is a bounder."

"But . . . what do you think I should *do*?" Sarah was beginning to feel that her friend lacked a deep enough understanding of the situation. "Don't you see—?"

"Of course I see. It's a dreadful situation, I admit. But Sarah, to be truthful, I don't care a fig. Let her run off with him—serves 'em both right!"

"Clara, you can't mean that!"

"I *do* mean it. Ask Fitz if I'm not right. *You* agree with me, don't you, Fitz?"

"Of course, love . . . that is, I expect I would, if I knew what you were talking about," he responded placidly.

"Oh! You haven't yet read the letter. Well, *read* it, you gudgeon," his wife said with affectionate impatience. "He *may* read it, may he not, Sarah?"

Sarah made an acquiescent gesture and dropped down on the sofa. "I can't permit Cory to do this to herself, Clara. She doesn't know . . . ! She can have no *inkling*—"

"Good Lord!" Fitz exclaimed, gaping at the note. "What a cork-brained wet-goose! Ned will be *livid*!"

Sarah sighed despairingly. "That's why we mustn't tell him about this. I've got to get her back, before *anyone* learns of this."

Clara sat down beside her friend. "Nonsense, Sarah. Let the matter go. You've been making yourself ill over the prospect of your marriage to North. Now you needn't go through with it. On the other hand, your silly little cousin is obviously beside herself with joy. Let her have him."

Sarah shook her head. "How can I? She's such an innocent. I can't permit her to fall into such a trap. She has no idea what marriage to such a man can mean. Besides . . ." Her voice faltered, and she turned away.

"Besides?" Clara prodded gently.

"I . . . I won't have Edward hurt this way!" Sarah admitted, her head lowered.

Clara put a hand on her friend's shoulder and patted it sympathetically. "Do you love him so much?" she asked softly. "My poor child, can't you think of *yourself* for once?"

Sarah merely shook her head again. Fitz chewed his moustache thoughtfully. "I can understand your wish to bring the girl back, I suppose, Sarah, but I don't see how you can expect to accomplish it."

Sarah turned to face him. "I want to go after them. But I don't know where they've gone."

"To Gretna, of course," Clara stated in disgust. "Where else?"

"Yes, my love, you're probably right," Fitz agreed, "but that's not much help. There are so many roads out of London. Who knows what route they may have chosen?"

"Can you help me decide which route is most likely?" Sarah asked, looking hopefully from one to the other.

"Sarah, you're not considering trying this *alone*!" Fitz was aghast.

"And in this fog!" his wife added promptly.

"As Edward would say, it's a mere nothing," Sarah reminded her, looking out the window where nothing but a white mist could be seen.

"The whole idea is impossible," Clara insisted. "You must realize how fruitless such a chase would undoubtedly be. They have several hours' head start—"

"Only a couple," Sarah said. "I must *try*, Clara."

Clara and Fitz exchanged looks. "Then we'll go with you," Clara declared, her husband's agreement having already been ascertained by the glance between them.

"Clara, no! I couldn't ask it of you."

"You haven't asked, my dear," Clara said, patting her hand.

"We can't permit you to go alone," Fitz said with unusual firmness. "It's out of the question."

Sarah couldn't trust herself to say a word. She merely swallowed and hugged her friend gratefully.

"Now," mused Fitz again, chewing his moustache uneasily, "if we could only find a clue as to their direction . . ."

"Perhaps," Clara suggested, not noticing either the sound of the front door or of the footsteps in the hallway, "if we read Cory's letter again, carefully—"

Edward appeared in the doorway, casually pulling off the greatcoat which he'd thrown over his riding habit. "Is there a letter from Cory?" he inquired, smiling at them comfortably.

Everyone in the room stiffened and looked at him in consternation. Edward, suddenly aware of their tension, glanced about the room. His eyes took in Sarah's face, and he felt an unexpected constriction of the chest. He'd not seen her since the day she told him about her feelings for Lord North—more than three weeks ago. The change in her was alarming. She'd grown thinner, her eyes were deeply shadowed and her skin so pale it was almost translucent. *"Sarah!"* he exclaimed impulsively, tossing his greatcoat over a chair and crossing the room in quick strides. He sat down beside her on the sofa. "What's wrong?" he demanded, taking her hands in his, his eyes searching her face.

"Nothing . . . nothing at all," she managed to reply, her voice a mere breath. "Cory is . . . quite well . . ."

"I wasn't talking about Cory, since I saw her only yesterday. It's *you* who concerns me."

"I'm . . . very well, thank you," she murmured, unable to meet his eyes.

Edward looked up at Fitz questioningly. *"Something* is out of order here," he said flatly. "It shows in *all* your faces." When Fitz didn't answer, he turned to Clara, but she, too, lowered her eyes. There was a moment of awkward silence while Edward stared at each of them. Then he dropped Sarah's hands abruptly and stood up. "I am evidently intruding. I beg pardon . . . of all of you." And he started from the room.

Sarah looked after him with a tortured expression, putting a restraining hand to her mouth to keep from calling out to stop him. But at the doorway he stopped *himself.*

"Wait . . ." he said, turning back. "I thought . . . I heard something about a letter from Cory. Has this something to do with *her*?"

Clara could stand this no longer. She expelled a breath decisively. "I think he has a right to know," she said to Sarah flatly.

Sarah winced painfully. "Clara! No!"

"If it's a letter from Corianne," Edward said, an eyebrow rising coldly, "I have *every* right—"

"The letter is addressed to *me*," Sarah countered desperately.

"I see." Edward hesitated for a moment and then strode back to Sarah's side. "If Cory is causing this difficulty—whatever it is—I wish, Sarah, that you would let me help." He looked down at her gravely. "I've tried to tell you from the first that I'm well able to . . . that I wish you could learn to *trust* me!"

"I . . . I *do* trust you, Edward," Sarah said stumblingly, her voice choked with emotion, "but this is not a question of—"

"Dash it, Sarah," Fitz put in, "*tell* him! Even at *school* everyone went to Ned when in a fix."

Sarah, finding three pairs of eyes fastened on her expectantly, shut out the sight by closing her own. "I can't," she moaned doggedly. "I *can't*."

Clara put a hand on hers. "Sarah, he's here as her *guardian*. You *must*!"

Sarah's eyes flew open, and she rounded on her friend in anguish. "No! It would be . . . *murder*, don't you *see*?"

"Murder?" Edward stared at her with dawning comprehension. "Has this something to do with *North*?" He seized Sarah roughly by the arms and pulled her up to face him. "Are you still afraid of a *duel*?" he demanded, wanting to shake her furiously, but restraining himself. "Damn it, woman," he muttered through clenched teeth, "*why can't you let me fight my own battles?*"

"I say, Ned," Fitz remonstrated, "that's not the way to speak to the lady. At least . . . I'd say it's a bit strong, isn't it?"

But neither Edward nor Sarah heard him. They stared at each other mulishly, eye to eye and chin to chin. Finally

Sarah wavered. She seemed to sag in his grasp. "Very well. If you want to kill yourself . . . *go* after her. Here!" And, pulling herself from his grasp, she held out the letter that had been clenched in her hand.

Wordlessly, Edward took it and went to the window. In the grey light, he scrutinized the page. *Dear Cousin Sarah,* he read, *this is the most Difficult Letter I have ever had to write, but I cannot in Good Conscience go off to find my Happiness without a care for the Pain I leave behind. Believe me, Dearest Cousin, I would not willingly Hurt you, but there is no Other Way! North and I have just Discovered that we Love each other quite Madly, and there was nothing else for it but to Run Off like this. North and I will be Husband and Wife within a day of your reading this Note. I am, of course, the Happiest of creatures; but I am most Regretful that I should have been the Unwitting Instrument to cause you Sorrow. However, as the old saying goes, Love, like a cough, cannot be kept hid, and it is better— is it not?—that North and I should be Wed rather than that the three of us should live ever after in Abject Misery. I hope that this Letter will at least provide you with Adequate Preparation against the Shock when the news comes out about our Nuptials. Please, please, find it in your Heart to Forgive your most devoted cousin, Corianne.*

As he read the words, Edward muttered a stinging epithet under his breath. When he'd finished, he remained standing at the window, staring out into the fog, his back to the others. They could discern no signs of his reaction except for his hand which was slowly crushing the paper into his tight, white-knuckled fist.

"Well, Ned," Fitz said at last, unable to stand the silence, "what do you think we should do?"

"Think? What do I *think*?" Edward said explosively, turning around and glaring at Sarah, who still stood motionless in the middle of the room. "I think, ma'am, that you've chosen yourself a *fine specimen* to be your bridegroom!"

Sarah, completely taken aback by this unwarranted attack, instinctively put up her defenses. "*I've* chosen? . . . I? It seems to me your *Cory* has done a bit of choosing, herself."

Edward's glare wavered. "Well, as to that, there's no denying the girl's behaved like an idiot. But she *is* a mere child from the country, completely inexperienced in dealing with *rakes* and *seducers*."

"Are you implying," Sarah demanded with trembling indignation, "that *I have* such experience? I would like to point out to you, sir, that although I've lived my entire life in the city, I have *yet* to be seduced!"

"Stop this nonsensical bickering," Clara interrupted. "There are more important matters to discuss in connection with our runaway pair."

"There's nothing at all to discuss," Edward said shortly. "I shall go after 'our runaway pair' at once. Then I'll deposit your *bridegroom*, ma'am, at your doorstep and take my charge back to her father."

"But how will you find them?" Fitz asked sensibly. "We don't even know their route."

Edward shrugged and strode to the door. "Martin," he shouted, "run down to the stables and horse the light carriage. Quickly, man. There's no time to waste."

Clara rose from her seat. "There's no point in rushing off without a plan, Ned. Where will you go?"

But Edward was already occupying himself with that problem. "Fitz," he asked impatiently, "what's the name of that sharp-nosed fellow North always has with him? Looks a bit like a jackal."

"I know whom you mean," Ftiz said, his eye brightening. "That is, I *expect* you mean Ingalls. Anthony Ingalls."

"That's the one. You don't happen to know his direction, do you?"

"Well, hardly. The fellow's not my sort, you know. However, we *could* learn it at the club."

"Not *we*, Fitz," Edward said bluntly. "Just I. I'll travel more quickly on my own." He picked up his greatcoat and put it on.

Sarah came up to him. "You will *not* go alone," she declared firmly. "I'm going, too."

"Whatever for?" he asked her coldly. "Can't you trust me to restore your bridegroom to you unharmed?"

Sarah ignored the thrust and grasped the edge of the capes of his coat in two trembling hands. "You'll be *killed*!

Perhaps I can stop some useless bloodshed if I—"

"The last thing I need," Edward said cuttingly, "is an hysterical female at my side." He loosened her fingers from his coat and pulled her to Fitz. "Here. Hold her 'til I've left."

Fitz reluctantly followed his friend's orders and held the struggling Sarah in his arms in a tight grasp.

"Edward, *please! Wait* . . . !" she cried. But he was gone.

Chapter Twenty

EDWARD, HATLESS AND with his open greatcoat flapping behind him, strode past Anthony Ingalls' surprised valet into the apartment. It was a small place, very bachelorish in its sparse decor and not very exemplary in its upkeep. Newspapers were strewn about the drawing room untidily, the remains of a meal were still to be seen on the dining room table, and an empty bottle of spirits lay carelessly on its side on a table in the corridor. But Edward took no special note of these solecisms. He had only one purpose in searching through the rooms—to find the gentleman of the house himself. It was not until he barged in through the bedroom door, however, that he found his quarry. Ingalls stood beside a bed littered with clothing, packing a portmanteau.

Edward came to an abrupt halt, his brows knit. "*Packing*, Mr. Ingalls?" he asked in sudden suspicion.

"What—? Who the *devil*—? How did you get in here?" Ingalls demanded with a start.

"My name is Middleton," Edward said, his eyes fixed on the other man's face. "We've met a number of times before. Forgive this unceremonious entrance, but I've precious little time to waste. I'm looking for your friend, North. I suspect you know his destination."

"See here, Middleton," Ingalls said, reddening, "you've no right to barge in here like this!"

"I don't think you heard me," Edward interrupted. "I have no time for the niceties. *Where has he gone?*"

"How the deuce should I know?" Ingalls answered sullenly, shifting his eyes from Edward's intense gaze.

"I think you do," Edward said threateningly, watching Ingalls closely. "I think this hasty packing has something to do with it, too. Where are you off to, old fellow?"

"To . . . er . . . to visit my uncle, if you must know," Ingalls improvised.

Edward took a step toward him. "You're lying. You're meeting North, aren't you? Where? And why? What have *you* to do with this?"

Ingalls backed away. Middleton was only a country bumpkin, but here in this small room he suddenly seemed *huge*. Ingalls was of average height, but his breadth could never be considered more than slight, and he did *not* excell in demonstrations of physical prowess or what were called "the manly arts." He had always been clever enough to talk his way out of situations which threatened to lead to fisticuffs. "Nothing . . ." he said hastily. "I don't know *anything* . . ."

"I'm convinced that you *do* ," Edward insisted, moving closer. "Where has your friend gone?"

"I don't know what you're talking about. I didn't know North had gone *anywhere* . . ."

Edward's right hand shot out and grasped Ingalls' neckcloth. "Where has your friend *gone*?" he asked again, this time more threateningly.

"Don't . . . *know* . . ."

Edward pulled the neckcloth tighter. Ingalls felt himself choking, and flailed his arms about helplessly. *"Gretna!"* he croaked in fear.

Edward loosened his hold. "By what route?"

"Old . . . North Road . . ."

That was all Edward had come to learn. He was about to fling the cowering fellow aside and go on his way, but some instinct held him. The fact that Ingalls was packing was a coincidence too significant to ignore. The fellow had reddened, stumbled and shown other signs of guilt. What *was* his involvement in this affair?

Edward tightened his hold on Ingalls' neckcloth again. "And where are *you* to meet them?" he demanded.

"No . . . nowhere . . ." Ingalls insisted desperately.

"At Gretna? Or earlier?"

"Gretna . . ." the fellow lied.

Edward nodded and let him go, smiling grimly. Ingalls was to be best man, no doubt. Well, Edward would let him make the trip. Ingalls would find, when he'd arrived, that there would be no Lord North to meet—that his lordship had been stopped somewhere along the Old North Road.

Itching with impatience to face Lord North, Edward dropped his hold on Ingalls and started for the door, leaving Ingalls leaning against the far wall of the room, panting for breath. But something in Edward's mind clicked warningly as he was about to step over the threshold. If Ingalls' part in this escapade was only to play best man, why was he so fearful? Why all the signs of guilt? Why the vehement denials and the lame excuses? *He* was not the one doing the eloping, yet he was behaving exactly as if he *were* abducting the girl.

Edward whirled around and advanced on Ingalls a second time. Ingalls, seeing him coming, groaned and held his hand to his throat protectively. "No, no," he pleaded. "Not again! I don't know anything else."

Edward held his hands up peacefully. "I don't intend to touch you. I only want to know what *your* part is in all this."

"I've told you. Nothing."

"You told me you're meeting them at Gretna Green. Why?"

Ingalls looked at him fearfully. "Just as a . . . surprise . . ." he said unconvincingly.

Edward grasped him again. "You're forcing me to this," he said, tightening the neckcloth just enough to frighten the man. "I don't see why you're so reluctant to tell me your plans. I know enough already to stop the elopement. There's nothing more to be lost by your giving me the whole story."

Tony made a final attempt to avoid answering. He shook his head. "I don't know . . . anything . . ." he gasped.

"I have no time to play games," Edward told him impatiently and tightened his hold. "If you're so afraid to tell me the truth, you must have more to do with this than I thought. If that's true, I'll have to deal with you as I intend to deal with your friend." He made his free hand into a threatening fist.

Ingalls, terrified, pulled back as far as he could. "No,

don't! Shouldn't hit *me*," he managed, his eyes bulging fearfully. "I'm supposed to *save* her!"

"*Save* her?" Edward scrutinized the fellow's face suspiciously. "What do you mean?"

"I'm going to *marry* her," Ingalls said hurriedly, taking advantage of the fact that Edward's hold on his neck had eased by pushing the large hand away.

"*Marry* her? But isn't *North*—?"

Ingalls laughed hollowly. "North? Make a runaway match? Don't be a flat. He's betrothed already."

Edward paled. So *that* was the scheme! North had not intended to marry Cory at all. He wanted to ruin the child and then have Ingalls come to pick up the pieces. He faced Ingalls with a sneer. "You slimy muckworm! You went *along* with such a scheme?"

Ingalls lowered his eyes and slid slowly down against the wall until he was seated on the floor. "I . . . there was no other way—" he muttered.

"No other way?" Edward asked, fury churning up inside of him. "No other *way*?" Roughly, he pulled the limp Ingalls to his feet. "Why, you damned milksop, there were a *dozen* ways you could have—"

"I know," Ingalls admitted, shamefaced and unresisting. "Go ahead—do anything to me that you think you should."

Edward pushed him away in disgust. "No, you're not worth it. I have a better target for my revenge." And he strode to the door.

"The Th-Three Forks Inn. North of Wolverhampton," Ingalls muttered.

Edward paused and turned. "What?"

Ingalls shrugged and hung his head. "That's where they'll stop tonight. I was to . . . arrive there in the morning."

"I see." Edward looked at the other man disdainfully. "Are you expecting any thanks for that? I'd have found them anyway."

Ingalls lifted his head. "Not expecting any thanks, Middleton. Just tell Corianne . . . I'm . . . sorry . . ."

Everything looked beautiful to Corianne as North's rented carriage rumbled northward. "Look, Jack," she exclaimed joyfully, "the fog is beginning to drift in. See it surrounding that clump of trees. Isn't it lovely? Like a fairy-tale setting."

North grunted. "It won't look so lovely to you if it thickens and keeps us from reaching the inn tonight. You won't want to spend the night freezing here in the coach, will you?"

She snuggled into his arms. "The fog won't stop us. Nothing will stop us, I'm certain. We're under the protection of a lucky star."

He ran a finger along the curve of her cheek. "You're a silly little romantic. A lucky star will be of little assistance if we can't see it."

But Cory would not be depressed. Her dreams were coming true, and it would take more than a little fog to dampen her spirits. She lifted her face to be kissed, and his lordship kindly obliged. It was only when his embrace seemed to pass beyond the bounds of propriety that she felt a twinge of misgiving. It was only a tiny twinge, quickly banished. She told herself that Jack's hand, passing lightly over the curve of her hip, had made only the slightest of slips, quite easily ignored and as easily forgiven.

But by the time the carriage turned into the inn yard of The Three Forks, Corianne was troubled and bemused. Lord North's behavior for the past hour had been far from gentlemanly, and although he'd turned aside her demurs with smooth banter, she couldn't help feeling uncomfortable. If they'd already been wed, she supposed she would feel no objections, but surely a *gentleman* would refrain from handling a girl so freely until the few days remaining of their single state had passed.

The inn was small and cosy, and a cheerful fire burned in the taproom, the first room that met Corianne's eye. A woman of ample girth was bent over the fire, feeding it some additional logs. The presence of another woman on the premises, and the welcome warmth of the fire, gave Cory a feeling of relief and contentment. She had no reason to be ill-at-ease, she thought, in such a clean and pleasant place.

Just then, however, the woman at the fire turned round. She was much younger than she'd appeared to be from the rear, and her features were coarse and vulgar. Her dress was cut far too low across a full bosom, and she wore a half-apron which looked as if it had never been laundered. At the sight of Lord North, the woman grinned lewdly. "Oh, yer lordship," she brayed from across the room, dropping a clumsy curtsey, "back again, are ye?" Every vestige of Cory's feeling of safety fled.

Lord North raised his quizzing glass and stared at the woman depressingly. His look was cold enough to wipe the leer instantly from her face. But the act did little to ease Corianne's discomfiture. Lord North was evidently a frequent visitor to this establishment, a fact which she instinctively felt was an indication (though she didn't know why) of some sort of depravity.

The innkeeper bustled in, all obsequiousness, and led them to a private parlor without ado. While Cory warmed herself at the fire, Lord North ordered dinner. The meal was soon brought in. It was simple but excellently prepared, and Cory, who was as hungry as a bear, thrust aside her misgivings and permitted herself to enjoy the food to the full. North, looking breathtakingly handsome in the glow of the candles on the table, kept the conversation pleasant and reassuringly impersonal. Soon the girl told herself once again that she had worried about nothing.

When they finished, the innkeeper entered, piled all the china on a large tray and set out a brandy bottle and two glasses. He lifted the tray to his shoulder and proceeded to bow himself out. "Your bedroom is ready whenever you should wish it," he said at the door. "G'night, m'lady . . . yer lordship."

Corianne's heart seemed to fall right down to her shoes. "Bedroom? *One* bedroom? What did the man mean?" she gasped.

Lord North shrugged and reached for the brandy bottle. "This is a very small inn, my dear," he said calmly, pouring the liquor into a glass. "There *is* only one bedroom available. However, it is large and quite luxurious for a country hostelry. I've stopped here before, you know, and found it quite to my liking."

"But, J-Jack! You surely must be *joking*! You can't

expect . . . you don't m-mean to suggest—!"

North smiled. "Don't be such a little Puritan, my love. Come, have a drop of brandy. It has a deliciously warming effect on the blood." He rose, the glass in hand, and came round the table to her.

Warming her blood was the last thing Cory wanted. She pushed back her chair, raised her arm and knocked the glass out of his hand. "I'm *not* a Puritan," she cried, her heart pounding against her ribs in fright, "but I won't share a bedroom with you tonight!"

North was completely undaunted by her act of rebellion. His smile widened, and he pulled her to her feet. "Why this unnecessary defiance, my sweet? We are to be married the day after tomorrow, are we not?"

"Y-Yes, but . . . we are n-not married *yet*! Please, Jack, if you are teasing m-me, I wish you would s-stop."

"I don't tease," North declared, putting an arm around her and tilting her face up to his. "You're delightfully young, my dear. It makes you very delectable, but your appalling innocence is a decided disadvantage. You mustn't be frightened. I promise I will use you with all gentleness."

"You will not use me at *all*!" Cory thrust him from her and backed away. "Call the innkeeper. Tell him to make up a room for me. A servant's room, if necessary. At *once*, please."

"Don't be childish, Cory. You're making a fool of yourself, you know."

"P-Perhaps I am," she said mulishly, very close to tears. "I s-suppose I'm not b-behaving like Mrs. Saxon or the f-fashionable London l-ladies—"

"No, you certainly are not."

"I don't c-care! If they behave as you expect m-me to behave now, then I don't *want* to be one of them! If you won't call the innkeeper, I *will*."

"It won't be of any use to call him, my dear. He's gone to bed."

She threw him a look of disbelief and started for the door. "There will be *somebody* in the taproom—"

He caught her in his arms. "No one is about, I assure you. When I stay here, the whole house is mine. I don't like intruders. There's no point in struggling, Cory. The innkeeper and the servants will keep to their rooms, whatever they hear."

Cory's breath caught in her throat, and she stared at North as if she'd never seen him before. There was something in his eyes—something heart-stoppingly icy—which she hadn't noticed before. Yes, this was the Frozen North she'd heard about but hadn't recognized until now. "You *planned* this!" she cried in sudden comprehension. "Oh, my God . . . you intended *all along* to . . . to . . ."

"Why not? You're a taking little creature, you know, and you flirted with me outrageously every time we met. Are you going to continue to behave in this ridiculously coy fashion, or are you going to admit that you are as eager for this adventure as I am?"

Cory's eyes widened. *"You never intended to m-marry me at all!"* she accused in a horrified whisper.

North snorted, tightened his hold on her, and pressed his mouth against hers. Cory, feeling the pain of complete desolation for the first time in her life, sagged in his arms helplessly. He had tricked her, lied to her and used her as no man ever had. Now he was going to *ruin* her!

This night would ruin her life forever. How could she have been so *stupid* as to have permitted such a thing to happen? *Well*, she thought with a renewed flash of spirit, *I won't let him do it without a struggle*. She stiffened in his embrace and bit his lip as hard as she could.

With a cry of pain, he dropped his hold on her. "You *imp of hell!*" he exclaimed in irritation, taking out a handkerchief and dabbing at the blood on his lip.

Cory looked around for a way to escape, but the only door in the room was directly behind him. She couldn't reach it without being caught. Desperately, she backed away from him across the room, farther and farther until the back of her leg struck the edge of a wooden bench. Caught off guard, she lost her balance and dropped down on it with a surprised cry of fear.

North laughed. "Had enough, my girl?"

Cory cowered into the corner of the bench but said nothing.

"Well, *I* have. It grows late. Come upstairs."

Cory didn't move.

North smiled. "I'll carry you, if I must. I don't think the task will be too much for me."

"D-Don't *touch* me!" Cory burst out. But seeing that her words had not the least effect on him, her last bit of courage died. She dropped her head in her hands and wept.

Her sobs kept her from hearing the door open, but North heard it. Angrily, he wheeled about. "I *told* you I didn't want—" he began. But it was not the innkeeper in the doorway. It was Edward Middleton. *"Damnation!"* he hissed under his breath.

Edward's eyes brushed past the startled North to the girl weeping miserably in a corner of the bench. "Cory?" His voice was taut with apprehension.

Her head came up slowly, and as her eyes took in the identity of the shadowy figure standing in the dimness of the doorway, a look of unutterable relief flooded her face. "Edward?" she breathed, her heart immobilized for a moment with joy. *"Edward!"*

She leaped from the bench and flew across the room, throwing her arms about his neck wildly. "You *found* me!" she cried, burying her face in his shoulder and bursting into fresh tears. "You've s-saved me! Oh, Edward, he . . . he didn't intend to m-marry me at all!"

Edward grasped her arms and held her at arms' length, scrutinizing her face carefully. "Are you all right?" he asked tensely.

"Yes, she's perfectly fine, bumpkin," North said drily. "You've managed to arrive in the nick . . . blast you."

Edward's eyes narrowed. He pulled off his greatcoat and tossed it aside. "Go into the other room, Cory," he ordered, his mouth tightening dangerously. "I have some private business with his lordship." His fists clenched, he pushed past her and stepped purposefully into the center of the room.

"Some *unfinished* business, isn't it?" North agreed, his mouth stretched in an icy smile. "I'm quite ready for you."

Cory screamed, and Edward stopped short, for North was holding out a small but evil-looking silver pistol. It was fully cocked and held not ten inches away from Edward's head, its muzzle aimed at a point right between his eyes.

Chapter Twenty-One

Edward had had a difficult trip. He'd had to push his horses to their limit on roads made dangerous by enveloping fog. The fog had caused him to lose his way twice, one misadventure taking more than an hour to rectify. He'd been buffeted by bitter winds and chilled to the bone by the damp November air. But through it all, he had been sustained by the anticipation of the immense satisfaction he would find in pounding the overbearing John Philip North to a pulp with his bare fists. Now, although it might have seemed to an onlooker (had there been anyone present to look on except a hysterical Corianne) that Edward's attempt to commit violence on the person of the Marquis had been effectively halted by a well-aimed pistol, Edward would not have agreed. No pistol would stop him now!

He felt absolutely no fear as he stared for a moment down the barrel of the deadly silver weapon. After a pause of only a fraction of a second—less time than it could take North to squeeze the trigger—Edward lunged at North's chest, knocking aside the arm that held the gun as his full weight came crashing against the surprised Marquis. The pistol flew from his grasp as the two men toppled over to the floor.

They rolled around, each one trying to get a firm grip on the other's throat. First a chair went over with a crash, then a basket of kindling, and then another chair. With each crash, Corianne screamed. North, his eye on the silver pistol still out of reach across the floor, rolled over—his opponent first under and then above him—in the direction of the weapon. When they neared it, he pushed his right hand roughly into Edward's face while he reached out with the left to grasp the pistol. But Edward saw the movement from the corner of an eye and managed to kick the gun aside. At the same moment, he swung his fist at the unprotected left side of North's face. North groaned and lay still.

Edward, breathless, got to his knees and, using a table leg to support him, pulled himself to his feet, his back momentarily turned to his opponent. North, watching with lidded eyes, pulled up on one elbow, grasped the legs of an overturned chair and heaved it at Edward. It caught Edward heavily on the shoulder and the side of his head. Dizzied, he fell to one knee. Instantly, North was on him again.

The two struggled on the floor again, neither able to loosen the grip of the other. North, beginning to tire, and with his jaw aching badly, cast about desperately for his pistol or some other weapon to use against the bulldog tenacity and strength of his opponent. His eye fell upon the glass that Corianne had knocked to the floor. It was just beyond his reach, lying against one of the table legs. With a sudden surge of effort, he swung himself over upon Edward and, pinioning his shoulder with one arm, reached for the glass with the other. Quickly he struck it against the table leg, breaking off the stem. Cory screamed a warning as North lifted the jagged edge and brought it toward Edward's throat.

Edward caught his hand at the wrist and held it off. This despicable trick was, for Edward, the last straw. Enraged, he forced North's arm back as far as he could, until the pain caused North to gasp and loosen his hold. That was all Edward needed. With a smashing right to North's face, he knocked him senseless.

This time he didn't take his eyes from North's prostrate body as he pulled himself up. His forehead throbbed from the blow of the chair, his shoulder was badly bruised, both his shins ached from the repeated impact of North's boots, and he'd sustained an ugly cut on the back of his hand from the broken glass. But he didn't want the fight to end. "Get up, damn you," he said to the fallen North. "Get *up*! I'm not through with you."

North didn't move. A terrified Corianne crept into the room and tugged at Edward's arm. "Please, Edward," she said quaveringly, "let's leave this p-place."

"I told you to go to the other room," he barked at her, his eyes continuing their furious watch over the fallen North. "Now, do as I say!"

Cory, shaken and chastened, backed away at once. But before she could cross the threshold, she heard North groan.

"Ah," Edward smiled frighteningly, "you're awake, are you? Get up, then. Get to your feet!"

North opened one eye, groaned again but did not move. Edward bent over him, grasped him by the lapels of his coat and shook him. "Get up, blast you!" But North lolled limply in his hold. Edward put both his arms under North's and hauled him to his feet. Keeping him erect by holding on to his neckcloth with his left hand, Edward raised his right fist to strike again.

"No!" Corianne squealed in agitation. "Edward, *don't*! That's *enough*!"

Edward's arm remained raised in its threatening pose for a moment, but then he let it drop to his side. "Very well," he muttered, "I'll let him be. It wasn't nearly the mill I'd hoped it would be."

He dragged North to a chair and let him fall into it. North slumped down, his legs outstretched awkwardly, his arms dangling down over the arms. One eye remained closed, for it was rapidly turning purple and swelling up alarmingly. The left side of his jaw was already dreadfully distended and discolored. With his one good eye, he looked up at Edward lugubriously. "I shou' ha' killed you when I firs' laid eyes on you," he said thickly, his mouth too bruised and stiff for proper enunciation. "We shou' ha' duelled then."

"Yes, we should have," Edward agreed. He walked slowly across the room to where the pistol lay gleaming in the firelight and picked it up. He studied it briefly. It was loaded and cocked. He sighted down the barrel in North's direction. "Do you still believe you could actually have killed me?" he asked, raising a quizzical eyebrow. "Well, my lord? Are you still so sure?"

There was a commotion at the door. "Edward, *don't!*" The cry didn't come from Corianne. Edward lowered the gun and turned around. It was Sarah in the doorway, looking at him in horror. Behind her, Fitz and Clara were gaping at him as if they'd never seen him before.

Edward laughed mirthlessly. "You needn't stare at me that way. I don't intend to shoot the damned blackguard."

Fitz stepped over the threshold first. "Well, you *were* pointing that thing at him, you know. Looked very much as if you were taking aim, although I never believed that you would actually—"

"Shoot an unarmed man in cold blood?" Edward finished drily. "How kind in you!" He looked over the three new arrivals with disdain. "No, you needn't worry. I leave that sort of thing to the nobility." He made an ironic bow in North's direction. "They have more experience at it."

"Ned!" Clara exclaimed. "He didn't try to shoot *you*, did he?"

"Didn't he?" Edward turned to Sarah, his once-so-breath-taking smile now a distorted sneer. "He's your husband-to-be, isn't he, ma'am? The man you've loved for so long? You must know him better than any of us. *Would* he try to shoot an unarmed man?"

Sarah looked up at him with a feeling of despondent confusion. This bitter irony was not what she'd expected from him. The sense of joyful relief she'd felt when she'd first glimpsed him alive and well as they'd burst in the door had been instantly dispelled by the realization that he was aiming a pistol at the obviously defeated North. She'd been appalled . . . and terrified. But now, on reflection, she knew she'd misjudged him. Edward would never shoot an un-armed man. But obviously her mistaken first impression had offended him. She wanted to apologize, but his caustic attack unnerved her.

"Well," he persisted angrily, "can't you answer me?"

She put a trembling hand on his arm. "Edward, don't. Please . . . I couldn't . . . I didn't mean . . ."

He looked at her witheringly and then shook her hand away. Turning, he crossed to North's chair. "And you, my lord . . . are you equally at a loss for words? Don't you want to tell your betrothed how courageously, how uprightly, how *nobly* you defended yourself?"

North fixed his good eye on Sarah. "Shou' ha' killed 'im that firs' day," he mumbled. "That very firs' day."

"Edward," Corianne whined suddenly, "I want to leave this place!" The entire drama, from the moment Sarah and her friends had come upon the scene, had taken a turn she didn't understand. Somehow, the fact that *she'd* been abducted had diminished in importance. Her humiliation and pain seemed a matter of little moment to anyone else. "I want to go *home*!" she cried pathetically.

"Yes, my dear, in a moment," Edward said, not taking his eyes from Lord North's face.

North was looking up at him with hatred. "I cou' ha' shot you down like a dog . . . as easily . . . and legally . . . as I'd shoot a sick horse . . ."

Edward laughed. "Do you think so?" He turned and walked to the wall behind him. Deliberately, he raised the pistol.

"Edward!" Cory squealed.

"Ned, what—?" Fitz began, startled.

"Fitz," Edward ordered, "take that candelabrum from the table and stand it on the bench against the far wall."

Fitz cast his wife a questioning look. She nodded imperceptibly, and he hurriedly followed Edward's order.

"Yes, thank you, Fitz. Well, North, which one shall it be? The one on the right? The left? Ah, the center one, eh? Good." He turned his face to the wall, waited a breath-stopping moment, whirled around and, barely taking aim, he fired. The center candle was instantly snuffed out. When the smoke had cleared, it stood erect and unmarked, but its wick was gone.

Edward tossed the gun into the fire and strode back to North's chair. "So you see, my lord, in a duel between us, it would not necessarily be *my* light that's snuffed out," he said quietly. "If you still wish it, I am willing to keep our duelling appointment any time you're ready." He gave North a mocking little bow and turned away.

Clara chortled. "He'll never fight a duel with you now."

"No, I don't suppose he will." Edward turned to Sarah.

"Well, there he is, ma'am. In a day or two, I have no doubt he'll be good as new. And all yours."

Sarah dropped her eyes from his angry, derisive glare.

Edward took her chin in his hand and forced her to look up at him. "Did you hear me, Miss Stanborough? Your betrothed, your heart's desire, your *love*! Look at him!" He made a scornful gesture toward North, who watched them balefully from the one good eye in his battered face. "The handsome rake . . . the attractive devil that women can't resist!" He looked down at her, his eyes burning wrathfully. "He's all yours now. I wish you joy of him."

He went quickly to the door, picked up his greatcoat and threw it over Corianne's shoulders. "Come, girl," he said, taking her hand and pulling her after him out the door. "We're going home. To Lincolnshire."

Chapter Twenty-Two

THEY DROVE, NOT speaking very much, through most of the night. Cory cried silently for the first few hours. Edward, wrapped in his own thoughts, did not try to console her. He was puzzling over his own feeling and the unreasoning way he'd ripped up at Sarah. Strangely, his mill with Lord North had done little to ease the anger that seemed to have built up in him. But why had he vented it on her? One would have thought that his rescue of Cory and his defeat of North would have eased his rage and given him some sense of satisfaction. But, inexplicably, a bitterness seemed to have lodged itself somewhere inside him and would not leave.

As the dawn came up, Edward drew up at an inn near Nottingham where, ignoring the curious looks of the innkeeper, he bespoke two bedrooms. He and Cory slept until noon when, by mutual agreement, they rose and took to the road again. By this time they were both feeling better. Eager for the sight of home, they welcomed every familiar detail of the landscape. Cory, her eyes beginning to shine, looked out on the wintry hills and wide fields stretching out beyond the carriage windows with a smile. A pale November sun lit the air, the wind had died down, and the leaves on the ground stirred gently in the wake of the carriage wheels. The countryside had never seemed so beautiful to her before. "I don't think I'll ever go to London again as long as I live," she remarked.

"Yes, you will," Edward predicted. "You'll forget your misadventures before very long, and you'll plead with your father to send you back."

"No, never. Besides, I won't have to plead with Father for long. I expect I'll have a husband to plead with."

Edward turned his eyes from the road to stare at her with eyebrows raised. "A husband? Really, Cory, you're the most inconstant creature. Only yesterday you were determined to marry North. Now you speak of someone else. Can you have found a new candidate as soon as this?"

She pouted. "You're unkind, Edward, to remind me of North. He was the most despicable monster, and I'm determined to put him out of my mind. I must have been *mad* to imagine that I cared for him. I was an ignorant child."

"I see," Edward said drily. "But you've quite grown up now, is that it? Overnight?"

"It can happen that way sometimes," she said seriously. "A shocking experience of that nature . . . it makes a woman more mature somehow."

"Does it indeed?"

"Oh, yes. It's *bound* to. It makes one learn . . . what is valuable and meaningful in one's life."

"Oh?" He smiled at her indulgently. "And what did you learn is valuable and meaningful in *your* life?"

"A great many things. Daynwood, for one. I shall always value it now—more than I ever did before. And Father. And Belinda. And . . . and you."

"Good. It's time you realized that one's greatest treasures are found at home."

"Yes, they are," she said with a sigh.

They rode on in silence until the landscape began to be recognizable. "Oh, look!" Cory exclaimed excitedly. "There's Swallow Road! We're almost home! Oh, Edward, stop the carriage."

"Why? What for?"

"I have something I must say to you. Something quite urgent. And I can't say it while you're holding the reins and watching the horses."

"Cory, if you're going to make another speech about your gratitude for my 'rescue,' you may save yourself the trouble. I've heard all I can stand on the subject."

"No, it's not that. It's about . . . something else entirely."

"Very well, then," he said obligingly and pulled the carriage to the side of the road. "Now, Miss, what is it?"

"It's about . . . a husband for me."

"Oh, yes. I'd forgotten. You began to tell me that you've latched on to a new prospect. I surmise that, this time, you've chosen someone a bit more acceptable."

She nodded eagerly. "The very best. Belinda has been telling me for *years* to consider him, but I didn't appreciate . . . until now, that is . . . his very sterling qualities—"

"*Sterling* qualities?" His eyes brimmed with wicked amusement. "That's quite a change for you, isn't it?"

"Don't tease, Edward. I'm very serious about this. I didn't realize, all this time, that he is the man I truly want, but now—"

He couldn't repress his grin. "But now, in your newly found maturity, it's all suddenly clear."

Cory nodded. "Yes. Exactly." She looked down at her hands. "I wish you wouldn't tease."

He patted her hands kindly. "Well, Cory, if I know your friend Belinda, it's Tom Moresby you're speaking of. I heartily approve, my dear, even if I seem to be teasing. There isn't a sounder, more reliable fellow in the county."

Cory giggled. "It isn't Tom. Belinda's caught him for *herself*!"

"You don't say! Clever girl, Belinda. But then, who—?"

She tossed him a coy glance. "Can't you guess?"

"I haven't the foggiest notion."

"Oh, Edward, you can sometimes be the most *mutton-headed*—!" She hesitated, eyed him askance, and then, in a burst of bravado, threw her arms about him.

He reared back, startled. "Cory! What—?"

"Don't you see?" she whispered into his ear. "It's always been you! I just didn't realize it. We shall be so *happy*, my love."

Edward was shocked into immobility. This turn of affairs had caught him completely off guard. For a moment, he had no idea of what he thought, what he felt, or what he should do. She was in his arms, as he'd so often dreamed she might be, her lips against his ear, her body soft and pliant against his. And he felt . . . what? Certainly not joy.

Not even triumph. He felt . . . *uncomfortable*!

A part of his mind wanted to laugh. This wasn't love—it was embarrassment! He was like an uncle discomfitted by the effusions of an overly emotional niece. He'd played the role for so long that it had become the truth! His love for Cory was nothing more than avuncular . . . a deep and protective affection. But mature love—the passion a man could feel for a woman he wished to wed—was something very different. It was something deeper, something that stirred the spirit to the core. Something like what he felt for—Good Lord!—for Sarah!

The thought struck him with a shattering clarity. *Sarah!* What a blind fool he'd been all these weeks. Everything that had happened now seemed bathed in a new light. He'd promised himself to put the London experiences behind him, but now he must think things over more carefully. Although certainly *this* was not the time for it. *Cory* was in his arms. He would have to take care of her first.

Gently, he removed her arms from about his neck. "Don't, Cory," he said softly. "You don't really mean these words at all."

"But I *do*! Truly! I mean every word."

He took her hand. "You've been badly hurt, my little one, and it was only *yesterday*. Your emotions are bruised, and they're searching about for a quick and easy cure. So they light on me. But when those wounds are healed—and they *will* be, if you wait calmly and quietly for some time to pass—you'll find that your feelings for me will return to what they were before all this happened. You'll look on me again as a dull, nagging old uncle whom you're merely fond of."

Her eyes clouded. "No! That's not *true*! I *love* you! I love you more than ever I loved North!"

"You only think so now . . . because your heart is so empty."

She blinked at him, two round tears spilling down her cheeks. "But I thought . . . I was sure that . . . Don't you love *me*?"

"Of course I do. I'm the fondest old uncle that ever was."

"Edward! Is that *all?*"

He grinned at her. "All? *All?* My dear child, when you

consider what I've been through these past two months in your behalf, you'll have to admit it is a very great deal."

But Cory would not be consoled. She turned away from him and stared gloomily out the window. Edward, not knowing what else to say, pulled at the reins and turned the horses back to the road.

Cory wept until she saw the gates of Daynwood from the window. "We're home," she sighed tremulously. "I suppose I'd better dry my eyes, or I shall alarm Papa." She sniffed bravely and wiped her cheeks with the back of her hand.

It was not often that Cory showed such thoughtfulness of others. Edward gave her an admiring smile. "That's the spirit," he said encouragingly. "Perhaps you *are* maturing after all."

They pulled up at the doorway. "Much good it will do me," Cory said with her old petulance. "There isn't a single man, either here or in London, who wants me now. I shall die an old maid. A miserable, lonely old maid."

With that grim prediction, she jumped from the carriage and ran up the steps. As he watched her go, her bronze-gold hair glinting in the faint sunlight and her slim ankles peeping deliciously from beneath her skirt as she ran, he doubted the truth of that prediction. He doubted it very much indeed.

And so he came home at last. Throughout his stay in London he'd said home was the one place in the world where he wanted to be. It was the place that had always given him contentment. He loved the work involved in the supervision of the land, in dealing with the tenants, in doing the accounts. He loved the outdoor pastimes and the indoor relaxations. He loved the smell of the stables and the damp fragrance of the fields in the early mornings. But there was no contentment in any of these things now. He couldn't seem to settle down. He couldn't concentrate on his work or take pleasure in any of his former amusements. It soon became clear that a large part of him had been left behind in London. He hadn't really come home at all.

It was Sarah, of course. Sarah's face came between him and everything he looked upon. He thought over everything that had happened during his stay in town in the light of his new awareness of his feelings, but nothing substantial was changed by it. Sarah loved North. Edward's feelings for her couldn't change that.

He tried to put her out of his mind, but he didn't succeed for a moment. He seemed to live *her* days rather than his own. It was ten in the morning—what was she doing now? Had she breakfasted? Was she in her sitting room writing letters? Would she ever write to him? It was evening—was she dressing for a ball? Would she go on North's arm? Did she really intend to wed him after all that had happened?

He lay awake at night, staring up at the ceiling of his room. Was *she* awake? Did she ever think of him? Did she remember the feeling of his lips when he'd kissed her that night so many weeks ago, as he remembered hers? Did North kiss her so? The possibility drove him wild.

How could she love that blackguard? *That* was the question that troubled him more than any other. Although he'd read that love was a powerful, overwhelming and irrational emotion, it was still inconceivable to him that a sensitive, intelligent, gently bred female could lose her head over an attractive scoundrel. Besides, marriage was something larger and more encompassing than mere infatuation. A person of sense should not give her *life* away on the basis of an irrational passion. Marriage required honesty, trust, reliability and tender regard. North would be able to supply *not one* of those essential qualities.

The more these thoughts bombarded his mind, the more he became convinced that he could not allow her to go through with the marriage. An idea, born of the pain of his unrequited passions and nurtured in the sleepless darkness of the night, grew in his mind. He would *abduct* her! He would return to London at once and drag her back with him to Lincolnshire, by force if necessary. North might be the man she loved, but *he*, Edward Middleton, was the man she ought to marry. He would surely be the better man for her in the long run—he must make her see that.

The following day, Martin came home from town with the baggage that Corianne and Edward had not been able to collect because of their abrupt departure. To the groom's complete astonishment, the Squire picked up his portmanteau and tossed it back into the carriage. "I'm returning to London, you see," he explained briefly.

"Returnin'?" Martin asked, gaping. "When?"

"Right now," Edward told the openmouthed groom.

He arrived in London early the following evening and made a quick stop at Fitz's apartments. The memory of his leave-taking of them had made him feel embarrassed and guilty. They had been too kind to him to deserve the bitter anger he'd exhibited when he'd left them that night at the inn. Besides, he wanted to see how Clara would react to his plan.

Fitz crowed with delight to see him. "Dash it, I didn't dare hope to see you again, old fellow! What brings you back?" he demanded, pumping Edward's hand energetically. "I was afraid we'd seen the last of you."

"We had the decided impression that you were angry with us," Clara said, kissing his cheek affectionately.

"Forgive me for that," Edward said, smiling his old, heart-warming smile. "I was angry at the world in general and myself in particular . . . but never at you."

"I'm glad of that, Ned. We'd like to *keep* this friendship, Clara and I," Fitz said, beaming at him.

"But you haven't told us what brings you," Clara reminded him.

"Sit down, please, Clara, for I fear I'm about to shock you. It's an abduction that's brought me."

"An abduction?" Fitz echoed, his smile fading. "Perhaps I'd better sit down, too. Is it Cory *again*?"

"No, no. It's Sarah. I've decided that I'm going to steal her away from that worm North. I can't permit her to wed him, you see. She'll be much happier married to me, though she may not realize it now." He looked sheepishly at their astounded faces. "Are you very much appalled?"

Fitz opened his mouth, but words failed him. He chewed his moustache for a moment and then tried again. "Ned, old fellow, haven't you *heard*? I mean, well, confound it, man, didn't you realize that Sarah isn't—?"

Clara dug a heel sharply into Fitz's foot. "What Fitz means," she improvised, giving her husband a warning look, "is that Sarah isn't . . . er . . . expecting you."

"No, of course she isn't," Edward said with a laugh.

"One doesn't warn a lady that she's about to be abducted. I intend to take her by surprise."

"But, Ned," Clara asked, looking at him closely, "what about Corianne?"

"Corianne?" Edward blinked at her impatiently. "What has *she* to do with this?" He waved the question aside, dismissing it as an irrelevancy.

Clara and Fitz looked at each other in amused wonder. "Nothing, I suppose," Clara murmured, hiding a grin.

"Well, what do you *think*? Have I lost my mind? Will Sarah rebuff me and have me tossed out the nearest window?"

Fitz gave a snort of laughter, but a sharp jab in his side, delivered cruelly by his wife's elbow, cut the laugh short. Clara bit her lip. "Who can say?" she said, struggling to keep her tone enigmatic. "But by all means, go and try."

Edward got up feeling decidedly encouraged, although he couldn't have said why. Fitz pumped his hand again. "Well, good luck, old chap. Be sure to let us know the outcome."

After Edward left, Fitz rounded on his wife. "Why did you step on my foot that way?" he complained. "What did I say?"

"You were going to tell him that Sarah broke with North for good on the night of the elopement, weren't you?"

"Yes, of course. Why *shouldn't* I have done?"

"And that North has left the country for an extended stay in Italy?"

"Yes, that too. Why not?"

"I think, my love," his wife answered, her eyes twinkling, "that the news had much better come from Sarah than from you."

"Don't see why," Fitz muttered, "but I'll take your word. You're the *connoisseur* in these romantic matters. But I don't see why you didn't tell him that we're packing to return home."

"Because it's entirely possible, my pet, that we won't return home just yet." She pulled him to his feet and whirled him around the room in a merry waltz. "Our presence may yet be required here in town."

"Our presence? Whatever for?"

"For a wedding, you gudgeon. For a wedding!" She gurgled happily and hugged her husband tightly. "Now all we have to do is to persuade Mama to watch over the babies for a few more days."

Sarah had spent the few days since the night at the Three Forks Inn in trying to recapture the feeling of serenity—wistful though it had been—that had been her usual mood before Corianne had come to stay. But she couldn't do it. She was not the same person she'd been two months ago. Two months ago, she hadn't really known Edward. He'd been merely a man in her dreams. Now the recollection of his face, his touch, his voice, his manner, his very *nature* was with her always as a distinct and permanent reality, filling her, in his absence, with a distinct and permanent pain. It was a pain she had to learn to accept, like a physical deformity. And, like a physical deformity, it made her life greyer and more difficult than it had been before.

She attempted, however, to resume her old ways of life. After she and Mama had sent the letters cancelling the betrothal party, she had again gone into her habitual seclusion. Her visits with Clara and Fitz were the only social activities in which she engaged, and even those would soon be at an end, for they intended to leave the next day. She was sorry to have to see them go, but perhaps, when they, too, had left her, she would be able to forget the events of the past few weeks and achieve some sort of emotional equilibrium.

She was completely startled when Madame Marie bounded into her sitting room with the announcement that a gentleman was waiting below to see her. "But who is he, Madame? You know I'm not receiving."

"I can't say. *Je ne parle pas*. My lips are sealed. *Fermé*. But you must go at once, Miss Sarah. It's important."

Sarah found Madame's air of suppressed excitement not only puzzling but annoying. However, she hadn't sufficient energy to quarrel. "Well, if I must," she sighed as she reluctantly started for the door.

"Wait!" Madame cried, running after her. "You're *never* goin' down wearin' that faded gown, are ye? And that cap—it's *hideaux*!"

"What's gotten into you, Madame?" Sarah asked. "I've no time now to change my clothes."

Madame Marie wrung her hands nervously. "No . . . not the entire *toilette*, o' course, but the hair . . . and p'rhaps yer Nor'ich silk shawl—"

"Don't be so foolish. I shall go down exactly as I am."

She marched out of the room, leaving Madame in a frenzy. "At least the cap!" Madame called after her. "At least take off the cap—!" But Miss Sarah paid no heed. "Oh, well," Madame consoled herself, shrugging her shoulders in Gallic acceptance, "it won't matter none." Her eyes lit up in hopeful anticipation of the results of the meeting down below. "From the look of 'im, he's missed her as much as she's missed him. I don't s'pose he'll mind her clothes. Or even that cap, if I'm a judge."

At the foot of the stairs, Sarah faced Edward dumbfounded. "*Edward*! What on *earth*—?"

He gave her a small, tentative smile. "I have to talk to you, Sarah. Urgently. Will you come for a ride with me in my carriage?"

"Of course we can talk, Edward, but come into the drawing room," she suggested. "Surely it will be more comfortable to converse in there."

"I'd rather talk as we ride," he insisted.

"But, Edward, I'm not properly dressed—"

"You look quite proper to me."

"And it's bitterly cold. It may even snow before long."

"Please, Sarah," he pleaded. "It will be more . . . private in the carriage."

"But we can be quite private here," she said reasonably, looking up at him wonderingly. "No one is here to disturb us."

Edward twisted his beaver hat in his hand irritably. Why was everything he attempted with this girl so deucedly difficult? "But your mother . . . she might—" he suggested in desperation.

"Mama has gone to one of her card parties and won't be back for *hours*."

He slammed his hand against the bannister in frustration. "Dash it, Sarah, how am I to *abduct* you if you won't *cooperate*?" he burst out in disgust.

"*Abduct* me? Edward, have you lost your *mind*?"

"No! Yes! I don't know . . . perhaps I have. Here, come into the drawing room. I feel like a damned fool standing about in the hallway like this."

He tossed his hat on a chair, took her hand, pulled the bewildered girl behind him into the drawing room and shut the door. "I *will* abduct you, Sarah, whether you like it or no," he said at once. "It's for your own good. So even if you force me to *carry* you, I'm quite prepared to do so. I only ask that you refrain from screaming—that might prove to be embarrassing."

The intensity and seriousness of his expression were at such odds with the ridiculousness of his words that Sarah had to laugh. "But, Edward, why should you *wish* to abduct me?"

He took both her hands and looked down at her intently. "Don't laugh, Sarah. I'm not joking. I can't let you marry that worm. He'd only make you miserably unhappy. I know you think you love him, but such feelings sometimes fade. I'll *make* them fade. I'll make you so happy you won't think of him again."

Sarah could scarcely make sense of what he was saying. Her pulse was racing madly, and she found it impossible to think calmly. She put a hand to her forehead. "Let's sit down here on the sofa, Edward, and see if we can make some sense of this." They sat down together, Edward looking at her expectantly. "Your offer is . . . very kind," she said. "It takes my breath away. But don't you know that I'm not—"

"Please don't say anything. Just *think* about what I'm suggesting. Please. Love *him* if you must, but *marry me!*"

Sarah's heart jumped up into her throat as the meaning of his words sank in. "Edward, I . . . ! Haven't you guessed by this time that I've *never* loved North? Not for one moment."

He couldn't quite believe his ears. "What? But you *said*—!"

"I lied. You would have fought that cursed duel if I hadn't."

"Sarah! Does that mean . . . you *aren't* going to wed him, then?"

"That's just what I told Lord North at the inn. When he ran off with Corianne, he forfeited any right to hold me to my promise. So you see, you needn't have concerned yourself about me." She smiled at him tenderly. "And there's no need to *abduct* me, either."

"No, I suppose not," he said, stunned. He dropped her hands, got up and took a restless turn about the room. He should have felt relieved—even happy—but he was aware only of a sharp stab of disappointment. "That's too bad," he muttered, staring out of the window. "All my plans, wasted." He shook his head in wry self-disdain. "I had looked forward quite eagerly to abducting you, you know."

She studied the back of his bent head for a long moment. "Must I be in love with North in order to be abducted?" she asked, timidly bold.

He wheeled about to face her, his breath caught in his chest. "*What*? Do you mean you *would* . . . ?" He crossed swiftly to the sofa, sat down and searched her face. The warmth in her eyes should have been enough, but he was afraid to believe what he saw. Taking her roughly by the shoulders, he pulled her close. "Sarah—?"

She slipped her arms about his waist and hid her face in his shoulder. "You idiot," she whispered into his coat, "I've loved you for *two whole years*!"

"Good God!" He lifted her face and peered at her in utter astonishment. "I can hardly make myself *believe*—"

"I can hardly believe this either," she said, smiling up at him tremulously. "You told me that . . . that you loved Corianne."

"It seems we've *both* said a great many foolish things." He pulled her to him, rested her head on his shoulder and rubbed his cheek against hers. "I never loved Corianne," he said softly. "I didn't know what love was . . . until you."

Sarah made a little, joyful gurgle in her throat and buried her face in his neck. All that was available for him to kiss was an ear, a bit of forehead, and a rather scratchy lace concoction covering her hair. "What is this thing on your head?" he asked dreamily.

That blasted cap! Sarah thought, lifting her head and wincing. *The most wonderful moment of my life, and I must look a fright!*

But Edward was gazing at her in the most lover-like, besotted fashion. If she looked a fright, he didn't seem to notice. "Do you remember the night you made me kiss you?" he was asking with his spectacular, devastating smile. "You put my arms around your waist, like this . . . threw your arms about my neck, like this . . . and said—"

She giggled. "I said, 'Kiss me, Edward, as if you really mean it.' "

He pulled her close and very expertly obliged. While he was preoccupied with the embrace, she gingerly lifted one of her arms from his neck, reached up to her head and pulled off the little lace cap. Then, behind his back—and without in the least disturbing this very satisfactory demonstration of his affection—she surreptitiously swung the cap by its ribbon from her right hand to her left and dropped it down behind the sofa.